GUN LAW

 This Large Print Book carries the
Seal of Approval of N.A.V.H.

GUN LAW

RALPH COTTON

THORNDIKE PRESS

A part of Gale, Cengage Learning

GALE
CENGAGE Learning·

Detroit • New York • San Francisco • New Haven, Conn • Waterville, Maine • London

GALE
CENGAGE Learning·

LIBRARY OF CONGRESS CATALOGING-IN-PUBLICATION DATA

Cotton, Ralph W.
    Gun law / by Ralph Cotton. — Large print ed.
      p. cm. — (Thorndike Press large print western)
    ISBN-13: 978-1-4104-4303-8(hardcover)
    ISBN-10: 1-4104-4303-5(hardcover)
    1. Large type books. I. Title.
PS3553.O766G84 2011
813'.54—dc23   2011033303

Published in 2011 by arrangement with NAL Signet, a member of Penguin Group (USA) Inc.

Printed in the United States of America
1 2 3 4 5 6 7 15 14 13 12 11

For Mary Lynn . . . of course.

PART 1

CHAPTER 1

Kindred, New Mexico Territory

Neither of the two men standing at the bar saw Sherman Dahl ride into town. They tipped shot glasses at each other, throwing back mouthfuls of fiery rye. Sliding their empty glasses away, they raised heavy mugs of beer and drank through an inch of cold silky foam.

"*Ahhh* . . . Damn, this is living," said one to the other.

The other man grinned and replied through a foam-frosted mustache, "You're by-God right it is."

Outside, Dahl stepped down from his tan dun and spun its reins to a wooden hitch rail out in front of a tack and saddle shop next door to the Lucky Devil Saloon. He pulled a Winchester repeater from its saddle boot. The tack shop owner wiped his hands on his leather apron when he saw Dahl step onto the boardwalk, but he looked on in disappointment as Dahl walked past his open door to the saloon.

Dahl levered a round into his rifle chamber and stepped back for a second while two cattle buyers walked out through the saloon's batwing doors. The buyers looked him up and down and moved on. One took a cigar from his lips and gave a curious nod.

"It doesn't look good for somebody," he said, noting the serious look on Dahl's face.

The two walked on.

At the bar, one of the drinkers, a former Montana range detective named Curtis Hicks, grinned and wiped the back of his hand across his foamy lips.

"Tell the truth," he said to his companion, Ernie Newman, "if it wasn't for me, you wouldn't be standing right here today, would you?" He poked a stiff wet finger up and down on the bar top as he spoke.

"I don't deny it," said Newman. "You were right about this place."

"Damn right I was right!" said Hicks. He took another deep swig of beer.

"I'm obliged," said Newman.

"Yeah? Just how obliged?" Hicks asked bluntly.

"As obliged as I should be," said Newman. He gave Hicks a guarded look. "But I ain't

10

kissing nothing that belongs to you."

"You know what I mean . . . ," Hicks said. He rubbed his thumb and fingertips together in the universal sign of greed. "Every act is worth its balance."

"I don't know what that means." Newman shook his head, sipped his beer. "The fact is, you was asked to bring a good man or two with you. So I might just have done you a favor standing here today."

"That ain't how I see it," said Hicks.

"See it how it suits you." Newman shrugged. "I'll do the same."

"You son of a bitch!" Hicks growled.

"Say it again. I dare you!" Newman's hand went to his holstered gun butt.

Both men heard the rustle and scuffle of boots as men cleared away on either side of the bar from them. The saloon owner ducked down behind the bar, crawling away in a hurry.

But before either man could make a move, Dahl's Winchester exploded from where he'd stepped inside the swinging batwing doors.

Dahl's first shot nailed Newman in the heart.

Hicks watched as the impact of the bullet flung Newman up onto the bar. He swung around toward Dahl, snatching his Remington from its holster. But the gun never cleared leather. It fell from his hand back down into a tooled slim-jim holster as Dahl's next shot hammered him backward against the bar and dropped him dead on the floor.

"Good Lord Almighty!" the saloon owner cried out, pulling himself up from the floor at the far end of the bar. Bullets had shattered the mirror behind him. Blood had splattered the wall. "Somebody's gonna pay for this!"

He'd jerked a sawed-off shotgun from under the bar and held it in his shaking hand, but when Dahl swung his rifle barrel toward him, the saloon owner turned the shotgun loose as if it were hot and let it fall to the floor.

Dahl lowered the rifle barrel, having levered a fresh round into the chamber. "Where's Ned Carver and Cordell Garrant?" It was a question for anyone listening.

"Cordell Garrant is dead," said a voice from a corner table. "He died a week ago from the fever."

Dahl swung around to face the voice as a man wearing a long swallowtail suit coat and a battered derby hat rose slowly from a chair, his hands chest high.

"Ned Carver left town three nights ago," the man said quietly. "Must've known somebody was coming for him."

"Nice try, Ned," said Dahl. The rifle exploded again. The shot flung the man backward from the table. His long coat flew open, revealing the sawed-off shotgun he never got the chance to draw.

"Holy Jumping Moses . . . !" shouted the saloon owner, seeing more blood splatter on the wall as customers once again ducked away and scrambled out of range.

Dahl noticed one man look past him, wide-eyed in fear, and realized there was a gun pointed somewhere behind him. He levered his own gun and swung in a fast full circle.

But he wasn't fast enough. He saw the big Russian pistol pointed toward him at arm's reach; he saw it buck; he saw the streak of blue-orange fire. He felt the bullet hit him high in the chest — heart level. A second bullet hit him no more than an inch from the first, and he flew backward, broken and limp, like some rag doll.

Dahl's rifle flew from his hand; he hit the floor ten feet back from where he'd stood.

"I'm Cordell Garrant," the gunman said.

He stepped across the floor toward Dahl, who lay struggling to catch his breath, his

13

right hand clutching his chest over the two bullet holes. He cocked the smoking Smith & Wesson Russian revolver in his hand and started to raise it for a third shot.

"Guess what. Ned was lying," he said with a flat grin. "I ain't dead."

Dahl managed to roll an inch sideways. His right hand dropped from his chest and reached inside his corduroy riding jacket. "No, he, wasn't. . . ." His voice was strained, but he made his move quick, swinging out a .36-caliber Navy Colt and firing.

"Damn it to hell!" the saloon owner shouted, seeing the bullet bore through Garrant's right eye and string a ribbon of blood and gore out the back of his head.

Garrant hit the floor, dead. Blood pooled in the sawdust beneath him.

Dahl let the Navy Colt slump to the floor beside him. He released a tense breath and felt the room tip sideways and darken around him. The pain in his chest seemed to crush him down into the floor.

Huddled in a corner of the saloon, a young dove named Sara Cayes stood up warily and ventured forward. Around her the stunned drinkers came slowly back to life.

"Oh my, he's alive!" she gasped, looking down at Dahl, seeing his chest rise and fall

14

with labored breathing.

"He won't be for long," the enraged saloon owner said. He snatched the shotgun up from the floor, shook sawdust from it and walked forward, raising it toward Dahl.

"You stay away from him, Jellico," Sara Cayes said, hurriedly stooping down over Dahl, protecting him. "Can't you see the shape he's in?"

"Get out of my way, whore," said the saloon owner, trying to wave her aside with the shotgun barrel. "All I see is the shape my place is in."

"He's unarmed, Jellico!" the dove cried out, huddling down even closer over Dahl.

"Suits me," he said, cocking both hammers on the shotgun. "Now get back away from him, else you'll never raise your ankles in this place again."

"She said leave him alone, Jellico," said a booming voice from the batwing doors. "While you're at it, empty your hand. Shotguns make me cross, especially when they're pointed at me."

The saloon owner, his customers and the dove all turned and faced the newly appointed town marshal, Emerson Kern. The lawman stood with a hip slightly cocked, his left hand holding open one of the batwing doors. His right hand lay poised around the

15

bone handle of a big Colt .45, holstered on his hip.

Jellico's eyes met the marshal's, and he immediately lowered the shotgun barrel straight down toward the floor, but he deliberately didn't put it aside. Sara Cayes rose a little over Dahl but remained in position in case the saloon owner tried anything.

"Marshal Kern, look what this murdering dog did to my place!" said Jake Jellico. He swung a nod around the blood-splattered saloon.

But the marshal was still interested in the saloon owner's shotgun, and the fact that it hadn't left his hand. He raised his revolver from its holster and cocked it toward Jake Jellico.

"If you don't drop the gun, I bet I stick a tunnel through your forehead," he said.

"Easy, Marshal," said Jellico. He stooped and laid the shotgun down on the floor. "You can't blame me for wanting to kill him, *armed* or *unarmed*."

With the shotgun out of play, the marshal lowered his Colt and walked over to Dahl. The young dove eased back and allowed him a better view of Dahl's face and the bullet holes in the front of his shirt.

"Not a big bleeder, is he?" said Kern.

"He's not bleeding at all," said a man

16

among the drinkers who gathered around closer.

Sara Cayes gasped slightly, noting for the first time bullet holes, but no blood.

"Step back, sweetheart," said Kern, touching the toe of his boot gently to the young woman's shoulder, pushing her aside the way he would a cat or dog.

Sara moved back grudgingly, yet she stayed stooped down near the unconscious gunman. Dahl lolled his head back and forth in the sawdust and murmured something under his breath. Even with him knocked out and helpless on the floor, Sara thought him to be the most handsome man she'd ever seen. *Too handsome for this place. . . .*

"What — what does this mean, Marshal?" she asked in a halting voice, staring at the bloodless bullet holes.

"What does this mean . . . ?" Kern echoed, squatting down beside her. He poked a probing finger down into a bullet hole and shook his head. "I'll tell you what it means." He stood up and looked around at the gathered crowd. "I'll tell all of you what it means." He gestured a hand around at the bloody aftermath of the gunfight. "It means the town of Kindred is going to have to get busy gathering up the guns if we're ever going to a respectable, upstanding community."

"Here we go," a voice whispered in the crowd.

"What's that?" Kern asked, taking a step forward toward the man who made the remark. "You got something you want to say, *Dandy?*"

"No, Marshal," said Ed Dandly, owner and manager of the *Kindred Star Weekly News*. He backed away as the marshal moved forward. "But it's *Dandly,* not *Dandy,*" he corrected.

Kern ignored him. "What I'm saying, gentlemen" — he settled back in place beside the unconscious Dahl — "is that this sort of thing is going to just keep happening so long as we continue allowing guns to be carried on the streets of this town."

"The marshal's right," said a voice.

Kern raised a boot and rested it on Dahl's shoulder. Sara tried to shove the boot away, but a cold look from the marshal halted her.

"I might not know what this was about," Kern said for all to hear. "But I can tell you straight up that it would not have happened if these men's guns had all been hanging on pegs in my office instead of hanging on their hips."

"For the record, is this where you're going

18

to tell us that as soon as our new mayor takes office, this sort of thing is going to stop?" Ed Dandly asked. He whipped out a pencil and a small leather-bound writing pad.

"Yeah, I'll say that," said Kern. "I'll say it, because it's the truth." Again, he took a threatening step toward the newsman. "The people voted Coakley into office to clean this town up, and by thunder, that's what he's going to do!"

But this time the newsman stood his ground, knowing he was doing his job.

"No need to come closer, Marshal. I can hear you just fine from there," Dandly said, scribbling as he spoke.

The marshal stopped, realizing that whatever he said or did now would be in the next edition of Dandly's weekly newspaper.

"So long as there are guns carried, there will be guns fired," Kern said stiffly. "There will be gunfights just like this, and people will die. Some of them will be innocent bystanders like all of you." He looked around the saloon from face to face. "Thank goodness, Mayor Coakley and I will be changing all this. That's what I'm saying."

Sherman Dahl moaned beneath the marshal's boot.

"Marshal, we need to get him some help,"

Sara Cayes said.

"You go do that, Sara," the marshal said. He looked around at the gathered townsmen and said, "Some of you drag these bodies out into the street, so Jake can get this place cleaned up and get to serving you again."

"I'm sticking with Sara and this man," said Ed Dandly, scribbling on the pad. "If he lives, I'll find out what this was all about."

"You do that, *Dandy*," said Kern. He gave the newsman a cold stare. "Maybe you'll find out what I said is true, if you'll look at it with your eyes open."

"I can assure you, Marshal Kern, my eyes are always open," said Dandly. "If men can't carry guns, what's to keep them safe?"

"Safe from what?" said Kern.

"Why, safe from the wilds, Marshal — safe from savages, safe from one another."

"That's the law's job," Kern said, tapping a thumb against the badge on his chest. "It's my job to keep all of you safe. That's what I was appointed to do, and that's what I *will* do."

"Without guns, who, or what, will keep us safe from you, Marshal?" Dandly asked, speaking boldly with his pencil and writing pad between himself and the lawman.

Kern gave him a smoldering look. "Safe

from *me?*" he said in a flat yet threatening voice. "What are you trying to say, *Dandy?*"

The newsman stood firm in spite of the marshal's harsh demeanor. "I'm not only talking about *you* necessarily, Marshal," he said. "I'm talking about the law and the government in general."

"You're saying you don't trust *the law?*" said Kern.

"Not entirely," said Dandly.

"You don't trust *lawmen?*" said Kern.

"That's correct," Dandly said. "Not beyond what's reasonable."

"You don't even trust the *government?*" the marshal said as if in disbelief. "What kind of a low, unpatriotic weasel are you, Ed *Dandy?*"

CHAPTER 2

Sherman Dahl awakened in a strange bed with a cool damp cloth pressed to his forehead. The two bullets had not rendered him completely unconscious, but their impact had knocked the breath from him so thoroughly that it had left him in a stunned haze. Nothing around him felt real.

"Are you feeling better now . . . ?" he heard a woman's voice ask.

He remembered lying on the sawdust floor, feeling two men lift his shoulders and heels and carry him from the saloon. After that a filmy darkness had engulfed him.

Feeling better . . . ? Dahl sorted through it as he opened his eyes and looked around slowly. He was in a small room. Pain pounded in his chest. Thin faded curtains stirred on a breeze through an open window across the room. Afternoon sunlight stood dim and slanted on the plank floor.

"Yes, ma'am . . . ," he said weakly. "I am

feeling *some* better." But that wasn't true. He felt as if a mule had kicked him in his chest. He continued to look around, getting his bearings.

Noticing the questioning look on his face, the young woman said quietly, "Don't worry, mister. This isn't one of the crib rooms over the saloon."

"Oh . . . ?" Dahl had no idea what she was referring to.

"What I mean is, you're not being charged for anything. I had them put you in a buckboard. I brought you here because I didn't know where else to take you. The doctor helped me with you."

"I see," Dahl whispered. Although he wasn't completely certain where he was, things were beginning to come back to him now. The gunfight, the explosions, the blood. He felt the impact of the two shots again in his chest. He pictured himself flying backward, in slow motion, like a man trapped inside a bad dream.

"I'm Sara Cayes," the young woman said. "You can call me Sara. I'm one of the doves from the Lucky Devil Saloon and Brothel. I was there when you came in shooting."

Dahl just looked at her. She was too young and too pretty to be a dove, he told himself. But who was he to say? He recalled seeing her in the saloon — catching a glimpse of her as she'd bent over him lying helpless on the floor of the bar.

"I remember you, ma'am," he said. "I'm obliged."

"It's Sara," she reminded him. She gave a light, pretty smile. "And you're most welcome," she added. "Those men you shot, Cordell Garrant and the others? They were all killers and thieves."

"Yes, ma'am, I know," Dahl said.

"Ma'am?" She gave him a look.

"I mean, *Miss Sara,*" he said, correcting himself.

"Good," she said. She patted his forearm. "I bet you have a name too."

He offered a thin, weak smile. The pain in his chest stifled his every movement.

"I'm Sherman Dahl, ma'am — I mean *Miss Sara,*" he said.

"Well . . . I am pleased to meet you, Mr. Sherman Dahl," she said, placing the damp cloth back against his forehead. "All the while you were asleep, you kept calling me Lilly."

"Oh . . . ?" He continued to stare at her.

"Is Lilly your woman?" she asked.

"Yes," Dahl said.

"I see . . . ," said Sara a bit coolly. She lowered the cloth from his forehead.

Dahl saw the slightest look of disappointment on her face. "That is, she *was* my woman."

"But not anymore?" she asked, looking at him expectantly.

"This past winter. The fever . . . ," Dahl said. He stopped there.

He didn't need to finish his words. She read the rest of it in the look on his face.

"I'm sorry," she said.

Dahl spread the front of his shirt open and looked down at his purple and swollen chest.

"Doc Washburn looked at you," Sara explained. "He said you have some crushed bones and a badly bruised heart."

"A bruised heart . . . ?" He sounded doubtful, but he closed the front of his shirt and allowed his body to relax on the feather mattress.

The two fell silent for a moment.

Finally Dahl asked, "Do you live here?"

"Yes, I do, sometimes anyway," she said. She looked around, paused, then shrugged and said, "I know it seems strange, a dove living away from the saloon where she works. But I like it here . . . it's quiet. It's right outside of Kindred." She gestured a hand toward the open window. Dahl could see Kindred in the distance, not too far off.

"You live here all alone?" Dahl asked.

"Yes," she said. "This was Widow Jefferies' place, but she died before I got here last spring. Most of the roof fell in last winter. The place is in bad repair. But I fixed this room up with things I found in the barn, and some belongings I brought in myself."

"It looks real nice," Dahl said, sensing that she wanted him to comment.

She smiled. "I think everybody needs a place to be, don't you?"

"I — I expect so," said Dahl, the pain in his chest all the more pronounced when he spoke.

She stood up from the edge of the bed. "I have some food cooking outside in a *chimnea*. I'll go check on it. I hope you like roasted rabbit and beans."

"Rabbit and beans sounds good," Dahl said.

Sara made her way to the door, but before she could turn the handle, the door burst open and Marshal Emerson Kern walked inside the room. He stood with a hip cocked, his right hand resting on his holstered revolver.

"Well," Kern said, staring at Dahl, "I see you're still alive." He looked Dahl over good. "I'm Emerson Kern, town marshal," he said. "And you'd be . . . ?"

26

"I'm Sherman Dahl." He cut a glance toward his rolled-up gun belt lying on a chair beside the bed. Draped over the chair back lay a Korean bulletproof vest the woman must have taken off him while he was unconscious.

"You won't be needing that gun," Kern said, seeing Dahl's quick sidelong glance. "They were all four outlaws with prices on their heads. That *is* what you were after, wasn't it? The bounty?"

"Yes, sort of," Dahl said. He eased down, but the pain in his chest remained intense.

"Sort of?" The marshal stared at him, tapping his fingers on his gun butt. "Are you a bounty hunter or not?"

"I'm working for the Western Railways Alliance," said Dahl. "They hired me to track down those four men. They derailed a train and robbed it . . . cost the lives of six passengers and two railroad employees."

"I see," said Kern, "and Western Rails Alliance didn't like the way the law was handling things. So they took matters into their own hands — hired you to get the job done."

"That's right, Marshal," said Dahl.

"That makes you a *hired gun,* then?" the marshal said bluntly.

"I consider myself a *fighting man,* Marshal," Dahl said. "Someone needs a person to fight for them, I'm for hire. This time it happens to be Western Rails Alliance."

"A fighting man," the marshal said with a wry smile. "But I take it you'd kill about anybody, for about any reason?" he asked.

"That's not how it is, Marshal," Dahl said.

"Yeah, I think that's exactly how it is," Kern said, a strong edge to his voice. He gave another thin smile. "Not that I care, mind you. What a man does is his own business. But you don't want to be coming back into my town, especially armed. You won't be welcome in Kindred."

"I understand," Dahl said quietly. "But what about my horse?"

"What about him?" said Kern.

"I'll need to come into town and get him," Dahl said.

"I could keep your horse, sell him to pay for all the mess at the saloon, all the burying that's going to have to be done."

Dahl stared at him.

"I *could*," said Kern. "But I'm not going to." He jerked his head toward the open window. "I brought him with me. He's hitched out front. There's a letter in your saddlebags attesting that you killed those four jakes. I signed it."

"Obliged, Marshal," Dahl said.

"Don't be," said Kern. "I figured if I brought your horse and the letter out to you, there'd be no other reason for you to step foot in Kindred. Am I right?"

"You're right, Marshal," Dahl said. "I'll get my boots on and —"

"Oh, I don't care about you being here in the widow's shack," said Kern. "This is outside of town. I have no say. But don't step inside the town line armed, you understand? Or are you and I going to get cross with each other?"

Dahl stared at him with ice blue eyes. "I don't plan on coming into your town armed or unarmed, Marshal," he said calmly. "That's enough said on it."

"Good, then, we're clear on the matter," said Kern, ignoring Dahl's cold stare. He looked around for a reason to change the subject and lessen the tense stillness between them.

"Is that the thing that keeps you alive?" the marshal asked, nodding at the frayed and patched Korean vest.

"It has, more times than once," Dahl said.

Kern shook his head. "What the hell will they think of next?" He turned to Sara Cayes. "What shape is he in?"

"Doc Washburn said his breastbone is broken — crushed is how he put it," she said. "It's awfully bruised." She touched a hand to the center of her chest to indicate where Dahl's breastbone had been hammered by the bullets.

"I bet it is," said Kern. He looked at the quilted vest, at the many patched-over bullet holes in its front, its sides. "But I expect he's used to that. Am I right, mister?" he asked Dahl.

Dahl stared ahead without reply.

"He shouldn't ride for a day or two, Doc said," Sara replied. "I told Doc I'd look after him here."

"Yeah . . . ?" Kern looked her up and down as if he was questioning her motives. "Well, do what the doctor says is best. Take care of your *hired gun* friend here. But see to it you get him back on his feet and send him on his way as soon as you can."

"Thanks, Marshal Kern. I will," she said, seeing him touch his hat brim toward her, then turn to the door.

Before walking out, he looked back and said to Dahl, "I'm happy I won't be seeing you again."

Dahl continued to stare at him from the bed without reply.

"A *fighting man* . . . ," the marshal murmured to himself. He shook his head as he walked out the door.

It was later in the afternoon when Dr. Fred Washburn knocked on the door to the widow's shack. Sara unlatched the door and let him inside. The large potbellied doctor with muttonchop sideburns took off a battered derby hat and walked over to the bed where Dahl sat leaning back against a pillow. He set his worn leather medicine case down on the stand beside the bed and laid his hat atop it.

"Well, young man, I can see you haven't let the pain keep you flat on your back," he said to Dahl. "That's always a good thing." He smiled. "The more you let pain stop you, the more it will stop you, I always say. Are you still spitting up blood?"

Dahl stared at him. "I didn't know I was," he said.

"Well, you were. I'm Dr. F. Washburn, young man. Who are you?" the big doctor asked, looming above the bed.

"I'm Sherman Dahl, Doctor."

"All right, then, Mr. Dahl, let's take a look at you," the doctor said. He spread the front of Dahl's shirt open for a quick look at his bruised and swollen chest. Then he pulled out a white handkerchief from his pocket

31

and said, "Spit on this. Let's see its color."

Dahl spit onto the clean handkerchief. He and the doctor both looked at it closely.

"Much better," the doctor said. "It was pinkish last time."

"I told him what you said, about his heart being bruised," Sara offered, stepping closer to the doctor beside the bed.

"That's right, as bruised as an overripe peach," the doctor commented, gazing down at Dahl as if he saw the doubt in his eyes.

"Begging your pardon, Doctor, I've never heard of a heart being bruised," Dahl said.

"You have now." The doctor gave a short grin. He looked around for an empty chair, but upon seeing none, he took a breath and said, "Mr. Dahl, the heart is a large muscle — I should know, I held many of them in my hands while studying medicine in Pennsylvania."

Sara stepped away, found a short wooden chair for the large man and pulled it over beside the bed. "Here, Dr. Washburn," she said.

"Thank you, Sara," said the doctor. He sank onto the small chair and rested his thick hands on his knees.

"The excruciating pain you feel in your chest is the same sort of pain you would feel pressing down on a small bruise on your arm, except it is a hundred times worse."

"I can't argue with that, Doctor," Dahl said. "It hurts when I move. But I've been hammered by bullets before."

"I can see you have." The doctor looked at the vest lying over the chair back. He had also noticed the scars and healed bullet wounds on Dahl's upper body when he'd first examined him.

"It'll go away," Dahl said.

"Yes, it will," the doctor agreed. "The breastbone will mend quick enough. If you lie still a few days, you'll let the bruising heal on your heart. If you don't take it easy, you could overwork your heart and get yourself buried alongside those men you killed."

"I'll take it easy a day or two," Dahl said. "But then I'll have to get on up and get back —"

He stopped himself. He had started to say *get back home,* but it had occurred to him that there would be no one waiting there for him — not anymore.

The doctor saw the change in his eyes.

"What's your hurry, young man?" he said. He gave a nod toward Sara and added, "You won't find more capable hands to take care of you than Sara's here."

Sara smiled and looked down modestly.

"No hurry, Doctor," Dahl said, "now that I think of it."

"Good, then," said the doctor, looking back and forth between the two of them. "I will warn you to keep out of Kindred whilst you're staying here."

"I've already been given a warning by Marshal Kern," Dahl said.

"A warning from Kern is a warning indeed," the doctor said. "If Sara here hasn't already told you, Emerson Kern was recently appointed to his job by our newly elected mayor, William Coakley." He gave Sara a look.

"No, I hadn't mentioned it, Doctor," Sara said.

The doctor continued talking to Dahl. "The thing is, Mayor Coakley ran on a platform of cleaning the streets of Kindred of all the riffraff cowhands and drifters who come here on their way back from a big drive. He won his election, then left town. Nobody's seen him for a week. Gone off celebrating, I suppose — damn politicians. None of them is worth a dead dog's ass."

Dahl only nodded. He ignored the remark about the new mayor and speculated, "I could find myself looked at as one of those drifters?"

"I expect nobody here knows quite how to look at you, Mr. Dahl," the doctor said. "That's why it's probably best you do as Kern says, stay out of what he now calls *his* town."

"I heard the warning. I won't be causing any trouble," Dahl said. "I don't care whose town it is."

"That's good." The big doctor pushed himself up from his chair. "Unless you need anything for the pain, I can say my job is through. I will check back on you in two days," he added. He wadded his handkerchief and put it away.

Dahl reached down into his trouser pocket and pulled out a gold coin. "Obliged for your help, Doctor." He held the coin out.

But the doctor held his thick hand out, refusing the coin. "Put your money away, young man. I'm not a doctor who takes pay for just looking at somebody and telling them what's hurting." He grinned. "You knew what was hurting before I even got here."

"I want to pay you, Doctor," Dahl insisted.

"All right, then. But for this amount, let me give you some more medical advice," the doctor said, taking the coin. "No gunfighting. No chopping wood. No hauling water . . ." He looked at Sara, then at the bed, then back at Dahl. "Anything else, I expect you'll do it whether I say so or not."

"Obliged again, Doctor," Dahl said.

Dahl and Sara watched the doctor leave.

When he was out of sight, Sara turned to Dahl and said, "Will you give me your word that you won't leave until the doctor comes back in two days and says you're well enough to ride?"

"I don't think I'm hurt that bad," Dahl said, "but yes, I promise."

Sara smiled, reaching behind her back and loosening the strings on her apron. "Well, if you're not hurt that bad, maybe . . ."

She had to let her words trail when someone knocked on the door. Without waiting for a reply or an invitation, a man walked into the room, pencil and paper in hand.

"Please keep that thought in mind," Dahl said to her in a lowered voice.

"There you are, young man," the man said with a wide grin. "The doctor just told me it would be all right for us to talk a little."

Dahl looked at Sara.

"This is Ed Dandly," Sara said, introducing the intruder. "He runs the newspaper here in Kindred." To Ed Dandly she said, "Mr. Dandly, this is Mr. Sherman Dahl. . . ."

CHAPTER 3

On the way back into Kindred, Dr. Washburn looked back along the trail and saw two men riding abreast toward town. As they drew nearer and reined their horses down to a walk, Washburn veered his buggy to one side, making room for them to pass him. The two dusty riders offered no sign of thanks for his courtesy. They rode straight ahead, stopped their horses and stepped down from their saddles out in front of the saloon.

Dr. Washburn rode on.

One of the men, a Missouri gunman named Tribold Cooper, rubbed the toe of his boot back and forth in the dirt, following a trail of blood that ran from the street to the saloon doors with his eyes.

"It looks like somebody in this cow-stop had themselves a bad day," he said. He loosened two horses hitched to the crowded rail and slapped their rumps. The horses turned and trotted away, their reins dangling in the dirt.

The other man, a gunman from Colorado Territory named Denton Bender, wiped a hand across his dry parched lips as he looked back and forth along the saloon boardwalk.

"Let's hope he didn't drink all the whiskey before he got sent to hell," he said.

"That would be my prayer for the departed, whoever he might've been," said Tribold Cooper. He spun his reins around the hitch rail, raised his rifle from its boot and wiped dust from its stock with his gloved hand.

Across the dirt street, Marshal Kern watched the two walk into the saloon. *It's about damn time. . . .* He gave a faint grin to himself, took his hat from a peg on the wall and walked out of the office, rifle in hand.

Inside the saloon, the two gunmen looked at an old swamper who stood on a chair wiping dried blood and matter from the wall with a wet cloth. Behind the bar the saloon owner called out to the newcomers from between the row of drinkers, "Don't let that blood scare you away, gentlemen. This is the most peaceful place on the frontier."

"Do we look scared to you, *idiot?*" said Cooper with a dark stare.

"Well, no, sir, you do not!" said the saloon owner, taken aback by the dusty stranger's sudden harsh remark. "I didn't mean to imply that you *were* afraid of anything. I only meant that this is out of the ordinary—"

"You need to shut up right now, barkeep, and fetch us a bottle," said Bender. "You've already made a damn poor impression."

"Sorry, gentlemen," said Jellico. He hurried away and snatched a bottle from under the bar.

Drinkers at the bar hastily scooted sidelong, making room for the pair among them. Cooper and Bender offered no sign of thanks, as if it were only natural for people to stand aside in their presence.

When Jellico placed a bottle of rye and two clean shot glasses in front them, the two men looked at each other with a smile of satisfaction.

Watching the nervous saloon owner fill their glasses, Bender instructed him, "Leave the bottle. Don't even cork it."

"Yes, sir," said Jellico.

The two stood staring coldly until the saloon owner walked away.

"Here's to *us,*" Cooper said, the two of them raising their glasses in unison.

But before either of them could touch the

glasses to their lips, Marshal Kern stepped inside the batwing doors and called out, "Don't drink that whiskey."

Other drinkers turned and looked on as the marshal walked across the floor. Cooper and Bender also turned to face him, their glasses still raised but halted for the moment. They looked at the shiny new badge on Kern's chest.

"You are asking a hell of a lot, Marshal," Cooper said with a guarded smile.

"I bet I am," Kern replied. "Jake, get me a clean glass and fill it. I want to have a nice friendly drink with my newly appointed deputies."

"You best hurry, barkeep," Bender said, gesturing a nod toward his raised glass. "If my arm gets stuck here, I'm blaming you."

Jellico acted fast. He snatched up a clean glass from a row of glasses, filled it and slid it over to the marshal.

Kern raised his glass and turned to the other drinkers who stood watching intently. Jake Jellico was poised behind the bar like an obedient hound.

"Fellows," Kern said to the drinkers, "I want all of you to meet deputies Tribold Cooper and Denton Bender. They'll be helping me clean up this town and making a respectable place for folks to raise their mud-ugly children."

The townsmen laughed at his joke, raised their glasses in a toasting gesture and welcomed the two strangers into their midst. Cooper, Bender and Kern gave each other a smile and a look and drank their rye in one gulp.

"All right, then," Kern said, setting his glass down and tapping it on the bar top for a refill. He looked along the bar and said, "All of you move down some. Give me and my deputies room to drink without smelling everybody's dried sweat."

Again the drinking men laughed; they made room along the bar and went back to their own conversations.

"Tell me I haven't hit the mother lode here," Kern whispered under his breath as the saloon settled back into its normal state.

"Yep, I've got to hand it to you, Emerson," Tribold Cooper said. "You've treed yourself the biggest cat in the canyon."

The three laughed quietly among themselves.

"Where's the other four deputies you talked about bringing in here?" Bender asked.

Kern took on a troubled look. "I'm afraid my plan took a bad turn earlier today," he said. "The four of them are dead. But it's nothing to worry about. I know plenty of others I can get to —"

"*Whoa,* hold on," said Cooper, cutting him off. "Did you say they're *all four dead?*"

"That's right. They are," said Kern, "but like I said, it's nothing to worry about. I can replace them as fast as I need to."

The two men looked at each other, both thinking about the dried blood spots they'd seen in the dirt out front.

Cooper said, "I take it these four didn't all die of natural causes, did they?"

"You know they didn't," Kern said.

"They must've had a posse on their tails?" Bender asked.

"Yes, in a manner of speaking," said Kern, trying to get away from the subject.

"In a *manner of speaking?*" Cooper said with a curious look.

"Some hired railroad gunman tracked them here and killed them," Kern explained, "even before I could swear them in and pin a badge on them." He shrugged as if it were of no concern. "But forget about them. I want us to talk about what we've got going here and how we —"

"*One* man killed them? All of them?" Bender questioned, clearly stunned.

"That's right. One man," Kern said, recognizing that the two weren't going to

42

let it go right away. "He caught them off guard and killed them."

"Who were these four gunmen?" Cooper asked.

"Curtis Hicks and some others," said Kern. Again he tried to pass it off with a shrug.

"What *others?*" Cooper asked bluntly, getting tired of Kern trying to play it all down.

"Ernie Newman, Ned Carver and Cordell Garrant," Kern said with a sigh. "Like I said, they got caught off guard."

"Damn!" said Bender. "You just named four of the toughest dogs ever let out of hell."

"No," said Cooper, "the man who killed them is the toughest dog ever let out of hell. What's the chances of getting him to work with us?"

"Don't think I haven't given it some thought," said Kern. "But the truth is if this fellow wasn't wearing a bullet-stopping vest, he'd be dead."

"I've heard of those vests," said Bender. "I expect anybody can be a tough dog if he's wearing one."

"Cordell Garrant put two bullet holes in this jake's chest," said Kern. "Either one would have killed him, had he not been wearing the vest. He's laid up outside of town licking his wounds right now."

Bender and Cooper looked at each other. Cooper turned to Kern with a slight grin. "Are you thinking what I think you're thinking?"

"Not if you're thinking I want you to go kill this man," said Kern, getting a crafty look on his face. "I'm thinking it's best we leave him be, let him clear on out of here."

"Suit yourself," Bender said. "But you change your mind, we can go put a few bullets in his head — make sure he's not wearing a bullet-stopping hat." He grinned at his joke.

Cooper said in contemplation, "What kind of man wears a bullet-stopping vest anyways?"

"One who's scared of getting shot?" Bender offered.

"Maybe scared," said Cooper, still wrestling the thought. "Maybe smart."

Bender shrugged. "It doesn't matter, scared or smart. They bury both kinds every day of the week."

Kern said, "I told him to keep out of Kindred. I'm figuring he'll cut on out of here soon as he's up and around."

"And if he's not?" Cooper asked.

"It makes no difference," said Kern. "Soon as you two get settled in, we're going to start collecting guns. Once the guns are gone we'll start putting pressure on these merchants and townsfolk, begin drawing us in some money."

"That's the kind of talk I like hearing," said Cooper.

"Me too," replied Bender. He lowered his voice even more and asked, "But why squeeze them for money a little at a time? Why not raid this place and take it all at once?"

"Because that's an outlaw's way of doing things," said Kern. "I'm through with that. We do it the way I'm saying — it's their government at work for them." He grinned. "It's as respectable as sugar on a pie." He sniffed his rye and tossed it back.

Sugar on a pie . . . ?

Cooper and Bender smiled at him.

Sara pretended not to be listening as Sherman Dahl and the newspaperman talked, Dandly asking questions about the gunfight and about the Western Railways Alliance for whom Dahl worked. Sara listened as Dahl answered, taking his time. He impressed her, appearing to be a man who was unaccustomed to answering to anyone about anything. She liked that about him, she told herself, as she busied herself straightening up the small room when she knew no straightening was needed.

As she listened to Dahl speak, she positioned herself in ways that allowed her to look at him without him knowing — catching glances like some young schoolgirl, she thought. But that was all right. She liked what she saw. She'd known many men during her time working the crib rooms above the Lucky Devil Saloon. For the most part they had all come to look the same to her. They paid their money, they lay down atop her and in a moment they walked away. Their faces were soon only blurry images in her memory.

But this one was different. Dahl was young, handsome and memorable. He had a gentlemanly bearing about him. He was quiet, well mannered and appeared to be easygoing in spite of the fact that she had witnessed him shoot down four men amid a hail of blazing gunfire. *Well, nobody's perfect. . . .* She smiled to herself.

Yes, he had killed them, she allowed herself to admit, but they were all four wanted men. In a way Sherman Dahl was a lawman only doing his job. She looked at the bulletproof vest hanging on the chair back and thought of what the outcome would have been if he'd not been wearing it. But then she forced herself to look away, not wanting to think about that.

Instead she wanted to think about the respectful manner Dahl appeared to have for everyone around him, even Ed Dandly, who was known to be a little pushy in his pursuit of the news. There was good in this man, she'd already decided to herself. There was gentleness and sincerity in his eyes.

Dahl had answered Dandly's questions regarding the shooting and the four wanted outlaws: who they were, what they had done and who had sent him to bring them to justice.

". . . And just how long do you plan to be with us here in Kindred, now that your job is finished, Mr. Dahl?" Dandly asked in closing. He continued to scribble down Dahl's replies to his preceding questions.

Dahl cut a glance to Sara Cayes before answering Dandly. "I've just promised Miss Sara I'd be here until the doctor tells me it's all right for me to leave," he said.

Seeing the guarded look Dahl and the young woman gave each other, Dandly stood up and closed his notepad and put his pencil away.

"I understand," he said. But before he turned to leave, he shot Dahl one more question. "Did the marshal tell you what is about to happen in Kindred in the next couple of days?"

"No," said Dahl. "He only told me to stay out of his town, and I agreed to do so."

"Yes," said Dandly. "But aren't you interested in knowing why he doesn't want you in Kindred?"

"No," said Dahl, "not particularly. I did what I came here to do."

"Kindred is going to be disarmed," Dandly said without regarding Dahl's explanation.

"Disarmed, huh?" Dahl sounded curious, but no more than mildly so.

"Yes, you heard me correctly," said Dandly. He gave Dahl a studious look. "What are your thoughts on something like that working here on this wilderness frontier?"

Dahl only shook his head. "It's not something I should comment on," he said. "I wish all of you the best."

"Two days from now anyone wearing a gun in Kindred will have to hand it over to the marshal," he said. "Do you suppose that he wants you to stay out of town because he knows how difficult it would be to disarm a man such as yourself?"

Dahl didn't like the question. "If a man *such as myself* were to go into Kindred, he

48

should abide by the law, whatever that law may be. I'm no troublemaker, Mr. Dandly."

"So, if you were to go into Kindred, you would turn your guns over voluntarily if called upon to do so?" Dandly asked.

"I won't be going into Kindred, Mr. Dandly, so I don't understand why you would ask me," Dahl replied, not wanting to give the newsman anything that could be misinterpreted or misquoted.

"Come now, Mr. Dahl," Dandly said. "Surely you don't mind giving your opinion. After all, you do make a living with your gun." He sounded a bit frustrated by Dahl's reluctance.

"Not in Kindred, I don't," Dahl said firmly. "In Kindred, my job is finished."

"I see," Dandly said quietly, realizing that he wasn't getting anywhere. He let out a breath and said, "In that case, so is my job here."

Sara stepped over to the door as Dandly turned to leave. Placing his hat back atop his head, Dandly smiled at her.

"You take good care of Mr. Dahl, Miss Sara," he said. "And a very lovely afternoon to you both."

As soon as Dandly stepped through the open door, Sara closed it quickly and slid the bolt into position.

49

"There, finally," she said, letting out a breath and leaning back against the closed door for a moment. "Now, where were we, Sherman?"

Dahl noted it was the first time she had called him by his first name.

"We both know where we were, Sara," he replied in a quiet tone. He scooted over slightly in the bed, making room for her beside him in spite of his painful condition.

CHAPTER 4

Three riders sat atop their dusty, sweat-streaked horses gazing down on the rock canyon below them. A stream of dust loomed behind a slow-moving, heavily loaded wagon. Three horses led the Conestoga-type wagon, and an empty place for a fourth horse gave the rig an off-balance appearance. Atop the wagon stood a row of arched wooden bows. But the canvas that had once covered the bow rib-work was gone, exposing the wagon's cargo to the harsh desert.

"I don't believe my tired eyes," said Jason Catlo to his brother, Philbert, and "Buck the Mule" Jennings. He handed a pair of battered army binoculars to his brother, keeping his gaze on the wagon.

"I want to look too," said Jennings.

Raising the binoculars to his eyes, Philbert said sidelong to the big dirty gunman, "Wait until you've been here longer, Buck the Mule. Not everybody starts right off borrowing another man's personals."

Jennings stared at him with a seething look, but he kept quiet.

Looking down through the smudged lens, Philbert chuffed a short laugh and said, "You're right, brother Jason, she is a fine little darling, that's for sure." His eyes moved along with the lens, drawing in close on the face of a young blond-haired woman seated beside the wagon's driver.

"Not the woman, Phil," said Jason Catlo. "I'm talking about that old wagon. That's a relic. I haven't seen one since I was just a boy."

"You look at what suits you, brother. I'll do the same," said Philbert.

He moved his eyes and the lens up and down the woman as she shook out her damp hair and pushed it back from her face. Her dusty sunbonnet lay folded on her lap.

"Let me see her, damn it," Jennings said, getting irritated trying to see the woman clearly with his naked eyes.

"Do not curse, Buck the Mule," Philbert warned him, raising a finger toward him for emphasis. "You can see her when I'm through looking."

"Let him look, Phil," said Jason Catlo, recognizing trouble a-brew in Jennings' eyes.

"I will," said Philbert, "soon as I'm finished." He chuffed again and said under his breath, "Honey, why don't you lift that dress on up, get some cool air on your knees? You could roast yourself in all this heat."

"All right, that's enough," said Jennings. "I want to see too." His big dirty hand went to the butt of the Colt holstered on his hip.

"Let him look, Phil," Jason insisted.

Watching the woman place the sunbonnet back atop her head and step down out of sight, off the other side of the moving wagon, Philbert chuckled, lowered the binoculars and rubbed his eyes.

"All right, Buck the Mule . . . your turn," he said. He handed the binoculars sidelong to the big, dirty gunman.

Jennings nervously raised the binoculars to his eyes and stared down at the distant wagon. Then he lowered the lens in disappointment and gave Philbert Catlo a scorching stare.

"She's gone," he said in a raspy growl, the binoculars squeezed tight in his broad filthy hands.

"Well, you can't expect a gal to wait forever," said Philbert. "I learned that coming home from the war."

"I'm riding down there, damn it," said Jennings. "I'm going to say 'Howdy-do' to her, big as day." He pitched the binoculars to Jason Catlo.

"*Is* you, now?" said Philbert, taunting him. "What about that big ol' flat-headed boy sitting beside her?"

"What about him?" said Jennings.

"You saw that long shotgun barrel sticking up beside him," said Philbert. "Suppose he was to raise it and blow a hole through you the size of Aunt Ethel's bloomers?"

"Then I expect I'll ride in and kill him before he can get it raised and cocked," said Jennings. He started to jerk around on his reins.

"Whoa! Hang on, Mule," said Jason. "We're all riding down there. But let's feel this thing out when we get a little closer. Maybe we'll stop and let you say 'Howdy-do.' Maybe we won't. It's all up to how quick he grabs on to that shotgun."

"Huh . . . ?" Jennings had a hard time grasping it.

The Catlo brothers looked at each other.

"If he seems a little shy and hesitates to arm up right off," said Jason, "we'll jump right in and help ourselves. Take whatever we want, wagon and all if it suits us."

"But if he arms right up just as soon as we get closer," Philbert put in, "maybe we'll ride on past them and leave them about their business." He grinned.

"It's our way to look things over good before we jump in," said Jason.

"Yeah, because there's nothing like a blast of buckshot to ruin a man's day," Philbert said, with a thin teasing smile.

The big dirty gunman finally settled a little and gave a grin himself. "Hell, all right. I'm with you two, whatever you think best."

"*Gracias,* Mule," said Jason. He turned his horse to the thin path leading down into the rock canyon. "Now let's all three find ourselves a good friendly face and go see what we've got there."

From the wagon seat, Charles Knox, traces in hand, looked down at his wife of six weeks, Celia Timble Knox, walking along beside the slow-moving wagon.

"That is not a safe thing to do," he said to her, lightly scolding her for stepping down from the wagon without waiting for him to stop the rig for her first. "Nor is it very lady-like," he added.

Celia Knox smiled up at him. She had scooped up a palmful of small loose rocks and was flipping them with her thumb as she spoke.

"Which is it that annoys you the most, my dear *husband?*" she asked with a playful smile. "Is it my lack of regard for safety, or my loose, unladylike abandon?"

"You know I'm right," Charles said. "Luckily there was no one around to see you."

"Luckily there was no one to see my *unladylike* behavior last night while we camped by the stream. Should I try to be more constrained from now on . . . ?"

Charles Knox looked away with the trace of a smile and shook his head. He failed to notice the first thin rise of dust looming on a trail higher up among the rocks.

"You beat all I have ever seen, my dear *wife*," he said.

"I should certainly hope so," she said, cocking a hand on her hip. She flipped a tiny rock up at him. The rock bounced from her husband's leg, off the front edge of the wagon and fell down the tail of one of the horses. The big horse didn't flinch. But Charles tightened his grip on the traces just in case.

"Don't be doing that, Celia," he said. "We don't want to spook these horses."

"These horses are too tired to spook, husband," Celia replied. She paused, then asked, "How much farther is it to Kindred?"

"Tomorrow by noon, we should be there," Charles replied, watching the trail ahead.

"Why don't you climb back up here? We'll find ourselves a way to pass the time."

"Oh . . . ?" Celia said coyly. "Should I wait for you to stop the wagon, or just *climb* on up, *unladylike?*"

Charles glanced around, then said, "Since there's nobody watching, climb on up this time."

"Aren't you afraid it's a little too dangerous?" Celia asked.

Charles put both traces in one hand and reached his free hand down to her. "Climb up to me," he said, his breath sounding a little excited. "I love watching you climb."

Celia let out a soft sigh. "Oh, all right, if you insist," she said with mock reluctance.

"Oh yes, I *do* insist," said Charles. "The sooner the better."

Celia gazed up at him, seeing the aroused look in his eyes. "You are naughty," she said, taking his hand.

The wagon rolled on.

When the Catlo brothers and Buck the Mule Jennings spotted the wagon again, the three were on a downward trail less than a hundred feet above. The man and woman in the wagon, thinking they were alone, leaned back on its stiff seat, locked in a lovers' embrace.

"Lord God . . . ," Jennings whispered as if in awe, staring down wide-eyed from the cover of a scrub juniper along the edge of the trail. "He's got her dress unbuttoned and everything."

Philbert Catlo gave a quiet chuckle and teased the big gunman. "Don't throw yourself into a staggering fit over it," he said. "That's the way men and women act when they're alone."

Jennings sat atop his horse, his breathing growing heavier and quicker as he stared down at the wagon below. Philbert drew his brother's attention to the big gunman's worsening condition.

"Jesus, man, are you all right?" Jason said in disgust, looking Jennings up and down.

"We're going to have to get him to a whorehouse, soon as we get to Kindred," Philbert said, "else our riding animals could be in danger."

"That's not funny," Jennings managed to say sidelong without taking his eyes off the couple below.

"Damn right it ain't," Philbert chuffed, he and his brother turning their horses back to the trail.

Before the Catlos nudged their horses forward, Jason said to Jennings, "Well, are you coming or not? You're the one who wanted to say howdy."

"Oh yes, I'm coming," Jennings said in a hushed, excited voice. "I wouldn't miss this for nothing in the world."

In the wagon, Celia Knox writhed and squirmed on the hard wagon seat until she managed to get her hands up between herself and her husband and push him away.

"Charles . . . stop, please," she said in a breathless voice.

"I — I can't," Charles said, his words ending between her damp naked breasts as he pushed his face back down between them.

"No, stop! I mean it, Charles," Celia said, pushing harder against his chest with both hands. "I heard something." She stared up warily along the higher trail above them.

Charles stopped himself and collapsed back beside her with a sigh.

"Okay, okay . . . ," he said. He pushed his hair back from his eyes and stared up along the trail with his wife. "I thought I heard something up there too, a while ago."

"You did?" Celia asked, one hand clutching the front of her unbuttoned dress. "Why didn't you say something?"

Charles sighed again and blew out a breath, collecting himself. "My mind was on other things," he said. He cut a glance to her, then looked back along the downward trail.

"You should have said something," she whispered.

"Don't worry," said Charles. "It was probably nothing more than a —" His words were cut short when they both saw three riders step their horses out onto the trail in front of them.

"Oh my God," Celia whispered, "they saw us." With no time to button her dress, she quickly tucked her naked breasts out of sight and clutched the front of the dress tighter.

"Hello, the wagon," Jason Catlo called out with a friendly smile. The three held their horses back a safe distance.

Charles grabbed the reins with one hand and jerked back on them, stopping the horses. At the same time he grabbed the brake handle with his other hand and yanked back on it. The wagon jolted to a clumsy halt.

Philbert Catlo held back a laugh and called out, "We didn't mean to interrupt anything."

"What do you want?" Charles Knox called out, shaken by their sudden presence. He realized he and his wife had heard something, and the thought of what these men had most likely seen gave him an ill and uneasy feeling.

"We're strangers to these parts," Philbert said, looking all around. "We appear to have gotten ourselves all turned round and lost." He gestured a thumb toward the big dirty gunman to his left. "Anyway, our friend here wanted to ride down and tell you both 'Howdy,' so here we are."

As Philbert spoke, he moved his horse forward a cautious step. The other two followed only a few feet behind him, spreading away from him slightly as they approached.

"Charles, tell them to stop," Celia whispered, clutching her dress shut.

"Stay where you are, mister," Charles called out in a forceful voice. "We weren't expecting company."

The three horsemen stopped at once. "We can see that, mister," Philbert Catlo called out respectfully, now less than thirty feet from the wagon. "We don't mean to cause any trouble. Like I said, we got all turned around is all." He averted his eyes away from Celia.

Charles nodded in the direction of Kindred. Beside him, Celia knew of nothing to do but hold her dress closed and look down until they left.

"Town is that way," Charles called out.

"Keep riding and you'll be there this time tomorrow."

"I see," said Philbert. He raised his hat and ran his fingers back through his damp hair. "That's a relief. We were afraid we'd really caused ourselves —" He stopped and stared, rising slightly in his stirrups for a closer look at the wagon. "Easy, stranger . . . ," he murmured in a frightened tone.

"What is it, mister?" Charles Knox asked, seeing the concerned look on his face.

Philbert said, "You weren't fixing to draw that shotgun on us, were you?"

"What?" exclaimed Charles.

"That shotgun beside your hand," Jason Catlo called out. "My brother thought you were about to throw down on us."

"Charles, please, let's go," Celia whispered to her husband.

Charles ignored her. He glanced to the side of the wagon seat, then smiled at the three worried horsemen.

"Gentlemen, that's not a shotgun," he said disarmingly. "That's only a broom." He put his hand near the up-stuck object and said, "May I show you?"

"By all means, please do," Philbert said.

Charles picked up a long broom by its handle and raised it for the three men to see.

"A broom," Philbert said with a dark chuckle. "Boy, do I ever feel foolish!"

"Me too," said Jason as all three men stepped their horses closer to the wagon. "Then where *is* your gun, sir, if you don't mind me asking?" he said.

"I don't carry a gun, gentlemen," Charles said. "I never have, and I never will. We — that is, my wife here and myself — believe guns are an evil we can live without if we all exercise mutual respect for one another."

"Now, there's a fresh and optimistic attitude if ever I've seen one," Philbert said. He stepped his horse closer, now with less caution.

"One that I for one greatly admire," Jason said, moving alongside him.

"Really?" Charles asked with a smile. "Well, it just happens that the town of Kindred has voted to ban guns. That's why the wife and I are going there. We think that the only way to ever rise above this violence is to —"

"Shut up, idiot," said Philbert Catlo.

His Colt came up from its holster. As a shot exploded from his gun barrel, a blue-orange blaze exploded beside him; the other two men had drawn their guns and fired. Charles Knox flew out of the wagon seat and landed dead on the ground, three bullets in him.

Celia screamed loud and long. Her screaming continued as she jumped from the wagon seat and flung herself atop her dead husband. The three gunmen sat on their horses watching her, their guns smoking in their hands.

"We did her a favor," Philbert said to the other two amid the woman's screaming and sobbing. "It's unnatural, a man thinking that way."

Celia pulled and tugged at her dead husband as if she still hoped she could wake him up. The front of her unbuttoned dress fell open; her pale breasts spilled out into the sunlight.

"Yeah," said Jason, "somebody would have had to kill him sooner or later."

Buck the Mule Jennings stared down at the woman, his mouth agape, watching her sob and scream and pull at her dead husband's bloody shirt. "She sure has pretty teats," he said.

CHAPTER 5

In the late afternoon Philbert and Jason Catlo stood in a shadowed rocky gully where they had taken the wagon out of sight from the trail. The wagon horses were dead; they'd unhitched them and shot them down. Their rifles were still smoking in their hands.

"I wish I knew something to do with this wagon," said Jason, looking it over. "These big prairie schooners are getting scarce. Soon, there'll be none of them left."

"Well now, won't that be a damn shame?" his brother said with sarcasm. "Maybe we ought to build you a barn to keep it in. You can come see it any time you take a notion."

"Stop goading me over it, brother," Jason warned. "I just happen to admire things like this. Is there something wrong with that?"

"Naw, not really." Philbert shook his head. "I just can't see it, is all. To me a *wagon* is a wagon. I can't make more of it than that."

Jason looked off toward an overhang of rock where they had dragged the woman and ripped her clothes from her, ignoring her pleas and sobs. A curl of smoke from a small campfire rose from under the overhang.

"It's getting dark," he said. "We best get some coffee and tend to our horses."

The two walked back toward the hastily made campsite where Buck the Mule waited for them with the woman.

"I told him to shoot her when he was finished with her," Philbert said. "Do you think the fool followed through?"

Before Jason could answer, a pistol shot exploded from beneath the overhang.

"Well, what do you know?" Philbert chuckled. "He finally did what he's supposed to do."

"You ought to stop crowding him so much," Jason said to his brother. "Buck the Mule Jennings is not a man to mess with."

"He's a thickheaded fool," Philbert said. "I don't know why we ever took him in with us."

"Because of what I just said," Jason insisted. "He's not a man to mess with. He'll kill anybody we tell him to. Shooting that woman proves it. When the time comes to chop down a bank guard or a stagecoach guard, he'll do it without batting an eye."

"So far," said Philbert, "I don't see us doing much business, bank, stagecoach or otherwise."

"We will, though, and soon," said Jason.

"Yeah, we better," said Philbert. He grinned. "I need some money for the finer things in life . . . whiskey, whores, poker . . ."

"What do you make of what the idiot told us before we shot him?" Jason asked.

"Which idiot?" Philbert asked.

Jason stared at him.

"Oh, the *no-gun* idiot," said Philbert. "I thought it was real intriguing."

"Intriguing enough to go see about?" Jason asked. "I figure if the whole town is unarmed, we might just find ourselves a soft spot and sink our teeth in it."

"We could do that . . . ," Philbert said, considering it as they walked on.

At the campsite beneath the rock overhang, Buck the Mule Jennings sat huddled beside the small fire, his hands wrapped around a tin cup full of steaming coffee.

"Did you shoot the woman like we told you to?" Philbert asked.

"Yeah, I shot her, like you *told me to,*" Jennings said in a sad and grudging tone of voice, his eyes on the flickering flames.

Jason gave his brother a slight smile. "See

what I mean — anything we tell him to do," he said, quiet enough that only his brother could hear.

"Yeah, I see," said Philbert, "if he *really did* shoot her." He said to Jennings, "Where's she lying, Buck the Mule?"

Jennings looked up from the flames at him. "Don't you believe me?" he asked.

"Oh, I believe you," said Philbert. "I just enjoy looking at naked dead women. Now, where is she?"

"She's over there," said Jennings, nodding toward the bush-covered edge of the overhang. "I stuck her under the brush with the man."

"Yeah . . . ?" Philbert said skeptically. "Well, I'll just go take myself a look-see." He stooped and picked up a burning stick from the fire, and held it up as a torch.

"Don't go over there," said Jennings. He stood up, tin cup in hand.

"Oh? Why not?" said Philbert.

"Because I don't want you to," said the big dirty gunman.

"That's not a good enough reason, Buck the Mule," said Philbert. He moved away slowly, keeping his eyes on Jennings.

Jason stepped back watching, keeping his hand poised near his holstered Colt. He was ready to cover his brother if he needed to.

"Easy, Buck the Mule," he cautioned the broad-shouldered gunman, seeing a look of rage come over Jennings' grimy, beard-stubbled face. "My brother just wants to make sure she's dead. It never hurts to make sure, does it?"

"I killed her, just like I was told," Jennings said.

Philbert held the burning stick down and illuminated the area below the brush. The flicker of firelight shone on the naked woman, a hole in the center of her back. The bloody body of the man was there too, and Philbert was surprised to see that Jennings had undressed him as well. Even more shocking, though, was the gruesome way the body was left.

"Jesus . . . !" he said aloud.

"What is it?" Jason asked, not daring to take his eyes away from Jennings.

"You'll have to come see for yourself," Philbert said in a disgusted tone of voice.

"I never done nothing to him," Jennings said, pacing back and forth beside the flickering fire like some irritated grizzly. "I never touched that man's eye! I only undressed him," he said.

Jason walked over and looked down with his brother at the naked couple. Jennings had broken the broomstick in half and jammed half of it down firmly into the dead man's right eye.

"What the hell . . . ?"

Jason and Philbert stared at each other, bewildered.

"Well, somebody sure impaled him," said Philbert.

"I know, but it wasn't me," Jennings insisted. "I only undressed him."

"But why'd you even do that?" Jason asked.

"Because, so they both could, you know . . . look just alike," Jennings said.

"Oh, I see," Jason said, placating the irritated, pacing gunman. They both noted that Jennings had arranged the man and woman together in some strange embrace.

Philbert whispered, "He's one crazy sumbitch, brother."

"Yeah, I can see that for myself," Jason whispered in reply. "Still, he'll do whatever we tell him."

The two walked back to the campfire, sat down and poured coffee into tin cups, carefully keeping their gun hands free.

Jennings still paced back and forth, seething, staring at them from across the fire. Jason and Philbert looked at each other.

"I didn't do nothing wrong," Jennings

said. He slung coffee from his cup to the ground.

"Nobody said you did, Buck the Mule," Jason said to him. "Now, why don't you pour yourself some more coffee, sit back down and take it easy for a spell?"

"Yeah." Philbert shrugged. "You did like any normal person would do. You stabbed a stick in a dead man's eye, took off all his clothes and wrapped his arms around a woman you shot." He chuffed to himself. "Sounds right as rain to us. . . ."

The three finished their coffee quietly and crawled beneath their blankets, each of them keeping a hand close to the butt of his gun.

The next morning, before the first rays of sunlight had mantled the horizon, they awakened, saddled their horses and rode away toward Kindred.

"If nothing else, it'll be fun seeing a whole town walking around unarmed," Philbert said, nudging his horse up into a trot.

No sooner were the three out of sight than, in the brush, consciousness came slowly upon Celia Knox in a haze of pain and fear. Her first thought was that she had just awakened from what she imagined to be the worst nightmare she'd ever had. But as shock and horror came back to her, she realized this had been no bad dream. This was real.

She felt Charles' cold forearm on her; she saw his pale, purple-tinted face only inches from hers. She did not realize that the broken broomstick was protruding from his eye until she had scooted back from beneath his forearm and stared more clearly at his lifeless face. When she did realize what she was seeing, her first impulse was to scream, yet she stopped herself and scooted farther away in spite of the terrible pain in the center of her back.

"Oh God . . . ," she whispered. A few feet away she spotted her dead husband's trousers lying on the ground. With all of her effort, she dragged herself over the downed brush and rocky ground and grabbed the trousers with a bloody hand.

Now, if she could just get those trousers on, she told herself, in her addled state. Once she had them on, pulled up and buckled around her waist, she'd be all right. . . .

Sherman Dahl watched Sara Cayes light a candle. His eyes followed her in the flickering glow as she carried the candle dish to

72

the bedside and set it on the small, wooden nightstand. He liked being with her — liked it so much it troubled him, he thought to himself.

"Her name was Lilly," he said to her, answering the question she'd asked as she'd walked to the table a moment earlier. "Lilly Jones," he said, "and yes, I cared a lot for her."

"I can tell you did," she said. She smiled and loosened her cotton gown, letting it fall around her ankles before she stepped out of it.

"Oh? How can you tell?" Dahl said, making room for her beneath the quilt beside him.

"You're gentle with me," she said. "I think you must have been gentle with her. I can tell how a man treats his woman by the way he treats me. Doves know a lot about men and their women. We should, as many men as we open our knees for."

"Don't talk like that about yourself," Dahl said quietly.

"But it's the truth," she said. "Isn't the truth what everybody wants to hear?"

"The truth might be best for us, but it's not always what we want to hear." Dahl looked into her eyes. He liked it there. "Anyway, I'm always gentle with women. At

73

least that's what I try to be."

"Always . . . ?" she questioned, giving him a look in the soft flicker of candlelight.

"You know what I mean," he said.

They lay in silence for a moment. Whatever troubled him about her surfaced enough for him to mention it.

"I'm not looking to replace her — Lilly, that is," he said quietly.

"I wouldn't *try* to replace her," Sara whispered. "I know I'm only with you while you're here."

"And when it's time to go?" Dahl said.

She smiled. "Then it's time to go," she said. "I understand that."

Satisfied, he let out a breath and whispered to himself, "Good. . . ." And he took her in his arms.

Maybe he *was* trying to replace the woman he'd lost. Maybe he knew it deep down, and maybe that was what had troubled him.

"I just want whatever time we have together to be good," Sara said, moving over and atop him, her lips close to his ear, "and *that is* the truth."

Dahl smiled in response.

Outside, from a trail flanking the widow's shack a half mile away, Tribold Cooper and Denton Bender sat atop their horses and started at the bedroom window, watching the candle glow fade and eventually go out.

"I bet I can guess what they're doing in there," said Tribold.

"Yeah," said Bender, "and here we are, like geese watching thunder." He spit in disgust. "We ought to ride over and shoot this man full of holes. To hell with what Kern says."

"No," said Tribold Cooper, "we do it his way, for now anyway."

"I can't see what the marshal's got in mind, the way he's talking," said Bender.

"I see what he wants," said Cooper. "He wants to bleed this town a little at a time instead of all at once. Once they're unarmed, he can put the squeeze on them hard as he wants to, any time he wants to. What can they do about it?"

"I expect that's one way," said Bender. "But I say, once we disarm this town, we need to rob it blind, burn it to the ground, then move on. Maybe ride over to Méjico, teach a few important words of *inglés* to some willing senoritas." He grinned. "Why be two-faced about it?"

"I agree," said Tribold, "but for now it's Kern's play. We're just the hired guns — I mean *deputies*," he corrected himself.

The two sat in silence for a moment, staring out at the dark silhouette of the widow's shack against the purple starlit sky.

"It wouldn't hurt to ride over and take a closer look, would it?" Bender asked. "Maybe even look in through the window?"

"I was just now thinking the same thing," Cooper said with a sly grin. "What Marshal Kern doesn't know won't hurt him. . . ."

Lying beside Sara, Dahl heard the slightest sound of hoof striking stone on a flat rocky stretch of ground beyond the shack, farther from town. He stiffened and held Sara in a way that signaled her to stay still.

After a second, she whispered in his ear, "What is it, Sherman?"

Dahl didn't answer. Instead, he touched his finger to her lips and gestured for her to stay put. He stood up from the bed, naked, feeling the pain in his chest, and stepped into his trousers.

Sara watched him slip his big Colt from its holster in the rolled-up gun belt. She heard the quiet, metallic click of the cylinder as he checked the gun on his way to the door.

On the rocky ground headed toward the shack, their horses at a walk, Cooper and Bender didn't see the door open in the black of night; they didn't see Dahl ease out onto the porch and stand with his back to

76

the front of the shack.

"Can you keep that damn hay burner from stumbling on every rock in the territory?" Cooper asked Bender in a harsh, angry whisper.

"He's all right now, damn it," Bender replied in the same tone of voice.

Dahl called out, "Who goes there?"

"Oh, shit!" said Bender. Instinctively, he drew his Colt and fired toward the sound of Dahl's voice before he could stop himself.

Identifying the flash of light from the gunshot as his target, Dahl fired three shots as fast as he could pull them off. One bullet streaked past Bender's head, another whistled past Cooper's side, so close that he felt the slap of its wind on his shirt. The third bullet struck Bender's boot heel as he turned his horse and batted his heels to its sides.

Dahl heard the gunman let out a squall as the impact of the bullet stung the sole of his foot and ripped his boot away. Then he heard only the sound of running horses headed out across the rocky ground.

"What was that?" Sara asked, rushing from the bed out onto the font porch, nothing but a sheet held to her bosom to cover herself. "Are you all right?"

"I'm all right," Dahl said, his arm going

around her as she stepped out the door. "It was nothing," he said, gazing into the darkness. "Leastwise, nothing I wasn't expecting."

"You — you're not going after them, are you?" she asked warily.

Dahl looked down at her, seeing her in the soft pale purple light of the moon, feeling the warmth of her against his bare chest. "What do you think?" he said quietly, his Colt still smoking in his hand.

The two turned and walked back inside. Dahl bolted the door behind them and followed her back to the bed.

CHAPTER 6

At dawn, Sherman Dahl walked out of the widow's shack and stood in its weedy, rock-strewn yard. He carried his rifle in the crook of his arm. To his left stood the main street leading into Kindred. To his right, a dusty trail ran out across the rocky flatlands. He studied the skyline of the town for a moment, then turned and walked in the direction of the flatlands.

The pain in his chest had diminished greatly; the purple skin color had already begun to lighten and heal. He could ride, he was certain. But he was in no hurry. He liked it here. He *liked* Sara Cayes, he told himself, and that was as much as he wanted to make of it.

Out beyond the front yard, he found the hoofprints of the two horses from the night before. At a point where he saw the prints turn full circle and head back the way they'd come, he stooped down, picked up the busted boot heel and looked it over in his palm.

Town Marshal, Emerson Kern . . . ?

No, not Kern himself, he told himself. Maybe someone he'd sent, just to keep an eye on things.

All right. . . . He could abide that. Kindred was the marshal's town. Kern had a right to send someone snooping if he thought it was necessary. In that case, Dahl thought, he was glad no one got shot last night. That could have complicated matters. After a moment he pitched the broken heel away, dusted his hands together and walked back to the shack. Silvery sunlight had begun to ascend, wreathing the eastern horizon.

When Dahl and Sara had finished breakfast, and the only two plates and eating utensils Sara owned were washed and dried and put away, they walked to the rickety, weathered barn where Dahl's horse stood in the only usable stall.

"I bought some hay and some grain from the livery barn," Sara said, gesturing toward the fresh pile and the small feed sack of grain sitting beside it. "The liveryman delivered it."

"You think of everything," Dahl said. Before he left, he would pay her for the hay, the grain and everything else she'd done for him. But now was not the time to discuss it.

"I try to," she said proudly. She walked over and untied the top of the grain sack, pulling out a small wooden scoop. "See?"

Dahl walked over, took the scoop from her hand and gathered up a generous portion for his horse. He walked to the stall, reached over the rail and poured the grain into a gnawed-down feed box. The big tan dun took to the grain.

"How long have you been coming here, getting this place back into shape?" he asked.

"For a while," Sara said, "but I don't know if you can call this getting it back into shape."

"All this, you've done with money you make at the saloon?" he asked.

"At the *brothel*," she said, keeping nothing back from him. "Jake Jellico's Lucky Devil is a saloon *and brothel*, remember?" she said.

"I remember." Dahl nodded, rubbing the dun's head as the animal munched on grain.

"Anyway," Sara said, "I managed to save back enough of my own money and get the bedding, the curtains, the plates and dinnerware. The rest was mostly just cleaning up and fixing up a few things."

Dahl looked at her. "You've done quite a

lot," he said. He wondered exactly why she'd gone to so much effort — what was motivating her — yet he wasn't about to ask.

But as if she had seen the question in his eyes, Sara began to explain. "I know it seems foolish, a dove coming here, spending her free time . . . her money doing all this." She gestured a hand to indicate the entire rundown patch of land and its weathered buildings. "But I figured, who knows, maybe someday things will change for me. I might not be a whore all my life." She smiled with optimism. "Does that make any sense?"

"Yes, it does," Dahl said. He knew few doves ever worked their way out of the brothels and moved on to more respectable lives. But it was not for him to say. He had started his adult life as a small-town schoolteacher. Look at him now, he thought. A man killer, a *fighting man,* a gun for hire available to the highest bidder.

The Teacher, some called him.

Sara shrugged. "Anyway, not everything we do has to make perfect sense. Have you ever done something just because it felt like the right thing to do?"

"Yes, I have," Dahl said, "but it seems like a long time ago." He offered a thin smile.

Sara saw the weariness in his face. She reached out and brushed a strand of his long wheat-colored hair out of his face.

"It probably wasn't as long ago as you think," she said, gazing into his cold blue eyes. Trying to fathom whatever secrets he kept there.

"Probably not, but it's been a while," Dahl said. He looked away for just a second, just long enough to keep himself from giving anything away.

But her eyes followed his.

"I'm not the person to say what's good and what's not." He turned his eyes back to hers. "Sometimes what's *good* take its time revealing itself to us."

"I know," she said softly. "But sometimes it's all we get . . . just knowing that *good* might be coming to us."

"I suppose," he said. He tried to turn away again, but this time she pressed a hand to his cheek and held his gaze.

"Were you in the war, Sherman Dahl?" she asked, her tone trying to keep the question as light as possible. She gave a slight smile. "You remind me of men I've known who were in the war."

"Oh, how so?" Dahl asked.

"Just a sadness, a seriousness or something," she said, still holding his face. She liked looking at him. He was a handsome man, she thought, appraising him. Hair the color of sunlight . . .

His eyes were pale blue and cold at a glance, but they warmed as she searched deeper into them. He wore a trimmed downturned mustache only a shade darker than his hair. The shadow of his beard stubble was a shade darker yet.

"Yes, I was in the war," he said. "Before the war I taught school. When the war had ended I went back and taught, for a time anyway." He paused as if wondering how much further to go about himself, his past.

"And . . . ?" she asked quietly, not pushing, but still encouraging him to take it as far as he felt comfortable.

"A band of men — the Peltry Gang — attacked the town where I taught school," he explained. "They burned the schoolhouse to the ground and rode away. I rode with a posse led by Sheriff Abner Webb, and we hunted them down." He looked away, then back to her and said, "Afterward, I never seemed able to get settled back into teaching. I've been a hired gun ever since — a fighting man, I call myself."

"Is — is teaching school what you want to do?" she probed gently.

His eyes snapped back to hers intently. "I

can think of no more noble purpose in life than to acquire knowledge for the sake of passing it along to a child," he said.

"Yes, then you do want to go back to teaching?" she asked.

His eyes seemed to withdraw from hers. "No, I doubt that I ever will," he said.

She stood waiting expectantly for more, but he turned away from her and gazed into the dark stall, one hand on the dun's muzzle.

"I see . . . ," she murmured finally.

He did not turn his attention from the horse until he'd heard Sara's footsteps leave his side and walk back to the house.

Inside, Sara sat at the table with her hands folded on her lap as he walked through the door and closed it behind himself. She looked up at him.

"Last year a man hired me to hunt down a gang of robbers led by Curly Joe Hobbs," he said. "The gang killed the man's young daughter during a bank robbery."

Sara looked on quietly. "I've heard of Curly Joe Hobbs and his gang," she said. "I heard they met their end, but I didn't know who killed them. I just thought it was a posse, I suppose."

"I killed them," Dahl said quietly. "I brought back Curly Joe Hobbs' head in a jar, just as I was asked. I brought the gang's ears back on a string."

When he'd finished he stared at her, awaiting her reaction.

"I see," she said, without changing either her expression or her position.

"I thought you ought to hear it from me, instead of from somebody else," Dahl said.

Sara nodded slightly. "I'm glad it was you who told me," she said.

"I can leave here today, if you want me to," Dahl said.

"I don't want you to leave today," she said, "unless it's what you want to do."

"I don't want you to think that I'm a good man," Dahl said. "I'm not. I doubt if I ever will be again."

Sara gave only a trace of a smile. "I'll be the judge of that. Thank you," she said. She gestured a nod toward the bulletproof vest still hanging on the chair back. "I have some spare quilting. Why don't I mend your shooting vest for you?"

In the afternoon, the Catlo brothers and Buck the Mule Jennings rode into Kindred from the south. Passing the widow's shack along the way, they looked across the rocky flatland and saw clothes drying on a rope line. As they rode by, staring from thirty yards away, they saw a woman pull a garment down from the clothesline and walk back to the house, folding the clothing over her forearm.

"Is that a *petticoat* she's carrying?" Jennings asked his two companions, riding a few feet behind them.

"Uh-oh," Jason said with foreboding.

"Don't go concerning yourself with it, whatever she's carrying," said Philbert. "You've run your string with the fairer sex for a while, the way I see it."

"What do you mean by that?" Jennings asked with a scowl, staring hard at Philbert from behind.

"Jesus, Buck the Mule . . ." Philbert chuckled and shook his head without looking back. "Don't you see you have no business around womenfolk? You beat them up, force yourself on them. Do things to them that would curdle bear's milk —"

"You poke a broom handle in their husband's eye," Jason cut in, staring straight ahead.

"I told you I never done that," said Jennings, getting irritated all over again about the matter.

"Then just who the hell did it, Buck the Mule?" Jason asked pointedly.

"I don't know, I don't know," Jennings

repeated. "But it wasn't me." His voice turned harsh with rage.

Concerned, Philbert let his horse fall back beside the big dirty gunman in order to keep an eye on him. "Hey. He's just funning you, Buck the Mule. We know you didn't do it. Hell, for all we know the woman did it to him."

"Don't say that. She never done it either," Jennings said, defending the woman he'd had his way with and then shot in the back. He'd grown irritated, and his grimy hand had poised close to his holstered revolver.

"All right." Jason shrugged. "He might have poked it in his own eye, just for spite," he said, smiling to himself, "knowing you were off *romancing* his woman."

"Yeah . . . ?" Jennings seemed to settle down a little.

Philbert looked at him and said, "Tell us again, Buck the Mule, about the first time your pa tried to kill you."

"I already told you," Jennings said. Now that he had settled down, his hand moved away from the gun butt and rubbed back and forth on his trouser leg as if to wipe his big fingers clean.

"Tell us again, Buck," Philbert urged, grinning, friendly.

"It's the sort of story we never grow tired

of hearing," Jason put in. He let his horse drop back, flanking Jennings on his other side.

"All right," said Jennings, "it wasn't nothing really. I was just a baby. He tired to hit me in the head with a smithing hammer . . . but my ma stopped him. She grabbed the hammer from him and cracked the handle across his nose. Broke it all to hell!" He gave a wide grin and threw his head back in a laugh.

Philbert and Jason gave each other a bemused look and laughed along with him.

"Now tell us about how you stabbed him when you got older," Philbert said.

"Well," said Jennings, "that was when I was six or seven years old —"

"Wait, hold it, look at this," said Jason, cutting him off. He gestured toward a new hand-painted sign nailed to a post standing alongside the beginning of the main street into Kindred.

In large letters, the sign read:

GUN LAW
BY ORDER OF MARSHAL
EMERSON KERN, NO FIREARMS
ARE ALLOWED WITHIN THE
TOWN LIMITS OF KINDRED
TOWNSHIP. ALL GUNS MUST BE

TURNED IN AT THE TOWN MARSHAL'S OFFICE FOR SAFEKEEPING. THIS LAW WILL BE STRINGENTLY ENFORCED.

"So, the idiot was right," Jason said, after reading the new sign. "They really are banning guns." He gave his brother a surprised grin. "Can you believe this?"

Philbert stared at the sign. He nudged his horse over and touched a finger to it, checking if the paint was dry.

"What does *stringently* mean?" he asked. He rubbed his finger and thumb together, seeing no wet paint on them.

"It means the same as —" Jason started to answer but stopped short, finding himself at a loss. "Hell, you know . . ." He shrugged.

"No, I don't know," said Philbert. "That's why I asked. I thought *you* might."

"Well, it means . . ." Jason gave up. "Hell, I don't know *what* it means, all right?"

"It means *strictly* enforced," said Jennings, sitting his horse off to the side, his big wrists crossed on his saddle horn, watching the two.

The Catlo brothers looked surprised.

"Well, I'll be damned," said Jason. "I believe he's right."

"Good work, Buck the Mule," said Philbert. He looked at his brother and said, "You should have known that."

"But I didn't," said Jason, getting a little irritated himself, "so let it go."

"It's gone, brother." Philbert grinned.

"The thing is, I can't believe this is true, a town with no guns allowed," said Jason. He looked Buck the Mule Jennings up and down appraisingly, then his brother, Philbert. Looking back at the new sign, he shook his head and said, "Can you imagine the kind of no-good murderers and thugs this *gun law* is going to draw from all over the territory soon as they hear about it?"

Philbert looked at Jennings, then at his brother. He stifled an outright laugh and chuffed to himself. "Hell, I shudder to think of it," he said.

The three turned their horses to the street and rode into town at a slow walk. They took note of a long line of townsmen standing out in front of the town marshal's office, beneath a large wooden star that hung above the open door. The townsmen held rifles, shotguns and handguns, respectively.

"Look at this," Philbert said in amazement, "they even stand in line to get rid of their shooting gear." He chuckled and turned to Jason, whispering under his breath, "Tell me, brother, have I died and gone to heaven?"

"If you did, we both died together," said Jason.

"Me too," Buck the Mule Jennings cut in, riding right behind them.

From the window of his office, Marshal Emerson Kern watched the three men file past. They gazed at the shops, at the bank and at the telegraph office. Their caged eyes moved across the people along the boardwalk like hungry wolves sizing up a flock of sheep.

He nodded to Tribold Cooper and said quietly, "We might have trouble coming."

"Yeah? What makes you say so?" Tribold had just taken a short-barreled shotgun from an elderly townsman and laid it on a table with a stack of other guns. He looked out the window with the marshal, but he was too late to catch a glance of the three gunmen riding by.

"Stop this line. Arm yourselves and meet me behind the saloon," Kern said.

"*Arm yourselves . . . ?*" an old townsman murmured. He gave the others in line a strange look.

Cooper and Bender nodded at the marshal's order.

"Marshal Kern, how will you know my

Caroline from all the rest?" the old man asked. He'd just handed over his shotgun and watched as it was slung atop the anonymous stack of guns.

"Caroline?" said Kern. "Your shotgun has a name?" he asked, bemused by the idea.

"Yes," said the old man. "Sweet Caroline's been with me longer than any woman ever made it. I want to know how you're going to recognize her in case I come to —"

"*In case* you want her back?" Kern asked, cutting him off in an intimidating tone of voice. "You mean *in case* you get drunk and mad, and want to cause harm to somebody?" He stared hard at the old man and said, "Because that's the very thing we're trying to prevent."

The old man scratched his head, befuddled. "I don't drink. I never get cross with anybody. Look at me. Do I look like I'm going to start trouble?"

"What's your name, sir?" Kern asked.

"Virgil. Virgil Tullit."

"Well, Virgil, we've all heard those arguments too many times to count," Kern said. He shook a finger at him. "This is for everybody's good old-timer. Don't be a hardhead."

"But what if I want to collect my Caroline and leave town?" the old man asked.

93

As Kern turned to the door, he said over his shoulder in a dismissing voice, "Well, we just won't *let* you leave town. We'll stick you in jail and sit on you until you starve to death. Because that's the kind of low-down snakes us local government officials are." He grinned and winked at the others in line. "Isn't that right, fellows?"

The townsmen laughed at his joke, all except for the old man, who scratched his head again and shrugged. "I still don't see how you'll tell Caroline from all the others," he said weakly.

"Don't even trouble your mind *thinking* about it," Kern said. "Let me do all the thinking around here. That's my job." He gave a wide, generous grin. "I've got everything on file, right up here." He tapped himself on the side of his head.

Cooper and Bender looked at each other and grinned as they picked up their gun belts, unrolled them and strapped them on.

"He's good," Bender said privately to Cooper as the marshal walked out the door.

"Oh yeah, he's a pistol all right," said Cooper, his smile disappearing as he buckled his gun belt and slid his Colt up and down to loosen it.

CHAPTER 7

Jake Jellico finished wiping down the bar top at the Lucky Devil Saloon and Brothel and glanced up just as three dusty gunmen walked through the batwing doors. Along the bar, the row of drinkers saw the hard, trail-bitten look of the men and instinctively made space for them.

"Oh, hell . . . ," Jellico murmured. All three were armed — a rifle hanging from each man's left hand, their right hands poised near a holstered revolver on their hip.

As the three lined up and laid their rifles on the bar top, the nervous saloon owner pointed a finger at a sign leaning against the broken mirror behind the bar indicating the new Gun Law.

"Gentlemen, don't take this the wrong way, but the town is disarming itself this very day. Until you turn in your guns at the marshal's office, I'm not allowed to serve you strong drink."

The three looked back and forth along the bar on either side of them in disbelief, seeing no guns on any of the other drinkers.

"I see it. I still don't believe it," Philbert Catlo muttered to his brother.

"Oh, it's true," Jellico said, thinking the words were directed at him. "There've been so many killings here that the town voted to put a stop to it. Getting rid of guns is the only reasonable way."

Philbert gave him a hard stare. "I was talking to brother Jason here," he said.

"Easy, brother Phil," said Jason, seeing the look on Philbert's face. "He didn't know. . . ."

"Indeed, sir," said Jellico, "I did not know, and I apologize —" He stopped suddenly as a stunned look of recognition came to his face. "Phil and Jason?" he said, looking back and forth between the two while Jennings stared blankly at him.

"That's right," said Jason. "What of it?"

"You — you're the Catlo brothers, aren't you?" Jellico said in a shallow and worried voice.

"Again, what of it?" Jason said with a cold expression.

"Nothing, I mean —" Jellico stammered. "Welcome to Kindred, that is. It's a pleasure and an honor to meet you fellows."

"Why's that?" Philbert asked bluntly, not letting the saloon owner off the spot he'd suddenly found himself on.

Buck the Mule Jennings crowded in closer and asked the frightened man, "Have you heard of me too?"

Jellico looked back and forth wildly, not knowing how to respond, or which question to answer first.

"Well — that is —" Jellico stopped and finally collected himself enough to ask, "Gentlemen, why don't I get all three of you a drink?"

"Because it's against the law?" Jason answered, still staring at him relentlessly.

With a terror-filled grin, Jellico reached under the bar and pulled up a bottle of rye and three shot glasses.

"I always say a law is like a fence," he mused, sweat beading on his upper lip. "It's no good unless there's room for a gate in it."

"What's this idiot talking about?" Philbert asked Jason.

"Damned if I know," Jason said. "Something about building fences — leaving a gate open." He laid his hand atop his rifle stock resting on the bar. "What are you talking about, idiot?" he asked Jellico.

"I have no idea," Jellico said shakily. He froze in place with a tortured smile; sweat ran down his broad forehead. The bottle of rye and the shot glasses stood on the bar top.

Unarmed townsmen sensed trouble and began to slink away and fade out the doors, front and rear.

"Gentlemen, if you will allow me to intercede on Mr. Jellico's behalf," a voice bellowed from the far end of the bar.

The three gunmen looked around as Ed Dandly walked toward them, his hands chest high, a notepad and pencil stub in his right hand.

"Now *this* idiot," Jason said, his hand still resting on his rifle stock.

Dandly ignored the remark as he approached with a cautious smile. Behind the bar, Jake Jellico still stood with the same look of terror on his face.

"I'm Edward Dandly . . . ?" the smiling newsman said, ending his words in a question suggesting that the three should have heard of him. He touched the brim of his derby hat. "I own the *Kindred Star Weekly News* . . . ? The town newspaper . . . ?"

Jason whispered to his brother, "Everybody in this burg is crazy as a loon."

"I like it," Philbert replied with a grin.

"Mr. Jellico was concerned that you gentlemen were going to . . . well, that you may have killed him, had he refused you service."

"Now, there's a thought," Philbert said. He and Jason looked at each other. Jason drummed his fingertips on the rifle stock.

"I expect we'll never know, now that he went ahead and jerked us up a bottle," Jason said. He looked at the shot glasses, then at Jellico and asked, "Are you going to fill them, or do we start all over?"

Philbert looked at a slim young man standing to the side, watching on with apprehension, a guitar leaning against his leg.

"Do you play that, or is it all that keeps you from falling over?" he asked.

"What . . . ?" The young man looked wide-eyed and stunned. Then he caught on and said quickly, "Oh. Yes, sir! I do play it!" He jerked the guitar up across his chest and began plucking a snappy tune.

"See? It's the whole town," Jason whispered to his brother.

"I just wish we'd moved here when we were both children," Philbert whispered in reply, turning his eyes to the filled shot glasses.

Jennings stood grinning at the guitar player, his big dirty fingers plucking an imaginary guitar on his chest.

Marshal Kern stood waiting impatiently for Cooper and Bender as more drinkers slipped out the back door of the saloon and wasted no time getting clear of the place. He heard the sound of guitar music start up inside. He paced back and forth until he finally saw the two deputies rounding the corner of the building, their gun hands swinging near their holstered revolvers.

"What took you so long?" Kern demanded in a stiff tone.

"We came as soon as we strapped down," said Cooper, gesturing at his gun belt. "What's going on anyway?"

"It sounds like the trouble has already started," said Kern. "Hear the guitar?"

"I hear it," said Cooper. "But it doesn't raise that much concern for me." He grinned at Bender. "What about you, Denton? Does that guitar sound like trouble starting?"

"Not so far," Bender said. "But you never know when a guitar player might fly into a killing rage." He returned the grin.

Kern glared at them. "I'm saying the music means the three have settled in and made themselves to home. That tells me that Jellico has served them whiskey. That's

100

against our new rules. If these men get away with it, everybody will start questioning our ability to enforce the gun law. Do you understand?"

The two stopped grinning. Cooper raised and lowered his Colt in its holster. Bender took his Colt out, checked it and lowered it back in place, keeping his gun hand resting on its butt.

"Tell us how you want to play this, Marshal," Cooper said. "We've got you covered."

"Well, I'm damned obliged to you both, *Deputies*," Kern said in a cutting, sarcastic tone.

The two men stood in silence.

"All right, now, let's go unarm these saddle bums, before we all three look like fools," Kern said. He levered a round into his rifle chamber and started to turn to the rear door of the saloon.

From a few feet away, one of the drinkers who had fled the saloon said in a hushed voice, "Marshal, those three ain't your everyday *saddle bums.*"

Kern turned toward a short, stout man standing half-hidden by a telegraph pole. "Who are you?" he asked. "I haven't seen you around town."

"I'm a liquor peddler, name of Giles Frame," the man answered. He raised a

101

bowler hat that appeared too small for his head. "I was about to discuss selling this place some whiskey when those three walked in. The big dirty fellow doesn't look familiar, but the other two are Jason and Philbert Catlo. I've seen them a time or two the past year, usually after somebody just got themselves killed for looking at them the wrong way."

"Jason and Philbert Catlo?" Kern asked, an ill look coming to his face.

"The *Catlo brothers?*" Bender asked, with the same disturbed look.

"Yes, that's them all right," said the peddler. "Take my word for it." Having giving his information, the peddler turned and hurried away along the alley, a hand holding his bowler in place. By now, the townsfolk had scurried away.

"Well, that'll do it for me," Cooper said. He started to leave in an awkward half run, half walk.

"Hold it," Kern demanded. "What the hell do you mean, that'll do it for you? We're going in there. I don't give a damn if it's the Catlo brothers or the *James brothers.* We're going to disarm them." As he spoke his rifle swung around toward Cooper.

"Not unless I know I'm getting something out of it once we're finished with them,"

Cooper said. "It would be different if we were planning to clean this town out in one big raid. I wouldn't stand for them getting in our way. But the way we're going about this thing, a little bit at a time, *huh-uh,* it's not worth getting shot at. Bender and I feel like we're working for wages."

"Yeah, like some kind of *real* deputies," Bender put in with a disgusted look. "We could do this anywhere."

"So what's in it for us?" Cooper asked bluntly.

"Damn it!" Kern clenched his teeth, considered the question despite his frustration. "All right. A hundred apiece if you end up killing them all three."

"What if we only kill one or two of them?" Bender asked, his hand still resting on his gun butt.

"That'd still be a hundred apiece," said Kern. "I'm not made out of money . . . not yet anyway."

Cooper looked at Bender and shrugged. "What the hell, we'll kill all three. It wouldn't make sense just killing one or two of them. We'd lose money."

"Are we ready?" Kern asked.

"Ready as rain," Cooper said, "now that Bender and I know we've got an interest in things here."

"Then let's go get it done," Kern said with grim finality in his gruff voice.

Cooper adjusted his gun belt and gestured an arm for Marshal Kern to lead them through the rear door of the saloon. "After you, Marshal," he said.

The Catlo brothers and Buck the Mule Jennings watched from the bar as the marshal walked in. The two deputies stepped through the door behind him and spread out across the width of the saloon. Jake Jellico was behind the bar, sweating in his feet. He held the bottle of rye in his hand, ready to refill the gunmen's glasses as soon they set them down empty on the bar top.

A few feet away stood Ed Dandly, his pencil stub and notebook still in hand. He turned toward the marshal with a worried look.

Kern noted the rifles lying atop the bar, the holstered revolvers at each man's hip. He stopped in the middle of the sawdust-covered floor and stood with his feet spread shoulder-width apart.

"In case nobody told you three, nobody gets served liquor in Kindred unless they turn in their guns," he called out. As soon as he'd spoken, he gave Jellico a cold stare.

Jellico set the bottle of rye down. He

raised his hands chest high and said, "Marshal, I mentioned about the new gun law. I just figured these men —"

"Yeah, *Idiot* here told us rightly enough," Jason said. He turned and raised the glass of rye toward Kern as if preparing to toast him.

"And if he hadn't told us, Marshal, this sign would have been a dead giveaway," Philbert cut in, nodding toward the sign leaning against the broken mirror.

"We can read," Jennings said, and then backtracked. "Well, they can anyway."

"Drink your whiskey, Buck the Mule," Jason said quietly to the big dirty gunman in an effort to push him out of the conversation.

"The point is, Marshal," Philbert said, "you knew we had firearms, and you and your deputies here came to take them from us. Ain't that about right?"

Cooper and Bender stepped in closer, each of them thinking about the hundred dollars apiece the marshal had offered them to kill these three.

"That's exactly right," said Cooper. "Use them or drop them is all we come to say." He nodded toward the rifles on the bar.

"Keep out of this, Deputy," Kern warned, well aware why Cooper was so eager to get the fighting under way.

"Use them or drop them . . . ," Philbert repeated. "What a clever thing to say." He took a step away from the bar, his brother right beside him. Jennings moved to the side, his big dirty hand poised to reach for his gun.

Before either the deputies or the marshal could make a move, Philbert's Colt streaked up from his holster. Kern saw the open bore of the gun barrel pointed at him.

Philbert stepped forward, a mirthless grin spread wide across his face. "The fact is," he said, "we have nothing but respect for this new *gun law* of yours." In a flash, his Colt flipped around in his hand. He held the gun out, butt first, much to the marshal's surprise.

"Damn it," Bender growled under his breath. Not only had Jason Catlo's fast draw caught them cold, but he knew he and Cooper had just missed out on making the three hundred dollars the marshal had promised them. He and Cooper stood watching as Jason Catlo raised his Colt slowly, walked forward and held it out to the marshal in the same manner.

"My brother speaks for me too, Marshal," he said. "We heard about the law from some pilgrims on the trail. We came here wanting to see it for ourselves."

Kern didn't trust the moves they'd made, but he stepped forward anyway, took the two Colts they held out for him and looked toward the rifles on the bar.

"Buck the Mule," said Philbert, "bring those rifles on over here, so the marshal can *relieve* us of them. I sense an uneasiness at work here."

"You have to admit," said Kern, "you Catlos are not known for surrendering your weapons without a fight."

"I don't look at it as *surrendering* our weapons, Marshal," said Jason. "I like to call it bowing to the advancement of civilization."

"I like that!" said Ed Dandly. He scribbled it down on his notepad.

Ignoring the newsman, Kern questioned Jason and Philbert. "So you fellows heard about our gun law along the trail, eh?"

"Yep," said Philbert.

"Good news travels fast, Marshal," Jason put in.

"So does bad news," Jennings said, stepping forward with the rifles from atop the bar. He glared at Dandly and said, "Write that down too."

"Yes, of course," Dandly replied, scribbling in order to placate the gruesome gunman.

"The fact is, Marshal," said Jason, "we're wondering if you could use our help. We saw the line backed up out front of your office. It must be a big job collecting every gun in town."

"You can't imagine," Kern said, feeling better now that the rifles and sidearms were out of the Catlo brothers' reach.

"Now that we're legal here," Jason said, "maybe we could all have a drink and talk about it?"

Kern looked at his deputies, then back at the Catlo brothers. "Yeah, sure, why not?" he said. He turned to Ed Dandly and shouted, "Get lost."

"But, Marshal, this is all news," said Dandly. "What are you trying to hide?"

"Cracking your head with a gun butt is news too," said Kern, ignoring the newsman's question. He stared coldly at him until Dandly relented and slunk away.

When Dandly was gone through the front door, the men all turned back to the bar. Philbert looked at the guitar player, who'd stood frozen in silence since the three lawmen walked in.

"Nobody told you to stop playing, did

they?" he asked the frightened young musician.

"No, sir," the musician said.

"Then *play, man, play!*" Philbert demanded, waving a hand in the air.

The shaky musician jerked the guitar back up across his chest and played intently.

Philbert turned to Marshal Kern and said, "I am what you might call *appreciative* of good music, although I have never had any gift for it myself."

CHAPTER 8

Some of the unarmed townsmen who had left the saloon moments earlier had now slipped back inside. Others remained on the boardwalk out front, staring in at the town marshal and his five companions through the dirty front windows. The ones who had ventured back in kept their distance, drinking quietly and warily at either end of the bar.

"This is what you end up getting once you've handed over your guns," said Virgil Tullit, standing on the street at the edge of the boardwalk. "I knew it was a mistake, damn it to hell," he lamented. "When these political snakes know you're defenseless, they start showing you their whole other side — the lying sonsabitches."

An airtight goods salesman and a mercantile store owner both gave the old man a look.

"Isn't that a little harsh, sir?" said the

goods salesman, a Missourian named John Admore. "How do you know they are liars?"

"Because they hold public office," Virgil said bluntly. "They all lie until they get big enough to hire somebody to lie for them."

"My goodness, you are *bitter*, sir," said the goods salesman.

"Being bitter doesn't make me wrong, does it?" the old man retorted with a sharp glint in his eyes.

"No, sir, it does not," said Walter Stevens, the mercantile owner. He and Admore looked at each other and stifled a short laugh.

"Come on, old-timer," said the goods salesman, "do you really think your new mayor Coakley and Marshal Emerson Kern had some dark sinister plan in mind for Kindred?"

"Mayor Coakley? Hell," said the old man. "Nobody's even seen him since he won his —"

"Gracious no," said Stevens, even before the old man could finish his answer. "All they want is to stop all the killing in our streets and see us live in peace. Is that so bad?"

"Yes, I'm certain they only want what's the best for Kindred," said the salesman.

"It might seem like they only want what's

best for us *right now,*" said Virgil. "But mark my words, young fellows, all they want is to take control of the town. And they're doing it *today.* Without our firearms, there ain't a damn thing we can do about anything. They can hand-feed us dung . . . We'll have to swallow it. If we don't swallow, it'll choke us to death."

The two men looked at each other, shook their heads and grinned. The line of townsmen waiting for the marshal and his deputies to return and collect their guns still stretched far down the street.

"Young fellows . . . ?" said Admore, turning back to the old man. "I hardly qualify as a *young fellow.* I'm forty-six years old, sir. I have two grandchildren and another on the way."

"Anybody who thinks this gun law is meant to protect us is either awfully young or awfully foolish," said Virgil. "I didn't want to come outright and call you both *fools.*"

"Well, that's courteous of you," said Admore, with a mock touch of his fingers to his derby brim. "I've never been called a fool in such a polite manner."

But Stevens would have none of it. He gave the old man a cross look.

"If you feel that way, why'd I see you

standing in line to hand over a rifle to the marshal's deputy?"

"That was my shotgun," the old man corrected him. "I reckon I lost my mind for a minute," he added. "I must've got worn down and started believing them myself."

"Oh . . . ?" said Stevens. He studied the old man's face as his fingers fiddled deftly with a gold watch chain hanging from his vest pocket. "So, what are you telling us, Virgil?"

The old man looked back and forth cautiously along the boardwalk. Then he opened the front of his coat a little and said, "I'm telling you I snuck Sweet Caroline back while the deputies were strapping up to come over here." Down in an inside pocket stood two pieces of the broken-down shotgun.

Sweet Caroline . . . ?" said Stevens, looking at the shotgun. His fingers fell from his watch chain. He and the goods salesman looked shocked.

"My goodness, sir!" said Admore in a hushed tone. "Do you realize the trouble you could be in, stealing a gun from the marshal's office?"

"Steal her, *my ass,*" the old man said, dismissing the allegation. Caroline's been by my side every night since I was nineteen

113

years old. I'm the only hands she's ever known. How many of yas can say that same thing about —"

"Jesus, you crazy old coot, get away from us," said Stevens, cutting him off. He looked around quickly as if they were being watched. "I don't want the marshal thinking I had anything to do with this!"

"Nor do I," Admore, his tone turning icy.

"See, Caroline . . . ?" the old man said to the two pieces of the shotgun under his coat. "They're already scared as rabbits, and this is just the first day." He closed his coat and shook a gnarled finger at them. "Shame on yas both. Already you're left without *courage* — the main thing this country was meant to give every man she ever birthed."

Admore looked all around and said to the gathered townsmen, "Does anyone know where Virgil lives? Can someone take him home? Please?"

"We're afraid he's not himself today," Stevens put in. "He's talking out of his head."

"Come on, Virgil, old fellow," said a young man who'd been standing nearby. "Let's get you home." He stepped forward, looked at the mercantile clerk and the salesman and said, "Don't worry. I know where he lives." As he spoke he reached out, closed the old

114

man's coat and smoothed a hand down the front to make sure the broken-down shotgun wasn't seen.

"Who the hell are you?" said the old man.

"You know me, Virgil," said the young man with a disarming smile. He cast a glance to the others. "I'm Billy. I live over that way," he said, pointing out across the flatlands in no particular direction. "I'll take care of him, you can bet," he said quietly to the two businessmen.

"You see that you do, young fellow," Stevens said with warning in his tone. "Virgil's not thinking clearly today, but he's one of us. Don't you forget it."

The mercantile man turned to the goods salesman. The two shrugged.

"It must be tough on an old-timer like Virgil, seeing things change so rapidly," said Admore. He shook his head in reflection. "How do you ever convince them that our leaders have our best interest at heart?"

Admore smiled. "And if we find out they *don't,* we simply vote them out of office when the time comes, and they have to go. What could be more perfect than that?"

"Exactly," Stevens agreed. The two watched Virgil Tullit and the young man walk out of sight.

Inside the saloon, huddled along the bar, the five gunmen and the marshal spoke hushed and guarded among themselves below the noise of the busy saloon. Kern fell silent for a moment and stared coldly at Jake Jellico, who walked behind the bar, snatched up an empty rye bottle and set a fresh one in its place.

"As I was saying . . ." Kern went on speaking once the saloon owner was out of listening range. "When I saw that this town elected Mayor Coakley because they wanted him to get rid of the guns, I said to myself, 'This is the place where I want to put down some roots.' " He smiled, reached out and filled each of their empty glasses.

"When will we have the pleasure of meeting this Mayor Coakley?" Jason asked.

Kern didn't reply right away, continuing to fill the glasses. Then he said, "He went off on a holiday soon after he won the election . . . sort of a celebration, I suppose."

Philbert gave him a look. "Did he go on a holiday, or did somebody kill him?" he asked.

"It was one or the other, I'm sure," said Kern.

"I don't know about putting down roots," Buck the Mule cut in, already feeling his shots of whiskey. He gave a crooked smile. "I'd sure like to *pull some up.*"

Kern gave Jason Catlo a guarded look of uncertainty.

"He's all right," Jason said under his breath. "My brother and I have gotten used to him."

"He'll do anything we tell him," Philbert cut in under his breath.

Seeing a flash of apprehension cross Kern's brow, Jason added quickly, "And in turn *we'll* do anything *you* tell us to do."

"Good. Because that's the way it's got to be," Kern said. He gave Cooper and Bender a glance as he spoke, making sure they heard him too.

The two deputies looked on in silence.

"I want all of you to ask yourself, do you want to spend your life on the run, looking back over your shoulder, or do you want to sit back and have the law work for you?" He gave a smile of satisfaction. "It'll take no time to get these townsmen shaped up and doing what we tell them to do. All the while they'll be thanking us for doing it."

"I don't mean to piss on your foot, Marshal," said Jason. "But why are they going to thank us for taking control of this town?"

Kern chuckled. "Because we're going to convince them this is the best and safest damn place to live on the whole frontier," he said. "Any time they question it, we'll remind them that they should be ashamed of themselves for not being grateful for everything we've done for them."

The gunmen laughed among themselves.

"You've put some thought into all this, that's for sure, Marshal," Philbert said, raising his shot glass in a toast to Kern. "I'm glad I'm on your side."

"Ain't we all?" said Tribold Cooper, raising his glass as well.

Kern nodded his appreciation. He tipped his glass to the men and emptied it. He looked all around at the unarmed townsmen standing at the bar, drinking, busy talking among themselves.

"All right," he said with a sigh, "we've left the line waiting at my office long enough to show them who's boss. Cooper, you and Bender take Deputy Jennings with you and get started collecting again. The brothers and I will ride along directly."

"You've got it, Marshal," Cooper said. He and Bender looked at Jennings. "Come on, Buck the Mule," he said, grinning. "Let's go take all the guns away from these trouble-making townsmen before they all start kill-

118

ing one another for no reason."

Philbert Catlo set his glass down and pushed himself back from the bar. He picked up his battered Stetson hat and dropped it atop his head.

"If you don't mind, Marshal, I'll go along with these three. Maybe it'll speed us up getting rid of all these terrible guns."

"Not at all, Deputy Philbert. You go right on ahead with them. That's the kind of attitude I like to see," Kern said with a laugh.

Jason nodded privately to his brother and turned to the bar beside the marshal. "Yeah, so do I," he said. "My brother is always one who can't wait to get his hands on a piece of work once he knows he has something to offer the job." He filled the marshal's glass. "Now let's talk some between us."

"Good idea," said Kern, turning beside him.

On the way to the marshal's office, Cooper and Bender both looked Jennings and Philbert Catlo up and down. Along the boardwalk, the line of townsmen had grown, trailing onto the dirt street and halfway down the next block.

"Let these idiots wait," Cooper said as the four men walked along. Again the two looked Philbert up and down appraisingly.

"Did you hear what he called them?" Bender asked.

"Idiots, right?" said Philbert.

"That's right. He called them idiots," said Bender. He paused for a second, and then said, "Isn't that what I heard you call the barkeep back there?"

"Yes, I believe I did," said Philbert, walking straight ahead. He shrugged. "We hadn't been introduced. Why, is he some kin of yours?"

"No, hell no, he's not," said Bender, his expression turning irritated. "It's just that 'idiots' is what we both usually call folks."

"Oh . . . ," said Philbert without looking at the two.

"So, how's that going to work out now that you and your brother are here with us?"

"And me too," Jennings cut in, not to be overlooked.

"Him too," Bender added.

Philbert not only turned and looked at them. He stopped in the street.

"Let me make sure I understand this," said Philbert. "You're wanting to know if it's all right, you and your pal Cooper here using the word *idiot,* the same word my brother and I use?"

"He's not asking your permission, Catlo," said Cooper, standing facing him, his hand poised at his side, "only your opinion."

"My *opinion* . . . ," Philbert chuffed. His gun hand was also poised, but not as tense or as deliberate as Tribold Cooper's. "My opinion is, if this is all we've got to worry about, we're in good shape here."

"It's about more than who calls who an idiot," said Cooper. "It's about you, your brother and your pal here riding in and jumping right into our feed trough feet-first."

"That's how you look at it?" said Philbert. "Us three just rode in and took over something you two started with the marshal?"

"Get this straight. You three didn't take nothing over," said Cooper. "The point we're making is that you're not going to either. This is something we got going for ourselves — ourselves, *only.*"

Along the boardwalk the townsmen looked on, not hearing the discussion, but wondering why it was taking so long to get their guns turned in.

"We understand that," said Philbert. "My brother, Jason, and I, and Buck the Mule here, have no interest in sticking around here, doing nothing the rest of our lives."

Bender shot Philbert a skeptical look. "We're not riding this on the short trail," he explained. "We're in it for the long ride, just

121

like Kern told us."

"What? Rob this place dry over the next ten or fifteen years . . . ?" Philbert chuffed again. "No, thank you. That's not the Catlos' style. If we were lazy thieves, we would all run for Congress, right, Buck the Mule?"

"Damn right . . . Congress," said Jennings.

"That's all Kern is doing anyway," said Philbert. "He's setting this up as something legitimate, when it's nothing but one more way to *steal*."

Bender and Cooper looked at each other, beginning to understand what the sharp young gunman was saying.

"We're not lazy thieves," Cooper offered in their defense.

"Maybe not, but you've thrown in with one," said Philbert. He thumbed back over his shoulder toward the saloon where Kern and Jason stood drinking. "At least the Catlos are *honest* thieves. We don't lie about what we are. We take what we want, all at once, and we ride on."

"So do we," said Triblold Cooper, "but this is something new. We figured, why not try it out? It's not even illegal, unless we get caught some way."

"Jesus," Philbret said in disgust. "You can say that about anything you've ever done. Nothing is *illegal* until you get caught and convicted of it. That's just the nature of things." He gestured a hand toward the line of townsmen. "Look at them, fellows," he said. "See anything familiar?"

"Like what?" asked Cooper, needing a clue.

Like what . . . Philbert took a deep breath for patience's sake. "Like, *they're all holding guns,*" said Philbert.

"We see that," said Cooper.

"Good," said Philbert. "What's the first thing you tell an armed man before you rob his bank, his stage line, his home, his whole damned family?"

"Drop your gun?" Bender offered, taking an interest in the question.

"Exactly," said Philbert. He gestured a hand toward the line of townsmen. "That's all this *gun law* is doing, telling everybody to drop their guns." He grinned. "Any *idiot* knows what comes next, don't they?"

Cooper raised the front of his hat and scratched his head. "Damn, Catlo, you're not going to be as hard to get along with as I thought."

"I have to admit," said Philbert, "I do have a way of growing on folks."

"Hold it, what's this?" said Bender.

The four turned and saw an old man appear from an alleyway, blood running down his forehead, his short-barreled shotgun in hand, waving above his head. Cooper quickly identified Virgil Tullit.

"He's not taking my gun!" Virgil shouted. "He's not taking my Sweet Caroline — !"

As the words left the old man's lips, the four deputies drew and fired in unison. Blast upon blast of gunfire streaked repeatedly, almost as one. Virgil fell back dead in the street, his shotgun flying from his hand. It landed across his chest, as if in a symbolic attempt to protect him.

"Damn, that was *fast,*" said Tribold Cooper, eyeing Philbert's smoking Colt.

"Thanks," said Philbert. He grinned. "You're not *slow* yourself." A cloud of gray-black smoke loomed up around the four gunmen.

CHAPTER 9

The townsmen broke from the line along the boardwalk and rushed to surround Virgil Tullit's bloody body in the dirt street. The four deputies stood staring without expression as Kern hurried from the saloon, Jason Catlo following behind him at an easy pace.

"My God," said a townsman, staring down at the bullet-riddled corpse. "Old Virgil wasn't going to shoot anybody. He never harmed a soul."

"Are these the sonsabitches we're handing our guns to?" another townsman asked under his breath.

"Maybe you," said another. "I'm not."

"Hold on, gentlemen," said Walter Stevens. "I care as much for this ol' man as any of you. But I have to say, he was acting quite odd earlier. He said he wasn't giving up his shotgun — even called it by a woman's name." He gave the others a skeptical look.

"Yes, damn it, he called it Sweet Caroline," said the town barber, Albert Shaggs. "So what? The gun was made in the Carolinas. What the hell's wrong with you, Stevens?" he yelled in the old man's defense.

"All right, I'm sorry," the mercantile owner said. "I didn't realize he always called it by name. I just found it odd, that's all. And the way he snuck it out of the marshal's office? Not turning it in like he was supposed to?"

A townsman who'd been in line looked at the others surrounding Tullit's body and spoke up. "Maybe it wasn't so *odd* after all. Maybe what's *odd* is us willing to hand over our guns if this is what we can expect from armed deputies, just for opening our mouths."

"He didn't just open his mouth, gentlemen," said John Admore. He gestured his hand down at the old man's bloody chest. "Let me remind you, he was waving a shotgun, and shouting that he wasn't going to let anyone take it."

"But he didn't point it at anybody," said Shaggs, a pair of grooming scissors in the pocket of his striped barber shirt.

"Not *yet,* he didn't," the salesman offered. "I was there earlier myself. I agree with

126

what Mr. Stevens said. The old man was acting oddly."

"Sure, you agree with Stevens," said the barber. "The two of yas have a special interest in common." He rubbed his thumb and finger together in the universal sign of greed.

"That is a *terrible* thing to say, sir," said the salesman, "and I resent it . . . on both Mr. Stevens' behalf as well as my own!" He sliced a sideways glance to Stevens as he spoke, making sure the mercantile owner saw him defending their honor.

"You might resent it, but let's hear you deny it," said another townsman.

Standing in their midst, Ed Dandly stared back and forth, pencil stub in hand, scribbling furiously on his notepad.

A few yards away, Marshal Kern stopped beside the four deputies. From all directions, more townsfolk ventured forward, drawn by the gunfire they'd heard.

"All right, what the hell happened?" Kern asked the four gunmen in a lowered voice.

Tribold Cooper spoke up first as he stood replacing the spent cartridges in his warm revolver.

"The old man came running at us with the shotgun," he said. "What were we supposed to do?"

"Kill him, that's what," said Philbert

before the marshal could reply. He smiled as he clicked his chamber shut on his gun and rolled the cylinder, reloaded, ready to fire. "Ain't that about the gist of what you were going to say, Marshal Kern?"

"Everybody saw the shotgun?" Kern asked cautiously, not replying to Philbert, but well aware that the reloaded gun in Philbert's hand was pointed loosely at his belly.

"We all saw it, Marshal," said Philbert and Cooper at the same time. "They all saw it too," Philbert added, nodding toward the townsmen who were now gathered in the street, looking in their direction, their assortment of guns in hand.

"This could get sticky," Marshal Kern said calmly, noting all the guns on the street. "Everybody stay back and keep quiet. I'll smooth it over."

"It's a pleasure watching him work," Cooper said to Philbert as the marshal walked away toward the crowd.

"He's only halfway there and I'm already inspired by it." Philbert grinned.

"All right, everybody back," Marshal Kern demanded, shoving his way through the tightly gathered crowd. "Give me room to see what's going on."

"Marshal, your deputies over there shot and killed Virgil Tullit," Ed Dandly said.

His writing hand was poised, awaiting the marshal's response.

"Was that shotgun in his hand?" Kern asked, gazing down at the short-barreled shotgun still lying across Tullit's bloody chest.

"Yes, it was," said Dandly. "Everybody saw it. Even I saw it from my office window."

That helps. . . . Kern breathed a sigh of relief to himself. He stopped and picked up the shotgun and broke it open.

"Is anybody gone to get Doc Washburn?" a townsman asked.

"Doc's off delivering a baby," said the barber. "But I'm qualified to tell you this man is dead."

"No, barber," said the townsman, "you're qualified to tell us he *needs a shave.* Doc Washburn is the only qua—"

"Damn it, *he's dead,* mister," Kern said, cutting the man off. "You could read a book through his chest."

The curious townsmen drew closer as if to see for themselves.

"Stay back, people," said Kern. "That was a figure of speech."

"Is it loaded, Marshal?" Ed Dandly asked, his pencil poised and ready.

Kern looked down intently at the empty shotgun in his hands. "Yes, it is," he lied instinctively.

"May I see for myself?" asked Dandly in an effort to check his facts before committing anything to paper.

Kern caught himself, realizing he needn't lie about the matter. "I mean, *no,* it's not loaded."

"It's easy enough to tell, Marshal," Dandly said with a crafty little grin. "Just look down at the —"

"Shut up, *Dandy,*" said Kern, cutting him off. "I know how to tell if a gun's loaded." He glared angrily at the newsman. "It's *not* loaded. But my deputies didn't know that when he came running at them, threatening them with it, now, did they?"

"Do you suppose they might have asked him first?" the newsman queried.

"Is that what you would have done, *Dandy?* Would you ask a man running at you with a shotgun if his gun was loaded?" Kern asked.

"It's Dandly, Marshal," the newsman corrected. "We're not talking about what I *might have done.* We're talking about what your men *did.*"

"My men did what any lawmen would do under these circumstances," said Kern.

Dandly wasn't about to let up. "Can you see why it might make the townsfolk a little reluctant to hand over their guns, seeing how quick it is for your deputies to draw and fire on a man with very little provocation?"

"He had a shotgun, you damn fool!" said Kern, holding the gun up close to Dandly's face. "Want me to spell it for you? *S-h-o-t-g-u-n!*"

One man spoke up from the gathered crowd. "Marshal, begging your pardon, but Ed Dandly is right. We're wondering about this whole thing now." He looked toward the four deputies, and at Jason Catlo, who came walking into the crowd. "We don't know any of these deputies who are working for you."

"What's that you're holding there, mister?" Kern asked in a tightly controlled voice.

"It's a Spencer carbine," said the man, Ben Clavens, a senior telegraph clerk.

"According to the law you're not supposed to be carrying a gun on the streets of Kindred."

Clavens said, "But I was there in line, turning it in, when all this started —"

"That's no excuse," Kern said with authority. "The law is the law. Now get yourself back in line to give it up, or my deputies will escort you straight to jail."

131

"Yes, sir, Marshal," Clavens said. He slunk back from the crowd.

"That goes for all the rest of you too," Kern called out. "This is a law matter out here in the street. The rest of you get back in line and give up those guns or go on about your business, whichever you were doing before."

Where the four deputies stood watching, Tribold Cooper leaned in closer to Philbert Catlo.

"See what I mean? Ain't he something to watch?" he said.

"I'm impressed," said Philbert, "and I don't impress all that easy."

"How come they're not getting back in line?" Jennings asked, staring back and forth along the street.

"I was sort of wondering that myself, Buck the Mule," said Philbert, his thumb hooked in his gun belt. He eyed townsmen moving away in every direction. Only a couple of them had gone back to the boardwalk out in front of the marshal's office.

From the widow's shack outside the Kindred town limits, Sherman Dahl and Sara Cayes had heard the powerful burst of gunfire a half mile away.

Dahl had risen from the bed and stepped

into his trousers. Instinctively, he'd slipped his big Colt from its holster and walked onto the rickety and weathered front porch, even though the gunfire quickly fell silent. He'd stepped off the porch barefoot as Sara ran to him from around the corner of the house, where she had been gathering kindling to raise a fire in the backyard *chimnea.*

"Don't go down there, Sherman!" she said in a frightened voice. "Please, you mustn't!"

Dahl turned as she ran to him. He caught her in his arm and held her to him. He felt her tremble out of control for a moment.

"Take it easy, Sara," he said soothingly. "I'm not going anywhere." He gestured toward what appeared to be a crowd gathering on the street in the distance. Each figure looked small and wavy in the heat and sunlight. "At first I thought it might have been an attack of some sort. Now I see it wasn't," he added. "It's over, whatever it was."

"It's Marshal Kern's town," she reminded him, gazing down the long dusty street from beside him. "Let him take care of it, whatever it was."

"Certainly," said Dahl, consolingly, realizing how terrified she was. "I wasn't going anywhere barefoot," he said to lighten the matter. "See . . . ?"

They both looked down at his feet. He smiled at her and drew her firmly against him.

"I — I just couldn't bear seeing something happen to you," she said. "I would think it my fault, having talked you into staying here."

"It wouldn't be your fault, Sara," Dahl said. "It's also Dr. Washburn's orders, remember? Besides, do I look like a man who would stay somewhere if I didn't really want to?"

She smiled, calming down, and she leaned her head against his chest.

"No, you don't," she said. "Now I feel foolish acting this way over a burst of gunshots."

"You needn't," Dahl said. "I've heard gunfire all my life. It still gets my attention."

"But I bet it doesn't scare you the way it just did me," she said.

"It might," Dahl said, gazing at the wavy figures in the distance, all of them standing still now, not in any hurry — no cause for alarm. He let out a tight breath. "It depends on the situation."

"You're just saying that to make me feel better," Sara said. She smiled, leaning her head against his bare chest.

Dahl only smiled thinly, looking off along the dirt street, still trying to discern the cause of the shooting.

"I only wish you could stay longer."

"Oh . . . ?" Dahl looked down at her and said, "What if I'm not always this easy to get along with?"

"You are, though," she said. "I can tell you are."

"Shhh," Dahl said, suddenly hushing her.

She fell silent, sensing urgency in his tone and in the way his arm tightened around her.

"Listen, hear that?" he said in a whisper.

"No," she said. They both stood listening intently beneath the purr of a warm wind. Staring toward a line of distant hills farther south of the town, she said, "Yes, I hear it now. What is it?"

"It sounds like someone in trouble," Dahl said. He turned to the house. "I'll get my boots."

"Should I get your horse?" Sara asked. "Am I going with you?" she called out as Dahl bounded quietly onto the porch and slipped inside the house with the sleek muscular ease of a mountain cat.

Sara didn't waste a second. She turned and ran to the dilapidated barn.

A moment later, Dahl stepped out onto

135

the front porch again, now in his boots, with his shirt on and his gun belt buckled around his waist. Sara stood holding the reins to his horse.

"I didn't think you'd want me to take the time to saddle him," she said, a bit out of breath, a canteen hanging by its strap from her shoulder.

"Thanks, Sara," said Dahl. He stepped off the porch looking toward the hill line. "Have you heard anything else?"

"No," she said, handing him the dun's reins. "Am I going with you?" she asked again.

Dahl glanced back along the dirt street and considered it for a second. There were still men moving about on the dirt street. The crowd that had gathered had now broken off in different directions.

"Yes, come with me," he said, not wanting to leave her alone.

Without hesitation Sara let him take her by her waist and lift her up over the horse's back. Reins in hand, Dahl swung up behind her and nudged the dun out across the sandy flatlands, strewn with rock, prickly pear, cholla and sage.

"Which direction do you think the sound came from?" Sara asked, scanning through the wavering heat and the sharp stabbing sunlight.

"We're not going to know until we hear it again," said Dahl. "That's *if* we hear it again," he added.

"It sounded like a child crying for help," Sara said.

"I know," said Dahl. "I figure anyone needing help will try to stick close to the trail leading them to town, if they can."

"So that's what we're going to do too?" Sara asked.

"Yep," said Dahl. He put the dun forward at a quick pace, hoping to get closer to the sound, should they hear it again. Sara gripped the dun's mane with one hand and reached back, holding firmly on to Dahl's thigh with her other.

"Are you all right there?" Dahl asked as they rode along across the rough terrain.

"Don't you worry about me, Sherman Dahl. I'm hanging on," Sara said bravely over her shoulder. "I'm not going anywhere."

CHAPTER 10

The woman had staggered down the trail from the hill line throughout the night and most of the morning. She had veered off the trail and walked barefoot through beds of prickly pear and spiky wire-brush until she'd collapsed in the thin shade of a dry creek bed. There she lay naked, save for her dead husband's bloody shirt, which she'd tied around her waist by the sleeves. The sound of gunfire had stirred her from a sleep so close to death that it awakened her with a start, even in her beaten and battered condition. Warm, fresh blood had oozed its way under a protective patch of dried, black blood from the bullet hole in her back. It trickled like a spider's touch down her spine into the blood-soaked shirt.

When she'd first cried out toward the sound of distant gunfire, she knew there was little left inside her that could resist the willowy arms of death. But that no longer mattered, something said inside her. No, she agreed, nothing mattered. . . .

Death would feel far better than this, she told herself. *Less painful. . . .*

She lay back on the rocky ground in silence and felt the endless blackness begin to swallow her up like some firm, gentle cocoon weaving itself around her.

She saw her husband's face, the way she last remembered seeing him alive, the traces to the team of horses in his strong hands. She saw his smile. Wherever death was taking her, Charles was already there, waiting for her. . . .

"Ma'am?" she heard him say, and she knew he must be joking with her. *"Ma'am . . . ?"* he said again. But she detected no playfulness in his voice. "Can you hear me, ma'am . . . ?"

She stirred slightly and murmured her husband's name. She managed to open her eyes and look up at the black silhouette of his face in the glare of sunlight. Then she realized it was not Charles looming over her.

Let me go . . . , she heard herself plead, not knowing if she said her words aloud or to herself.

Yet, even as she wanted to be turned loose and left to die, something else inside her spoke to her. If she only wanted to die, why then had she struggled so hard, so long, to get to this spot? *Good question.* . . . She felt herself slip backward again, deeper into the painless darkness.

"She's alive, but just barely," Dahl said, touching his wet bandanna gently to the woman's badly bruised and battered face.

Sara held the unconscious woman cradled in her lap as Dahl attended to her with water and cloth.

"There's not much we can do for her out here," Dahl said in a rush, having seen the bullet hole in the woman's back when they'd found her moments earlier. "We've got to get her into town to the doctor."

They both looked back toward the street into town, a thousand yards away, the short distance they'd gone before spotting the woman lying in the creek bed thirty yards from the main trail.

"You go, take her on the horse," said Sara. "I'll walk back."

Dahl drew his Colt from his holster and handed it to her butt first.

She gave him a curious look.

"I can't go armed into Kindred," he said. "Hold on to it for me."

She nodded, took the gun in her hands and looked it over as Dahl scooped the unconscious woman up carefully into his arms.

"Do you think Kern is going to give you trouble anyway?" she asked.

"He shouldn't, not under these circumstances," said Dahl. "I'm unarmed. That's all his gun law calls for."

"Yes, you're right," Sara said, "under these circumstances . . ." But she sounded apprehensive, following him to the horse. "Be careful all the same."

"I will, I promise," said Dahl. "And you be careful too." He nodded toward the Colt in her hands. "Do you know how to use one of those?"

"I cock it. I point it. Then I pull the trigger," she said. "Nothing to it."

"Right, nothing to it," he said, wasting no time getting the limp woman up onto his horse's back as carefully as he could. He leaned her forward onto the dun's neck, then swung up behind her and turned the horse toward town.

Please be careful. . . . For a moment, she stood with the gun in both hands and watched him ride away in a low stir of dust. Then she sighed and started walking back, letting the heavy Colt hang from her right hand, swinging loosely back and forth with each step.

141

■ ■ ■ ■

Dr. Washburn had just arrived back in town and stopped his buggy in the alley behind his office when Dahl rode up with the half-naked woman leaning unconscious against his chest. The large doctor hurried down from his buggy seat and ran over to Dahl as he reined the big dun to a sliding halt.

"My goodness, young man!" the doctor said. "What have we here? That's not Sara, is it?"

"No, it's not Sara, Doctor," said Dahl. He stepped down from the horse's bare back and pulled the woman into his arms. "Sara and I found her lying along the trail south of here. She's back-shot. I hope I'm not too late getting her here."

"Bring her into my office. We'll see," the doctor said. He hurriedly swung open the gate to his backyard.

He rushed ahead of Dahl and the woman and opened the rear door to his office.

"Straight ahead, on your left," he said, directing Dahl down a hallway. "I see you haven't listened to me and stayed off your horse," he said as Dahl moved quickly past him.

"I had no choice, Doctor," said Dahl. "I

142

had to get her here fast."

"I understand," the doctor said, pointing Dahl toward a treatment gurney set up in the middle of a small room. "Lay her on her side. Let me see her back wound," he said.

Dahl put the woman down carefully while the doctor jerked out of his black linen suit coat and rolled up his shirtsleeves.

Washburn clasped the woman's wrist between his thumb and finger to feel for a pulse. At the same time, he leaned down and looked at the bullet hole in her back, only an inch from her spine. Fresh blood trickled down onto the gurney. The two stood in silence for a moment.

"She's alive. Good," the doctor said finally, his black necktie hanging loose around his opened white collar. He laid her hand down and turned her wrist loose.

Dahl watched the large doctor hurry about the room, gathering medical supplies and instruments.

"What can I do to help, Doctor?" he asked.

"You can stay out of my way," the doctor said flatly.

Dahl stepped back.

"You took a chance coming here after the marshal warned you against it," Washburn said without stopping as he laid down a clean pan and filled it with a solution from a green bottle.

"I had no choice, Doctor," Dahl said, staying back out of the way. "I came unarmed, if that's any help."

"Might be," Washburn said. "But you still want to keep yourself out of sight and get out of here quick as you can."

"I'm gone as soon as you tell me to go, Doctor," Dahl said. "Not before."

"All right, *go,*" the doctor said.

Dahl just looked at him.

"I mean it, *go,*" the doctor repeated. He gave Dahl a serious stare. "There's nothing you can do here for me, or for her," he added, gesturing a nod down at the woman. She managed to loll her head a bit and half open her eyes.

"All right, I'll leave," said Dahl. But before he turned toward the rear door, he asked, "Did you hear shooting earlier?"

"I heard it," said the doctor. "I was on my way back from birthing a baby east of town. Don't know what it was about, though." He glared at Dahl as he picked up a small sponge and a clean white cloth. "Are you leaving, or what?"

"I'm gone," Dahl said. He started to turn away.

"If you want to do something good, send Sara here to help me look after this woman," the doctor said. "From the looks of her, I doubt a *man's* face is the first thing she wants to wake up to."

"What do you mean, Doctor?" Dahl asked.

"What do you *think* I mean?" the doctor replied in a grim tone.

Down the street in the marshal's office, Kern and Jason Catlo looked out the window as Jennings, Philbert and Bender waited outside for more townsmen to show up with their guns. They stood behind a table, which was piled high with all of the guns that had been turned in before the shooting.

"They'll come back," Kern said hopefully. "They're spooked right now, but they'll come back. I might need to go remind them all that the law is passed, and there's nothing they can do but comply." He nodded with confidence. "But they *will* be back."

"I hope you're right," Jason Catlo said, looking away, the trace of a smile spreading across his face. "There is nobody who wishes this plan more success than I do."

"Me too," Jennings said in a thick voice, overhearing the two.

"Oh, it's going to work," said Kern. "I can safely promise you *that*." He folded his hands behind his back and gazed back and forth along the street.

Small groups of townsmen stood along the first street, huddled together in conversation. Some still held the guns meant to be turned over to the lawmen. Others stood empty-handed, having already given up their weapons before the shooting had given everyone pause to reconsider the new law.

Among one group, the town blacksmith, a fellow named Erkel Fannin, stood with a big Remington pistol in his hand. A large Dance Brothers revolver stood behind his waistband, its hand sticking out from behind the edge of his long leather work apron.

"I don't trust it anymore," he said to the four men gathered near him. "I'm taking my guns back to my shop and burying them down deep under something."

"But you voted for this law, Erkel," said a real estate speculator named Dan Marlowe. He shook his head. "What about those of us who were first in line and got rid of our firearms?"

"All I can say is shame on you," said the blacksmith. "It was all a mistake. I'm keeping my guns."

"If it's a mistake, then we need to get the mayor and the three town councilmen to repeal the law," said the real estate man. "Until then, you have to abide by the law as it stands."

"You're on the town council, Matheson," the blacksmith said to a thin bald man who stood with his hands in the pockets of a long black duster. "How long does it take to get a law off the books once it's on?"

"I've never seen it done, but it shouldn't take long at all," said the councilman, who also happened to be managing president of the Great Western Bank and Trust Company. He considered it for a moment, then said, "On second thought, I'm afraid it might take a while." His brow furrowed. "We have to call a special meeting, get all three of us there and the mayor of course, soon as he gets back."

"Damn, who knows how long it'll be before Coakley gets back?" the blacksmith said. "Can't it get done without him?"

"I don't see how," said the councilman. "Coakley was councilman before he was elected mayor. Now we're one councilman short until the next council election. When Coakley gets back, he can appoint someone temporarily. But all this takes time."

"Where is Councilman Matthews?"

Stevens asked.

"He's off salmon fishing somewhere north of here," said Matheson. "I expect he'll be coming back in another week or two."

"A week or two?" said the blacksmith. "We need help from our local government now! What if he and Mayor Coakley neither one ever come back? What if Coakley fell down a hole and broke his damn neck?" he asked.

"Then the next elected town official will be the marshal when Kern's appointment runs out," said the councilman.

"Jesus," said the blacksmith, "what a mess."

"These are all things we didn't consider before passing the law," the councilman said. "See, the mayor *appointed* the marshal to office until the next town marshal's election." He used his fingers to guide him as he spoke. "Then the marshal has to run for office like everybody else. Until then he's an appointee —"

"Damn it," said the blacksmith, "can't you and Councilman Myers repeal the law by yourselves? Mayor Coakley said if it didn't work out, we could strike it from the books."

"I'm afraid Mayor Coakley spoke a little hastily," said Matheson.

"In other words, he's a lying son of a bitch," said the blacksmith.

"Crudely spoken, but *yes,* perhaps," said the councilman. "Although I believe that the marshal may have the power to appoint an interim councilman under these circumstances, even though he's an appointee himself."

The blacksmith and the other townsmen all stared at him as if he'd spoken in tongues.

"I'm keeping my guns," the blacksmith said flatly. "I must have been out of my mind."

Denton Bender walked into the marshal's office through the rear door, making his way back inside after using the jake.

"It looks like the town doctor is back from delivering somebody's whelp," he said.

"Oh?" said Kern. "Well, we didn't need him before, but we might before this is over." He looked at Jason and said, "Care to join me, Deputy?"

"Sure, where we headed?" said Jason Catlo.

"We're going to go remind some of these good citizens that they are breaking the law."

"Hell, let's go do it," Jason said eagerly. He gave his brother, Philbert, and the others a grin. "Think you ol' boys can handle all this action until we get back?" He

149

gestured all around the quiet office.

"We'll do our level best," said Philbert, working a chewed-down matchstick around in the corner of his mouth. He pulled the brim of his battered hat down low above his eyes.

CHAPTER 11

When the marshal and Jason Catlo had left the office, Denton Bender walked over to the window and looked out, watching the pair cross the dirt street.

"Looks like the town doctor must have his hands full today," he said over his shoulder.

"Yeah? How so?" asked Philbert Catlo, the words hanging loosely from his lips. He leaned back, his hands folded behind his head, perched on the corner of the gun table.

"I saw him and another man carrying a half-naked woman in through the back door. Looked like she'd been back-shot. She was limp as a Chinese soup noodle."

Philbert sat upright on the desk corner. He pushed his hat brim up with a finger and looked over at Buck the Mule Jennings.

"You don't say," he said quietly.

Jennings' face twisted instantly to one side. He batted his broad eyes nervously.

"You don't say," he repeated.

Tribold Cooper stopped sorting through the pile of guns for a moment and looked up.

"Is there something wrong with you, Buck the Mule?" he asked, sounding a little irritated with Jennings' peculiar ways.

"Nothing you want to fool with," Jennings said with a strange look on his face. His big hand went to the butt of his gun.

"Oh, is that a fact?" said Cooper, his hand reaching for his own gun.

"Easy now, Buck the Mule," said Philbert, standing up from the corner of the table, the matchstick clenched in his teeth. He turned to Cooper and said, "Pay him no mind, Tribold. He's been inside too long."

"Maybe you best air him out some," said Cooper. "He's headed to the point where there's no coming back with me."

"Good idea," said Philbert, not wanting to argue with Cooper right then. "Come on, Buck the Mule!" he said in a loud, strong voice, hoping to jar Jennings enough to get his attention. "Let's you and me take a walk."

"I want to see the woman," Jennings said in a strange voice.

"What woman is he talking about?" Cooper asked, his hand still in place on his gun

152

butt, even though Jennings had dropped his to his side.

"He's just rattling," said Philbert. "There's nothing to it." He walked over and gave Jennings a slight shove.

"I'll go, Philbert, but don't push me," Jennings warned him stubbornly.

"That's not a push," said Philbert, "that's a friendly nudge."

The big gunman turned and walked out the door, Philbert right behind him. Cooper and Bender looked at each other as soon as the two had left.

"That is one crazy sumbitch, right there," Bender said.

"Which one?" Cooper asked. He dropped his hand from his gun butt, now that the two were gone.

"*Both,* now that I think about it," said Bender.

"What the hell was Kern thinking, hiring a bunch like that to help us collect guns?"

"If you ask me, Kern was scared and didn't know what else to do with them," said Cooper, "so he hired them, figuring they'd throw with us and do what he says."

"But they won't, will they?" Bender asked, needing some guidance.

"Hell no," said Cooper. "Men like the Catlos and their idiot, skull-busting pal won't listen to anybody for long." He gave a short, dark grin. "Neither will *we,* as far as that goes."

After leaving the marshal's office, Kern and Jason Catlo walked across the dirt street and straight up to the blacksmith and the other townsmen, who were still gathered in a circle talking.

"It looks like your turn-in line has slowed to a halt ever since your gunmen shot down poor old Virgil," the blacksmith called out.

"We're called *deputies,* mister," Jason Catlo said before Kern could reply. They stopped only a step away from the gathered townsmen

"He's right, Erkel," said Kern. "How dare you call my deputies *gunmen?*"

"They're carrying guns," the blacksmith retorted, not backing down an inch. "They shot a man down in the street. They sure seem like *gunmen* to me."

"They are the only men on this street besides me who have a legal right to carry a gun," said Kern. He gestured at the big Dance Brothers revolver sticking out of Fannin's waist, and at the big Remington hanging in his hand. "What does that make you, Erkel Fannin?"

"It makes me —"

The blacksmith's words stopped short as Jason Catlo grabbed him by the bib of his leather apron with both hands.

"Under arrest," Catlo said, finishing his words for him. His knee jolted up sharp and hard into the blacksmith's crotch. The blacksmith snapped forward, jackknifed at the waist, any fight he might have had clearly gone out of him.

But it wasn't enough to satisfy Jason Catlo. He stepped back, sliding the big Dance Brothers pistol from the blacksmith's waist as the big man hung there, suspended, helpless.

"Plea-please!" Erkel Fannin managed to groan in a tight and strained voice.

The townsmen watched in stunned horror as Catlo stepped back, brought the big revolver around full-swing and swiped it across the top of the blacksmith's head.

Kern was just as stunned as the townsmen by Catlo's action. But he recovered quickly in order to show who was in charge.

"My deputy is following orders. Let this be a warning to you. Any of you illegally carrying guns run the same risk as Erkel here." He pointed down at the knocked-out blacksmith lying sprawled in the dirt. "The *law* is the *law,*" he added, looking all around slowly.

155

"Marshal, I'm appalled!" said Council-man Matheson. "Our blacksmith here has never raised a hand in violence toward any-one!"

"Raise your hands up out of your coat pockets, mister," said Jason Catlo.

"What? I beg your pardon, sir!" said the outraged councilman. "I happen to be a town official."

"We don't play favorites, do we, Marshal Kern?" said Catlo, stepping forward toward Matheson.

"Well, no," Kern said unsteadily.

"Now raise your hands, scarecrow," Jason said to the councilman. "Else you can join the blacksmith staring at pissants."

Matheson glanced down at the black-smith's half-open crossed eyes gazing across the dirt. Blood ran from a split welt on top of his head.

"I — I have a small Uhlinger pistol here," said Matheson, raising his hands from his coat pockets.

"A hideout gun. Shame on you, Council-man," said Jason Catlo with a devilish grin. "What kind of example does that set for the young folks of this town, an elected town official *prowling the streets, armed,* in clear violation of the gun law?"

"Easy, Deputy," Marshal Kern warned,

seeing that Jason Catlo was about to take it too far.

"I'm sorry, Marshal," Catlo said, "but this just makes my blood boil." He looked back at Matheson, the small gun butt peeping over the edge of his coat pocket.

"It's not even loaded, Deputy," Matheson said in a trembling voice. "I brought it along just to turn it in, I swear!"

"Loaded . . . unloaded. I don't give a damn," Catlo said, shaking his head in feigned disgust. "I ought to beat your teeth out just for the hell of it," he said.

"Wait a minute, Deputy," said Kern, just as Jason took a step toward Lyndon Matheson. "Maybe something good can come out of this." He looked at the shaken councilman and said quietly, "Councilman, a good word from you would help us get these people to abide by the law."

"I'll do anything to help you, Marshal!" said Councilman Matheson. "I *live* to serve my community." He raised the Uhlinger slowly from his coat pocket, stepped forward and laid it on Kern's outstretched palm. Catlo looked ahead, drumming his fingertips on his holstered Colt, the big Dance Brothers pistol hanging from his hand. Fannin's blood dripped from the pistol's handle.

■ ■ ■ ■

From the window of the marshal's office, Tribold Cooper and Denton Bender had seen everything taking place in the middle of the dirt street.

"Looks like the good citizens are starting to change their minds," said Cooper, watching the councilman address everyone on the street. Three townsmen lifted the knocked-out blacksmith and carried him toward his shop a block away.

"Yeah, I see that . . . ," said Bender, pleased to see the townsmen who still carried their guns start to make their way back to the marshal's office to form another line. "There's nothing like a good talking-to to straighten things out. We might start getting busy here after all."

Dr. Washburn removed the .45-caliber slug from the unconscious woman's back and dropped it into a small metal pan. He folded a soft cotton cloth, placing it on the gurney, and turned her onto her back atop it, allowing a few minutes of drainage before re-cleaning and dressing the wound.

He pulled a sheet up above the woman's bruised and naked breasts, and then looked at her swollen purple face and shook his head.

"You're a *double-shot* patient indeed," he murmured down to her.

He stepped over to a table and took a silver flask from his black medical bag. He unscrewed the cap, shook the contents around and gave himself a thin smile.

"Here's to me," he toasted himself wryly. "For a job well done."

He threw back a drink, let out a short hiss and threw back another. He started to screw the cap back on the flask, but stopped himself as he heard the back door open and close.

"Who's there?" he asked, walking out of the surgery room and down the hall toward the rear of the house, open flask in hand. "Is that you, Sara?"

"No, Doctor," said Philbert Catlo, both he and Jennings stepping into sight, as if coming out of hiding. "It's just us deputies," he said with his wide, friendly grin.

"Deputies . . . ?" the doctor questioned warily. "Where are your badges?"

"Badges?" Philbert slapped a hand to his chest. "You've got me there, Doctor." He continued with his wide grin. "We've been so busy, we haven't had time to pin any badges on yet." He cut a look to Buck the

Mule Jennings and said, "Remind me to make a mental note of it. I'll tell Marshal Kern first thing — *deputies need badges.* Okay?"

"I will . . . ," said Jennings, staring hard at the doctor as he spoke.

"What is it I can do for you?" the doctor asked bluntly.

"We heard tell that a woman was brought in, back-shot and naked, Doctor," said Philbert.

He stared at the doctor. "Of course we need to know any time something like that has happened to somebody, even if they're not from here."

Not from here . . . Washburn considered the deputy's words, but he put on his poker face. These two weren't from here themselves. How would they know the woman wasn't *from here?*

"So . . . how is she?" Jennings asked, leering past the doctor and down the hall toward the surgery room.

"She's dead," the doctor said somberly, the flask still in his hand, uncapped. "Why do you think I'm standing in here drinking all by myself?" he added for believability's sake.

"Dead, huh?" said Philbert. He clicked his cheek and winced. "Damn, that's a terrible thing, Doc."

"All the way dead?" asked Jennings.

The doctor just looked at him, then at Philbert, who shook his head a little, letting the doctor know not to expect much from Jennings.

"Who was she, Doc?" Philbert asked. "Where's she from? What happened to her?"

"She died before I could find out," the doctor lied, straight-faced. "She was badly tortured, raped, beaten, shamelessly treated . . . then shot in the back when they were through with her." As he spoke he stood watching Jennings' face contort and flinch.

"That's a terrible thing, for sure," Philbert repeated, shaking his head, trying to keep the doctor from seeing the guilt on Jennings' face. "But if she told you anything at all that might help us find the low-down snakes who done that to her, we need to know."

"I wish I could help you, Lord knows," said the doctor. "But she died no sooner than I got the bullet out of her back."

"All right, then," said Philbert with a showy sigh of regret. "May she rest in peace, the poor darling." He started to turn toward the rear door. But he caught himself and said suddenly, "We'll take a look at her body, then be on our way."

"I'm afraid I can't let you do that, Deputy," the doctor said, undaunted. "I never allow anyone to see the body until after someone has cleaned it up and —"

"Why's that?" asked Philbert, cutting him off. "Is it bad luck or something?" He shot the doctor another grin. "Because if it is, me and Deputy Buck the Mule here are not what you call real superstitious. Are we, Buck the Mule?"

"Not a lick," said Jennings.

"Besides, we're deputies," said Philbert. "We're supposed to look at dead bodies." He eased his gun hand up and rested it on his gun butt.

"I like to look at them," said Jennings. His big hand also went to his gun butt.

"Don't hurt our feelings, now, Doctor," Philbert said, his voice sounding dark and sinister, like the low hiss of a viper.

While the doctor stood staring, unsure of his next move, the rear door opened and closed again. This time, Sara Cayes walked into sight.

"Hello —" she called out. But she stopped cold at the sight of the two gunmen, who appeared to be facing off with the large grim-faced doctor. "Oh," she said, looking back and forth between the three.

"Sara, you go back home," Dr. Washburn said, trying to play down the urgency of the situation. "I'm afraid my patient didn't make it."

"Oh, I'm so sorry," Sara said. Sensing something was amiss, she backed away and said, "If you need me for anything else, just send for me." She started to turn to the door. But Philbert Catlo would have none of it.

"Hold on there, little lady," he said. His hand came up holding his Colt loosely pointed between her and the doctor. "We're getting ready to take a look at the dear departed. Why don't you just come along with us?"

"Who are you?" Sara asked.

"I'll ask all the questions," said Philbert. He gave Jennings a nod. The big dirty gunman stepped forward quickly and took Sara by her arm.

"Yeah, you keep your mouth shut and come with us," said Jennings. He looked her over and asked, "Are you from here?"

When Sara didn't answer right away, Jennings shook her roughly.

"No, I'm not from Kindred," Sara said, "but I live here now." She looked him squarely in his broad, vacant eyes. "I work at the Lucky Devil Saloon and Brothel."

163

"You're a saloon whore," Jennings said with a leering grin.

"Yes, I'm one of the doves there," Sara said.

"Sara is also a good citizen of Kindred," the doctor put in, seeing the lewd expression on the big gunman's face as he continued looking her up and down, desire in his eyes. "She's been a big help to me more times than I can tell you."

"I bet she has," Jennings said, breathing close to Sara's cheek.

"Whore or not, we've got no time for this," said Philbert. He wagged his gun loosely back and forth. "Let's see this dead woman."

CHAPTER 12

Inside the surgery room door, the two gun-men, Sara Cayes, and Dr. Washburn all stood staring at the sheet-covered body on the gurney. Washburn managed to hide his surprise when he saw that the sheet was not as he had left it, but had been pulled all the way up over her head, covering her entirely. One of the woman's bruised purplish arms hung limply off the edge of the gurney.

"There, I told you she's dead. Now let's all let her rest in peace," Washburn insisted, keeping himself in check.

Sara let out a slight sigh when she set eyes on the sheet-covered body, she herself believing the woman had died.

"The poor thing . . . ," she murmured.

Jennings turned Sara loose and stared down at the covered face of Celia Knox.

"Can I see her?" he asked Philbert, sound-ing a little excited.

"That's why we're here, Buck the Mule,"

said Philbert, giving the doctor one more quick, distrustful look. He took hold of the top edge of the sheet, lifted it and looked down, immediately recognizing Celia's bruised and swollen face.

After a moment, Jennings reached out a dirty hand and started to lay it on the woman's naked, battered breast.

"All right, that's enough of this!" said the doctor, stepping forward, outraged. "Deputies or no deputies, I won't allow you to disrespect the dead in my presence! Get away from her, the both of you!"

"Damn, Buck the Mule," said Philbert with a dark chuckle. "What the hell is wrong with you?" He dropped the sheet back down over the woman's face.

"I only wanted to touch her," said Jennings in an angry, childlike voice. He glared at Philbert. "What's wrong with that?"

Philbert just stared at him for a moment, a bemused expression on his face.

"Okay, *Deputies,* you've done your job. You've seen her," Washburn said firmly. "Now go report her death to the marshal."

"We will," said Philbert. He stepped away from the gurney, then turned to the doctor as he slipped his Colt back into its holster. "Who brought her here?"

"A young man who is convalescing in a

house outside town," said Washburn, offering them no more than he had to on the matter. "He found her and brought her here."

"Oh," said Philbert, "he found her like that, all beat up and shot, that is?" He gave a short, sly grin. "Well, well, who's to say he didn't do it to her?"

"I'm to say he didn't," Sara cut in instantly. "I was with him when he found her."

"And she was still alive when you both found her?" Philbert asked.

"Yes, barely," said Sara. "The man who found her with me is Sherman Dahl. We both found her. He brought her here on horseback. Then he came back and sent me to help the doctor look after her."

"But she said *nothing* about what happened to her?" Philbert asked.

"Not a word," said Sara. "She was in no condition to say anything."

Philbert considered it, and decided that there was no way he and his brother and Buck the Mule Jennings would be connected to the woman.

"Too damn bad," he said with a trace of his usual smile. "I always want to get my hands on a sumbitch who does something like this, eh, Buck the Mule?"

"Yeah, me too," said Jennings. "Choke the

167

sumbitch to death." He opened and closed his big, dirty hands as he spoke.

"Let's go talk to the marshal . . . ," Philbert said to Jennings. He gave a touch of his hat brim toward the doctor and Sara. With no apology for their earlier behavior, he gave Jennings a slight shove toward the hallway.

As soon as the rear door closed behind the two men, Sara turned to the doctor with a stunned look on her face.

"My God," she said, "where did Kern find —"

"No time to talk!" the doctor replied in a rushed voice. "Go lock the back door."

Sara did as she was told. When she returned to the surgery room, Dr. Washburn had thrown back the sheet from the woman's face and stood staring down at her intently

"Don't worry. They're gone," he said to the battered face. "You can stop pretending."

Sara gasped in surprise to see the woman's eyelids flutter slightly and try to open against the dark swelling that surrounded them.

"Oh my!" Sara said. "She's not dead."

"No," said the doctor, "she's still with us. Aren't you, dear?"

The woman made a moaning sound that

168

would have to do for the moment.

"Did you hear us talking from the hall-way?" the doctor asked. "You covered yourself when you knew we'd be coming in?"

With much effort, the woman managed to nod her head slightly. "I — I recognized . . . the voice," she managed to say in a weak and raspy voice. "They . . . did this."

The doctor and Sara Cayes gave each other a troubled look.

"They're nothing but murdering, back-shooting rapists," Sara said, horrified.

"They are also Marshal Emerson Kern's *deputies*," said the doctor, "at a time when Kern is disarming this whole town."

Jennings stopped dead in his tracks on the way back to the marshal's office, turning to Philbert. "You go on. I've got to go to the jake."

Philbert looked at him, recognizing the tightly drawn expression on his face.

"Has that little strawberry dove got you all steamed up, Buck the Mule?" he asked in a lowered voice.

"Don't you say nothing like that to me," said Jennings, getting upset. "I told you I have to go to the jake. That's *all* I have to do."

"All right, go on to the privy," said Philbert. "I'll be at the marshal's office. I want to tell Jason about the dead woman." He grinned. "He's going to be *real* surprised to hear it." He walked on as Jennings veered away toward the privies in the alley behind the row of shops and buildings.

Inside the surgery room, Dr. Washburn and Sara Cayes stood over the woman on the gurney as she came around. She'd managed to hold her swollen eyes open long enough to tell the doctor a little bit about what had happened to her and her husband out on the high trails. When she'd finished, Sara leaned in close and held her hand.

"You rest now," Sara said. "Doc Washburn and I won't let anything happen to you."

But as the woman drifted back to sleep, Sara gave him a worried look. After they'd walked a few feet away, Sara whispered, "What if they come back?"

"She mustn't be here for long, Sara," the doctor whispered in reply. "Can you keep her at the widow's shack?"

"Of course I can keep her there," said Sara. "Sherman won't mind sleeping on the floor. Neither will I."

"Bless you, Sara," Washburn said. He patted her shoulder. "I'm going to put her in my buggy. With the top up, nobody will see her in there."

"All right," said Sara. "I'll go make sure there's nobody snooping around back there."

While the doctor walked back to the gurney, Sara hurried to the rear of the house and looked through a window. At the hitch rail, the doctor's buggy still sat where he'd left it. But Dahl's horse, which Sara had ridden bareback from the shack, was missing. She finally spotted the big dun hitched near the open door of a barn thirty yards from the doctor's backyard.

When she looked more closely, Sara recognized Buck the Mule Jennings peep out from the shaded darkness of the open doorway. A chill went up Sara's spine. She turned and hurried back to the surgery room just as the doctor had started to scoop the wounded woman up into his arms.

"Doc Washburn, wait," she said. "There's a trap waiting out back."

"A trap . . . ?" Leaving the injured woman on the gurney, he turned and followed Sara to the rear window and looked out.

"There, see him?" Sara said, the two of them huddled at the edge of the window curtain, peeping out.

"Yes, I see that low-down scoundrel," said

171

the doctor. He looked all around to make sure the big dirty gunman was alone. Pulling his face back from the edge of the window, he sighed in frustration.

"One thing's for certain, we can't send you two off to the widow's while he's back there waiting for you to come get the horse."

"Yes," said Sara. "Once I get close enough for him to grab me, he plans on pulling me into the barn."

"That's clearly his plan," said Washburn, his rage growing. "If only I were a younger man, I'd go give him the thrashing he deserves." He clenched his fists at his side, his shirtsleeves still hanging loose and unbuttoned.

"No, you stay right here," said Sara. "He'll leave in due time, once he sees I'm not coming for the horse." She looked back out for a second, seeing only the toes of Jennings' boots in a slice of sunlight at the open barn doorway.

"You're right, of course," the doctor said, letting his anger settle a little. "We can outwait him. He has no interest in the woman now anyway. His only concern is to get you within his reach."

"While he's in the barn," Sara said, "I'm going to slip out the front door and go tell Sherman what's going on."

"Yes, certainly, you go ahead. He needs to know," the doctor said. "I'll wait here with this poor woman."

"Will you both be safe, Doctor?" Sara asked.

"Oh yes, we'll be safe," said the doctor. "I have a loaded gun in a desk drawer. Don't worry about us."

"Then I'm gone, Doctor," Sara said. She turned and walked toward the front door.

"You be careful, child," the doctor said, walking right behind her.

After he'd made certain that Sara had slipped unnoticed along the street toward the edge of town, Dr. Washburn went to his office and took a .36-caliber Navy Colt from a bottom desk drawer. He hefted the gun in the palm of his hand.

"It's sure been a long time since I've come calling on you," he said to the blue brass-trimmed revolver.

Sherman Dahl stood leaning against the door of the widow's shack, his Winchester rifle propped against the doorjamb, when he saw Sara cross the town limits and step into the weedy rock-strewn front yard.

"I was starting to worry about you," he said as Sara walked up toward the porch. Recognizing the worry on her face, he asked, "Are you all right? Is the woman going to make it?"

"I'm all right," Sara said. "The woman is alive. That's as well as can be expected, the shape she's in." She stepped onto the porch and said, "Two new deputies came to the doctor's office. She played dead while they were there. When they were gone, she told us she recognized their voices. They're the men who did all this to her."

"Deputies, huh . . . ?" Dahl appeared only slightly surprised.

"Yes, *deputies*," Sara repeated. "Thank God they thought she was dead. I believe if they hadn't, they would have killed not only her, but the doctor and me as well."

Dahl only nodded, gazing past her and in the direction of the doctor's office on the main street.

"Where's my horse?" he asked quietly.

Sara drew a tense breath and let it out slowly. She told him everything, about how Buck the Mule hitched the dun near an open barn door in order to lure her in close enough to grab her.

"He has my horse," Dahl said flatly.

"Yes, to lure me in," she repeated. "But it didn't work, and see? I'm okay," she added quickly, not liking the change she saw coming over Dahl's icy blue eyes.

"And these are the marshal's deputies?" he asked.

"That's what they said," Sara replied. "I believe them." She quickly changed the subject, getting down to business. "I'll bring the woman here in Doc Washburn's buggy as soon as things settle a little."

"Yes, as soon as things settle down," he said. He stared in the direction of Kindred, attempting to make out the doctor's office and the barn behind it in the far-off distance.

"What is it?" she asked, seeing him grow more distant from her.

"I'll be right back," he said. He picked up his rifle from the doorjamb and walked off the porch.

"Wait," Sara said. "Where are you going?"

"Where do you think?" Dahl replied over his shoulder.

"But you can't go into Kindred *armed*," she said. "You agreed not to!" she called out as he walked away across the front yard, the rifle lying back over his right shoulder.

"I agreed to when I considered Kern to be the law. If his deputies did that to the woman, Kindred has no law. I owe them nothing."

Sara stared at him as he walked away. "Should I — Should I come get the woman?"

"Give me five minutes. Then come get her," Dahl said.

From the darkness of the barn's open doorway, Jennings watched as the tall sandy-haired figure walked along the alleyway, a rifle propped over his shoulder. When he saw the man walk to the dun and begin to unhitch the animal, he stepped out, his big hand on his holstered revolver.

"Hey, you," he said. "What the hell do you think you're doing? You can't take that hor—"

Dahl's rifle swung off his shoulder and crashed down on the big man's right collarbone. Dahl heard the bone snap like seasoned hickory. Jennings' head snapped sideways with the impact of the blow. As he tried to straighten up, the tip of the barrel stabbed him full force in the V of his chest where his ribs joined. His breath exploded from his lungs.

Dahl looked down at the big gunman, who lay gasping in the dirt. He then unhitched the dun and led it away toward the widow's shack.

On the way, he saw Sara slip along the alleyway toward him.

"You said five minutes," she said with the

trace of a smile.

"It went a little quicker than I thought," Dahl said. He looked along the street toward the marshal's office where a long line of townsmen had once again formed. He shook his head. "Go get the woman in the buggy. I'll wait right here."

PART 2

CHAPTER 13

It was near dark when Buck the Mule Jennings dragged himself up on the hitch rail and staggered along the alleyway to the street. He had just turned the corner toward the marshal's office when Philbert Catlo approached him, looking him up and down.

"Great guns, man, what happened to you?" he asked, catching the big gunman before he fell and helping him lean against the front of a building.

"I . . . fell," Jennings lied in a strained and ragged voice. He clutched his right collarbone with his big left hand. "I'm all broken up here," he said, his big head cocked painfully to the right.

"You *fell* . . . ?" Philbert said in disbelief. "And broke your collarbone . . . in the jake?" He recoiled back from the injured gunman and looked at both his hands.

"No . . . not in . . . the jake," said Jennings. "But when I walked . . . out. I stumbled over a hitch rail."

"Oh, I see," said Philbert. "They put those things in the damnedest places."

Jennings stared at him, unable to tell whether or not Catlo was mocking him.

Philbert stepped closer. "Anyway, I came looking for you. I thought you fell in." He stifled a laugh. "Turns out I wasn't far wrong."

"It's not funny," Jennings managed to say. He straightened up a little.

"Do I need to take you to the doctor?" Philbert asked, still taunting the big gunman a little.

"Hell no," Jennings growled. "There's nothing he could do. It's just a broken bone."

"Right, just a broken bone," said Philbert. "I don't know what I was thinking."

"Did you tell Jason about the dead woman?" Jennings asked.

"Not yet," said Philbert. "I'll have to tell him when we're alone. The marshal's office has been crowded ever since I went back. These rubes can't get rid of their guns quick enough, ever since brother Jason parted the blacksmith's hair with a gun barrel."

"So, we're not going to tell the marshal about the dead woman?" Jennings asked.

"Jesus, Buck the Mule," said Philbert,

"did you get hit on your head? Of course we're not going to tell the marshal anything."

"Why not?" Jennings asked.

"Because . . ." Philbert lowered his voice as if letting the thick gunman in on a secret. "We're not really lawmen, Buck the Mule. We're only setting this town up for a big letdown."

"Hell, I know that," said Jennings, sounding irritated. "I just think it might look funny, us going to the doctor and asking about the woman, then not telling Kern about it."

"Let brother Jason and me do all the serious thinking," Philbert said. "You concentrate on sidestepping those hitch rails."

Jennings glowered at him.

"Right now, let's get back to work collecting these guns," Philbert said. "I don't know what the marshal or Jason, either one, has in mind, but whatever it is, it's going to go a lot better when these rubes aren't able to fight back." He turned and nodded back toward the marshal's office where men still stood in line, guns in hand.

"Yeah, that's what I can't wait to see," said Jennings. He turned and walked stiffly alone behind Philbert. He managed a slight grin, considering the possibilities awaiting them in an unarmed town.

They arrived at the marshal's office, and stepped inside. Jason Catlo placed an older muzzleloader rifle down atop the table and looked up. Denton Bender and Tribold Cooper carried guns from the table into a back room, which had been set up for temporary storage of firearms until a more permanent place was established.

"Damn, what happened to him?" Cooper asked, noting the stiff twisted way Jennings walked into the office.

"He fell in the jake," Philbert said.

"Damn . . . ," said Cooper, taking a step back, his nose wrinkling.

"No, I didn't," Jennings said. He cut an angry glance at Philbert. "I can speak for myself."

"Excuse the hell out of me," Philbert said. He shrugged and walked away.

"I stumbled over a hitch rail," Jennings said in a voice that was more of an angry growl. "Anybody got anything to say about it?"

The gunmen just look at each other.

"Yeah, I do," said Philbert, realizing that all the big man could do was make threats. "You should've stuck with falling in the jake."

With his collarbone broken, Jennings' gun

hand hung helpless down his side. All he could do was stare ahead in a smoldering rage. "I didn't fall in no damn jake," he said, "I fell over a hitch rail."

Bender stepped over to where a townsman stood in the open doorway, a shotgun and big Colt saddle pistol under his arm.

"Come back tomorrow," he said to the townsman, shoving him backward out the door. He slammed the door in the man's face. "I've worked hard enough for one day," he chuckled.

Outside, the townsman looked around at the few others in line. Some of them had been standing for over three hours.

"Notice how the fewer guns there are left, the more belligerent they're getting with us?" he said.

"Yeah," said one man who carried a ten-gauge long-barreled goose gun. "I also saw the blacksmith's head where one of them cracked him with his own gun barrel."

"Being made to stand in line ain't the worst thing that can happen to a man," another townsman said as the line began to break up for the night.

"No, but standing a man in line is where it all starts. Once he's standing in line, it's easy to point that line any direction *they* want him to go in."

"*They . . . ?*" another man said, irritated by his long wait only to be turned away. "I'd like to know who the hell *they* is?"

"I've got a feeling you'll know soon enough who *they* is," said another.

"We all will, *soon enough,*" added a third.

Inside the marshal's office, Kern having still not returned, Bender and Cooper stood on one side of the big gun table, looking across at the Catlo brothers and Buck the Mule Jennings. Bender finished examining a Starr revolver and tossed it on the table.

"The way this thing is shaping up," he said, "Tribold and I figure this town will be unarmed by noon tomorrow. Right, Tribold?"

"That's what we figure," said Cooper.

"Yeah? What then?" Jason Catlo asked, sounding the two out before telling them anything.

"Of course, that don't mean there won't be guns coming in and out of town with travelers until word gets around that guns aren't allowed," said Copper. "But as far as guns in Kindred go —" He stopped and grinned. "Hell, this goose is cooked."

Jason allowed himself a thin smile. "Yeah, I still can't believe these folks were stupid enough to be talked into this."

"I know what you mean," said Cooper. "It makes me wonder what's waiting in the future, especially for bank robbers."

Jason Catlo liked what he was hearing. He and his brother gave each other a nod. Jennings stood clutching his broken collarbone, mumbling curses under his breath.

"I expect robbing banks will get taken over by the government, just like everything else. Once folks everywhere are unarmed, all the law will have to do is get everybody's money into banks and rob every bank at once."

"Without having to fire a shot," Philbert said, grinning.

Bender chuckled, getting it. "Because what the hell can anybody do about it?" He shrugged and laughed. "Nobody will be *armed!*"

The five gunmen cackled and hooted for a moment.

"Rob every bank at once, eh . . . ?" said Tribold Cooper, considering it. "I like the sound of it."

"The government won't even have to say where the money went. Just say, 'Hey, all you rubes, the banks have been robbed. Now go home and start all over again.' " He laughed as he rolled his eyes. "The idiots won't be able to do nothing about it!"

" 'Cause they won't even have guns!" Philbert added, laughing loudly.

After a moment the laughter settled.

"But that's the future," Cooper said in a more serious tone. "What about right now?"

"What about it?" Jason Catlo asked.

"Are you Catlos willing to sit back and squeeze this town for nickels and dimes?" Bender asked.

"We hate to," Jason said, still not jumping out front until he knew where the two men stood on the matter. "It might look a little more respectable. But it's still robbery. I always say 'whole hog or none.' He patted his holstered Colt. "Until people like Kern and this Mayor Coakley figure out how to rob every bank at once, I say take what you can and ride on." He paused.

"But that's just the Catlo way of thinking," said Philbert, tapping his fingers on his gun butt. "How do you boys have it figured?"

Cooper and Bender both looked at the closed front door, then all around as if to make sure they couldn't be overheard.

"I have always wondered how it would feel to rob a town dry with all the time in the world — no bullets whistling past my head," said Cooper.

"Funny thing," said Jason Catlo, "we've always wondered that ourselves."

Darkness had fallen when Marshal Kern walked into the office of the *Kindred Star Weekly News*. Ed Dandly sat at his desk behind an oaken handrail. When he saw Kern, he stood up and took off his glasses.

"Well, Marshal," Dandly said, "I saw your deputy whip the townsmen into shape for you — quite *literally,* I might add."

"The blacksmith broke the gun law," Kern said, walking over to the gate in the handrail. "Any time a new law like this comes on the books, somebody has to be made into an example. This time it happened to be Erkel Fannin." He shrugged. "He was just doing his *civil duty.*"

Dandly glanced at the pencil stub and notepad lying on his desk. He started to reach down and pick them both up, but then he thought better of it.

"The irony is that Fannin happened to be one of Mayor Coakley's strongest supporters of the gun law," said Dandly. He gestured toward the printing press that took up a large corner of the room behind the handrail. "I plan on mentioning it in next week's edition of the paper."

"Do you really?" challenged Kern. "Which

189

side are you going to be taking?"

"Which *side?*" Dandly questioned. He gave Kern an indignant look. "Neither *side,* Marshal." Again he pointed toward the ink-splattered iron and wooden machine standing in the corner. "The press takes *no sides.* The press only prints the facts as it sees them to be."

Kern also gave a glance toward the large machine. Where Dandly's look had been one of admiration, the marshal's was one of scorn.

"That big stinking machine only spits out what you tell it to," he said. "So, I'm going to ask you again, which side are you —"

"Speaking of Mayor Coakley," Dandly said, cutting the marshal off, "has anyone heard from him? Any idea when he might be returning to Kindred?"

"I have no idea," Kern said, hearing an implication of sorts in Dandly's tone. He stepped through the oaken handrail and let the gate flap on its iron spring behind him. "Why are you asking me?"

"I'm asking you because you are the next highest seat to the mayor," Dandly said. "Do you find something wrong with me doing my job?"

"No," said Kern, "not as long as your job doesn't interfere with what I'm trying to do here." He stopped a few feet away from Dandly. "I'd like to think that in your job and mine, we could both do a lot to help each other. In turn, we'd both be helping this town go in the right direction."

"Hunh-uh," said Dandly, shaking his head. "My press doesn't take sides, Marshal. When the next edition comes out, it will talk about the new gun law and how it's being received. I will print the facts — the truth and nothing but the truth. Let the chips fall where they may."

"That's too bad," said Kern.

Too bad? Dandly stared at Kern. "Marshal, I have always said, what good is a reporter and his press if he doesn't print every side of a situation, in spite of his personal opinion?"

"I understand," said Kern. "But I look at it another way. I say, what good is a press or its reporter unless they do exactly the way I tell them to do?"

Dandly gave a slightly bemused grin; Kern grinned along with him.

"My goodness, Marshal, you can't be serious —"

Before Dandly got the words from his lips, he felt a deep searing pain shoot deep into his chest. His eyes went down to the front of the marshal's fist, which stood firmly

191

against the center of his chest.

"Shhh, be quiet now," Kern said softly, almost soothingly.

Dandly gasped; his eyes bulged as the marshal's fist pulled away slightly. He saw the blood-smeared knife blade slide halfway out of his chest, then plunge back deeper inside him, this time probing, this time finding the center of his heart.

"Let's just sit you down right here, *Dandy*," Marshal Kern said calmly, easing the man around to his chair and following him down with the knife's handle gripped firmly in hand. He stood over the newsman until he saw life fade away from his bulging eyes. Then he turned loose of the handle and took a breath. Finding none of Dandly's blood on his hands as he inspected them and wiped them together, he turned and left the office, a job well done.

Across the street from the newspaper office, the young man stood watching from the darker shadow of an alleyway. His belly growled with hunger. He was beginning to think the marshal would never leave. Now, as he saw the marshal walk along the boardwalk back toward his own office, he eased out of the shadows and slipped across the empty street, hearing only the music from the saloon wafting in the night air.

He made his way inside the newspaper office, slipping a club from his coat and starting across the floor. He didn't like doing this, but he had no choice, he told himself. He walked toward the man who sat staring straight at him, a look of terror on his face. But as he drew closer, he saw the knife in Dandly's chest, the circle of blood surrounding it.

"My God . . . !" he murmured to himself, looking all around. But he wasted no time. Within seconds he'd burst through the handrail gate, rifled the desk drawers and come out with an apple and a piece of bread wrapped in a piece of paper. He wolfed down the apple and the stale bread as he raked up a handful of change and a small pepperbox derringer Dandly kept in a desk drawer.

The young man turned the gun back and forth in his palm and checked to make sure it was loaded. *All right . . . !* It was about time he found himself a gun, even though this one wasn't much, he thought. He tossed the club aside, stood up and dropped the coins into his pocket. The old man's shotgun would have been better, but Virgil Tullit wouldn't give it up.

The young man took a deep breath and

swallowed the last of the apple that he'd eaten, core and all. He tucked the small pepperbox down into his pocket and smoothed his hand over it; he turned and hurried back out the rear door into the alleyway. He had a lot to do tonight on his way out of town. He wasn't going hungry anymore. *That's for damn sure. . . .*

CHAPTER 14

Dahl and Sara Cayes stood over the bed where the injured woman lay sleeping. As soon as Sara had put her into bed, she'd driven the doctor's rig out of sight into the barn behind the widow's shack and hurried back to the house before Dahl had arrived.

"Was there any trouble?" she asked Dahl, who still held his rifle in hand.

"None to speak of," Dahl replied. He offered no more on the matter.

But moments later, when the doctor arrived on foot, his black medical bag in hand, he looked Dahl up and down and said, "I saw what you did to the fellow outside the barn. Ought to be upset with you for going against my warning and overtaxing your bruised heart." His somber expression changed and a smile spread across his face. "But I'm not."

Dahl only looked at him.

"Are you feeling all right, after that?" the

doctor asked.

"Never better, Doc," said Dahl.

"What did he do, Doctor?" Sara asked.

"Nothing that low miserable miscreant didn't have coming to him, Sara, I can promise you," the doctor said. He'd already stripped off his linen coat and started rolling up his white shirtsleeves. "But enough about that ugly incident. Let me see how my patient is doing."

An hour passed as the doctor redressed the bullet wound in the woman's back. Sara stood beside the bed with a pan of warm water and clean gauze; Washburn treated the countless punctures, cuts and scratches covering the woman's feet and calves, caused by the torturous prickly pear and barrel cactus she'd trudged through.

Dahl sat cleaning his big Colt and his Winchester rifle at a wooden table in the corner of the room. They were ready to be used again — the most current bullet holes patched tightly and sewn over with cotton cloth — his bulletproof vest hung from the chair back. When he laid his guns aside and looked over toward the bed, he saw the woman try to sit up, but Doc Washburn placed a hand on her shoulder and pressed her back down gently.

"You lie still now, young lady," the doctor

said. "We're not here to harm you. I'm a doctor. Remember me, from earlier?"

The woman blinked and stared, at first with uncertainty, but then with relief as she recognized Washburn as the man she'd seen when she'd awakened in the surgery room.

"We're not . . . in the same room," she said, looking around her dim-lit surroundings with swollen eyes.

"No, we've moved you," the doctor said, raising her limp wrist between his thumb and forefinger, checking her pulse as she spoke. "We thought you'd feel safer here, away from the men who did this to you."

The woman looked from the doctor to Sara Cayes, who stood watching with a pan of water in her hands. Sara smiled at her.

"You do remember telling us about those men, don't you?" Doc Washburn asked her, making sure the story hadn't only been delirious ramblings.

"Yes, I remember telling you," she said, tensing at the thought of the three men.

"And everything you said was true, then?" Washburn pressed. "I mean what they did to you and to your husband?"

"Yes, all of it . . . is true," she said, her voice still a bit shaky. She collapsed back onto the pillow, but remained conscious.

"You can still identify them?" Washburn

asked, hoping to keep her awake and talking for a while longer.

"I heard their voices . . . I saw their faces as best I could. . . ."

"I understand," said Washburn. "You're a mighty brave and courageous woman." He patted her shoulder. "What is your name, ma'am?" he asked.

As Washburn spoke, Dahl stood up from the table. He walked over and stood behind the doctor and Sara, looking down at the injured woman.

"I'm . . . Celia Knox," the woman said, sounding more alert than she had a moment earlier. "My husband is —" She caught herself. "I mean *was* Charles Knox." Her swollen eyes welled. "We were . . . coming here to Kindred."

"Do you have folks here, or friends maybe?" the doctor asked.

"No." She shook her head weakly.

Washburn glanced at Sara, then asked Celia, "What brought you and Charles here?"

"We . . . we heard about the new gun law," she said. "We wanted to live . . . somewhere like this. Where we could raise a family . . . not be afraid to walk the streets."

Sara set the pan of water down and moved closer to Dahl. He slipped an arm around her and turned her away from the bed while the doctor continued to talk to Celia Knox.

"I keep wanting to tell her not to worry, that the law will see to it these men are punished," Sara said under her breath to Dahl. "Isn't that what we tell people, that the law is going to bring them justice?"

"Yes, ordinarily," Dahl said quietly, "but not this time."

Sara looked at Dahl's saddlebags sitting on the floor near the hearth, one flap unbuckled and hanging open. Next to it lay his saddle, his blanket rolled and tied behind the seat.

"Are you . . . leaving?" she asked.

"No," Dahl said, "not yet."

She looked at him and said, "I mean, I knew you'd be leaving eventually. I'm not trying to keep you. If it's time for you to —"

Dahl placed a finger on her lips, gently hushing her, his arm still around her waist.

"I'm not leaving," he said.

"But your saddle, your belongings," Sara said.

Dahl turned her loose, stooped down and flipped the saddlebags closed and buckled the flap. "I needed some things," he said.

Sara looked at the box of .45 caliber bullets sitting on the table. She looked back at

Dahl, who stood watching her.

"You're riding into Kindred?" she asked.

"I thought I might, as soon as the woman can be moved somewhere safer," Dahl said coolly.

"Are you going to . . . ?" Her words trailed; she wasn't sure what she had started to ask him.

"I'm going to talk to the marshal," Dahl said. "He might not know what his new deputies did."

"Just *talk* to him?" Sara asked, sounding a little worried.

"Yep, just talk," said Dahl. "We have to give the law the benefit of the doubt sometimes, if we expect it to work for all of us."

He picked his Colt up and slipped it down into his holster, which was rolled up in his gun belt on the table.

"And if you find out he does know what kind of men his deputies are?" Sara asked.

Dahl gave her a trace of a smile. "Then I'll stop giving him the benefit of the doubt," he said.

"But you won't take the law into your own hands, will you?" Sara asked, looking for some reassurance.

"Into my own hands . . . ?" Dahl repeated. He considered it. "That's a complicated question, Sara," he said at length. He turned away with no further word on the matter.

Overhearing part of their conversation, the doctor walked over and stopped at the wooden table. He looked down at the bullets, the Winchester lying cleaned and freshly oiled.

"This woman can be moved again if need be," he said firmly to Dahl. "If these men learn that she's here, they'll come to kill her."

"I know that, Doc," said Dahl. "Is there another place where you can hide her?" he asked.

"I have something in mind," said the doctor.

"Good," Dahl said. "It looks like she might be leaving here anytime."

In the dark hours of morning, three sudden blasts of gunfire caused Marshal Kern to bolt up from the cot in the back room of his office. He yanked his boots on and grabbed his rifle, which leaned against the wall beside him.

Along the rear wall of the building, Tribold Cooper had jumped up from his blanket and hurried through the open door of one of the cells where he'd bedded down. The other four deputies followed suit, grabbing rifles and revolvers as they rushed into the main room of the marshal's office.

"What the hell was all that, Marshal?" Cooper asked.

"I don't know," Kern said crossly. "Think we ought to stand here and jaw about it 'til somebody comes and tells us?" he asked with sarcasm.

"It was a fair question, damn it to hell," Cooper barked.

"So was mine," Kern growled.

He levered a round into his rifle chamber and looked at the others through sleepy eyes in the glow of a candle lamp on the wall.

"Everybody's up, Marshal," Jason Catlo said. Behind him stood his brother, Philbert, and Buck the Mule Jennings, the big dirty gunman still crooked at the neck with his shoulder hunched up in pain. Denton Bender was the last to walk out into the main room, his rifle held loosely in his left hand, his right hand steadying him with a firm grip on the barred cell door.

"Jason Catlo, you come with me. Thanks to what you did to the blacksmith, everyone's scared of you," Kern said, thinking quickly. "The rest of you stay here with the guns, in case they've come to revolt on us."

"An *unarmed* revolt," Philbert said with a chuff. "It doesn't seem like it's worth waking up for."

"If that's why they woke us up, they won't wake us again," Jason said in a grim voice. He slung his gun belt off his shoulder and down around his waist. He buckled the gun belt, adjusted his gun and holster and hurriedly looped the tie-downs around his thigh.

"Let's go," Kern said.

The two walked out onto the dark street, immediately setting eyes on torches and lanterns held in the air by a group of men gathered out in front of the mercantile store a block away.

"Here comes the marshal!" a voice called out as Kern and Jason Catlo walked closer.

"Don't worry, Marshal Kern. We've caught the sumbitch!" another voice cried out beneath a waving lantern.

"Be ready, Deputy," Kern said to Catlo, who walked quickly beside him. "There's no telling what these flat-headed rubes are up to."

"You're covered, Marshal," Jason said confidently.

"What sumbitch is that?" Kern called out to the voices on the street.

"The sumbitch who's been pillaging our stores all night long," a voice called out in reply.

Kern and Catlo saw a slender man hurled

to the ground a few yards in front of them. An ax handle rose in the air and came down hard on the man's back. A scream resounded from the man on the ground.

"All right, take it easy," Kern called out as he and Catlo walked into the light and looked down at the young man lying in the dirt.

"Take it easy, hell!" said the barber, Albert Shaggs. Excitement caused his voice to tremble. "This dirty little bastard killed Ed Dandly! Stole his gun and has been on a rampage."

"But we stopped him!" said Walter Stevens. "Caught him in my mercantile!" He stepped forward and raised the hickory ax handle above the frightened young man.

"I said take it easy, Stevens," Kern said. He stepped in and grabbed the ax handle before the mercantile man could swing it again.

"I'm sorry, Marshal," said Stevens, "but look at my doors." He swung an arm toward the front of his store where the door had been pried open. Scraps of splintered and broken wood lay strewn on the boardwalk.

"I understand," said Kern. "Did you say he killed Ed Dandly?" He stepped over and stamped a boot down on the young man to hold him in place.

"He sure did, Marshal," said Shaggs the barber. "He stabbed him in the heart. Dandly's sitting dead at his desk right now, a knife in his chest."

"I didn't kill nobody," the young man said.

"Shut up," said Kern.

"Say, this is the young man who was supposed to lead old Virgil home," said John Admore, getting a better look at the young man in the flicker of torch and lantern light.

"My God, you're right, John!" said Stevens. "Now I wonder what he was up to with poor old Virgil."

The young man hung his head and refused to look at anyone.

"I found this on him," said Shaggs. He jerked the small pepperbox derringer from his pocket and held it out to the marshal.

"It's Dandly's, Marshal," said Stevens. "He always kept it in his desk. His initials are carved in the handle."

"I know he meant to turn it in, Marshal," said Shaggs. "He just never got the chance to."

Kern examined the small pistol in the flicker of dim light and saw *E.D.* crudely carved into the gun's thin bone handle.

"I'll be damned . . . ," he murmured, carefully keeping his face from betraying his private thoughts. "Poor Ed Dandly is dead, then. . . ."

"Yep, but thank goodness we've caught the rascal who killed him," said Stevens.

"Yes, thank goodness for that," said Kern. He stooped and dragged the young man to his feet. As soon as the man got his footing, Kern gave his rifle barrel a vicious swing and struck him hard in the heel of his right foot. The young man cried out and almost fell, but Kern caught him and held him up.

"I did that to save your life, boy," he said. "I know how a young fellow like yourself is prone to making a run for it. That busted heel will keep you from getting shot trying to get away."

The young man whimpered in pain.

"That's real considerate of you, Marshal," Jason Catlo said with a sly grin. "Want me to toss him in a cell?"

"A cell?" said Albert Shaggs. "What for? He needs to be hung from a rafter, *tonight!* I'm talking about right this minute!"

"I bet you thought I was talking to you, didn't you, barber?" Jason Catlo said with a short, friendly grin. He stepped over in front of Shaggs, patted his shoulder and left his hand lying there.

"Well, I — No, that is," Shaggs said, remembering how quickly the blacksmith had gotten himself in trouble with this same deputy. "I — I won't say nothing else," he said meekly.

"Now, that's good of you," Jason said. He turned back to Kern and said, "What do you say, Marshal? The jail?"

"Yes, take him there, Deputy," Kern said. Considering the matter quickly, he realized that the best thing that could happen would be for the townsmen to hang the young man. Once they'd hanged this hardcase thief, there'd be no second-guessing about who had killed Ed Dandly.

"Let's go, *murderer*," Jason said, giving the limping young man a shove toward the marshal's office. He left Kern behind to finish questioning the group of townsmen who'd gathered.

"I — I didn't kill nobody," the young man said to Jason Catlo as he limped along. "I swear, he was stabbed in the heart when I got there."

"Do I look like I care, boy?" Jason said, shoving him again. "I ought to shoot your sack off for making me get up from my warm blanket."

"The sheriff was there," the young man said. "I had to wait for him to leave before I could go inside to rob the man! The sheriff's the one who killed him — he has to be. He was the only one there!"

"You're lying to me, boy," Jason said with a short chuckle.

"No, I'm not lying! I swear I'm not," the young man pleaded. "You've got to believe me! The sheriff killed him."

"You know how *I know* you're lying?" Jason laughed as he shoved him forward again. "Because that man you're calling a sheriff is not a *sheriff* at all. He's a town marshal."

"Hunh . . . ?" The young man gave him a strange puzzled look. "That makes no sense. . . . I don't understand."

Jason, still laughing, shook his head. "I'm just kidding you, boy," he said. "Don't you know when you're being jackpotted?"

"Deputy, please," said the young man. "I didn't kill him."

"I bet you didn't rob the hell out of him either, did you?" Jason Catlo grinned.

"All right, yes, I did rob him. I stole an apple and some stale bread from his desk. I was hungry. Haven't you ever been hungry?"

"Oh yes, I have," said Catlo. "I'm hungry right now. But I can't eat nothing because I'm busy hauling you off to jail." He gave the young man a harder shove and watched him limp along the dark dirt street.

CHAPTER 15

Inside the marshal's office, the other deputies looked the young man up and down as he staggered and stumbled through the door and caught himself on the edge of the desk to keep from falling.

"Who's the scarecrow?" Philbert asked.

"He's a candidate for a hanging," said Jason. "He killed the newspaperman."

"Is that all?" Tribold Cooper asked Jason, studying the young man's face closely. "That's nothing to hang a man over."

"Yeah," said Philbert, "I didn't think killing a newsman was even a *crime,* west of the Mississippi."

"Yep, it is these days," said Jason. "But that's not all he did. He robbed the newsman's office, burgled the mercantile store. Who knows what else?" he said. He reached out and thumped the young man on his head. "He might have even skinned another man's chicken, for all I know."

"So he's a thief?" Philbert said in mock shock and horror. "Why didn't you say so right off?" He stared at the young man and said, "You mean you go around stealing people's stuff? How dare you!"

"Yeah," said Tribold Cooper. He eyed the frightened young man coldly and said, "We all hate a damn thief worse than anything."

Bender stepped forward to join the razing. He stood staring coldly at the young man.

"What the hell's your name, *thief?*" he asked with angry contempt.

"I'm — I'm Billy Nichols," the young man stammered in reply. "I didn't kill anybody," he added quickly. I stole some food. I was hungry —"

His word stopped short as Tribold Cooper backhanded him sharply across his face.

"*Ohhh!* Good shot, Cooper!" Philbert laughed, watching the thin young man fly backward off the corner of the desk into Bender's waiting arms.

Bender shoved the young man back into the reach of Cooper, who backhanded him again. This time the young man fell to the floor, blood running freely from his smashed lips.

Cooper grinned, opening and closing his gloved right hand. The other four deputies stood watching as the young man groveled on the dusty floor.

"Damn," said Cooper with a grin of satisfaction, "I could smack this boy around all day long, daylight to dark."

"That's enough for now," said Jason, reaching down and pulling Billy Nichols to his feet, then leaning him back onto the desk edge. "So, Billy," he said, "how do you like the way we treat dirty low-down *thieves* here in Kindred?"

Nichols shook his head, trying to steady his senses after the hard backhanding Cooper had given him.

"I . . . I'm not a thief," he insisted. "I was hungry. I hadn't eaten in —"

"Huh-uh, now, no excuses," said Philbert. He quickly jammed his fist into Billy Nichols' thin midsection. Nichols jackknifed at the waist and hung there holding his stomach with both hands, gasping for air. "No man ever has an excuse for stealing," Philbert concluded.

"Pay attention here, damn it, boy," Bender shouted at Billy Nichols. "He's telling you all of this for your own good." He grabbed the young man by his hair and yanked his face up toward Philbert.

"Thank you, Deputy Bender," said Philbert. He glared into Billy's eyes. "Thievery is the worst and lowest thing a man can do," he hissed. Then he looked around at the others and kept himself from grinning at the cruel way they were taunting the helpless young man.

"Better listen up, lad," said Cooper. "This is the bitter gospel truth you're hearing. You know what they always say, 'If it wasn't for thieves, hell would be half empty.'" He finished his words with another hard slap across Nichols' face.

Bender grabbed Nichols to keep him from falling. Even Buck the Mule got involved, in spite of his crooked neck and broken collarbone. Without warning he raised a big boot and slammed it into the young man's unsuspecting back.

"Jesus, Buck the Mule!" said Philbert, jumping aside as Billy stiffened upright instantly, then crumbled to the floor. "I felt that one myself," he chuckled.

"If I was ever prone to being a no-account, low-down, underhanded thief, God forbid," Jason Catlo said, "I believe that kick alone would have cured me of it."

Philbert stooped and pulled the young man to his feet and leaned him back against the desk.

"What about it, Billy?" he asked him mockingly. "Do you think you might want to give up these sinful ways of yours and get on the right path in life?"

"Pl-please don't hit me," the half-conscious young man said.

"Don't hit you?" Philbert said in mock surprise. He turned to the others. "Hear that? Now he's accusing us of hitting him . . . and all of us servants of the law, just trying to show him the error of his ways."

"You should be ashamed, boy," said Bender.

"You ain't seen any hitting yet," said Cooper, adjusting his black leather glove up tighter onto his wrist. "I'm just starting to get warmed up."

"Whoo-ee," said Philbert, wincing as the back of Cooper's hand lashed out again. "I would not want to be a thief around this bunch if I was you, boy. With a little time I believe they could save your soul."

As the men stood laughing, looking down at Billy Nichols, who lay gasping for breath on the dirty floor, the front door opened and they all turned to face Marshal Kern.

Kern stared down at Nichols' bloody face for a moment.

"He tried to escape," said Buck the Mule, standing with his sore neck cocked, almost touching his hiked-up shoulder.

"I can see that," said the marshal. He

looked up with the trace of a grin. "Some young men never learn 'til it's too late."

"We tried to tell him the errors of his ways," said Bender. "Tribold wore a glove out on him."

"Didn't help, huh?" said Kern, joining in on the merciless taunting.

"Not a lick," said Philbert. He stooped and once again raised the young man to his feet.

"They're wanting to hang him," Kern said, looking Nichols in the face.

"Are we going to let them do it?" Bender asked.

"Lynch my prisoner? Hunh-uh," said Kern, shaking his head. He turned toward the young man, moving closer to him. "Don't you worry, boy. They'll have to kill every one of us before they drop a loop around your neck. There's not a man here who wouldn't give his life to save yours. Is that right, Deputies?"

"Damn right it's right," said Philbert. "We're lawmen. We stand up for the law, no matter what."

"You *do* believe that, don't you, boy?" Kern said.

Nichols didn't know what to make of the question. He stared in disbelief for a moment, seeing the hard faces staring back at him.

"I — I suppose so . . . ?" the battered young man finally said with a lost and fearful look.

Kern smiled and said, "In that case, it's best that they go ahead and hang you, boy. You're too damn stupid to live, let alone be a thief."

The men all laughed as Philbert nodded at Jennings, who grabbed Nichols by his shoulder and dragged him back toward the row of cells in the rear of the building. The big dirty gunman pushed the young man into the back room, shoved him into a cell and slammed the iron door. Nichols fell to the dirty cell floor and lay there.

"You better get some rest," Jennings said in a hushed voice. "When you wake up, I'm going to beat you some more."

Back in the office, Jason gave Kern a look and nodded toward the front door.

"Let's talk," he said. "Brother Phil, we're not going to want to be disturbed for a few minutes."

"Got you," Philbert said.

Kern gave Bender and Cooper a nod to let them know everything was all right.

"Let's go, then," he said to Jason, turning toward the front door.

The two walked outside in the predawn purple light. A block away they saw the torches and lanterns move back and forth as the townsmen milled and congregated, too excited to return to their homes. Around the corner of the building, Jason and Kern stopped and looked back and forth, making sure they were alone.

"The boy says you killed the newsman, Marshal," Jason Catlo said in a guarded tone.

"Oh yeah?" said Kern with a slight smile that didn't quite hide the tense impact of Catlo's words. "Well, I wonder whose ass he's trying to save."

"Don't try playing me and my brother, Philbert, for fools, Kern," Jason warned, standing face-to-face. "All the wrath you've seen me bring down on others can easily fall right onto you."

"Don't threaten me, Catlo," said Kern. "I've been straight with you, your brother and that crooked-necked lunatic you travel with. As far as killing Ed Dandly goes, once they hang this young jake for it, the matter is done and over with."

"I don't give a damn about a dead newsman," said Catlo. "What I'm thinking about is how you've told me and my brother that you're in this thing for the *long* ride. But as

216

I look around, I see some of Kindred's main men disappearing or turning up dead. It makes me think you've got some fast, *shorter* ride in mind . . . only you ain't exactly sharing it with Philbert and me."

"It's just like I'm telling you," said Kern. "Once the guns are in our hands, we're going to —"

"You're starting to make me cross now, Marshal," Jason said, cutting him off. Kern felt the tip of a gun barrel in his belly. He heard the click of a hammer.

"All right, take it easy," said Kern, ready to give in. "I had this deal all set up for Ned Carver, Cordell Garrant, Curtis Hicks and me. But that damned gunman rode in and killed them."

"What about Cooper and Bender?" Jason asked.

"Carver and Cordell said to bring them here," Kern replied. "They said we needed two more men to rob this town good and proper."

"So, the *long ride* idea was just you shining everybody on. What you wanted to do in the first place was rob this town in one big raid and get out of here," Jason said.

"All right," Kern admitted, "that is what I had in mind. I had Hicks kill the new mayor and get him out of our way. We were all set to do it when this Dahl fellow rode in and upset everything."

"The newsman?" Jason asked, the gun barrel still in Kern's belly, but less forcefully now. "This Nichols kid is right, you killed him?"

"Yes, I killed him, so what?" said Kern. He shrugged. "The son of a bitch wouldn't give an inch. What good is the news if it's not the news you want to hear, eh?" He managed a slight grin even with the gun in his ribs.

Jason lowered the gun and uncocked it.

"Anyway, there you have it," said Kern. "This gun law is the best thing could ever happen for people like us. I figured I'd never get a chance like this again. I — I guess I might've got a little *too* excited."

"I suppose you did," Philbert said with empathy. He patted Kern on his shoulder. "That's understandable, a situation like this. . . ." He gave Kern a patient grin.

"Yeah . . . ?" Kern stared at him.

"Well, you've come clean and told me everything, right?" Jason asked, actually kneading the marshal's shoulder a little as he spoke.

"Oh yeah, that's everything," said Kern. "And I have to say, I feel better getting it all off my chest."

"I bet you do," said Jason, still smiling. He brought his pistol up, flipped it around into his palm and struck Kern solidly on his cheek with the butt.

"Oh, Jesus . . . ," Kern groaned, and fell back against the building. Jason caught him by his shirtfront and jostled him to keep him from passing out.

"I know that hurt," Jason said. "I know because that's the same way a lawman named Earp once smacked me in Ellsworth." He still smiled.

Kern was only half conscious from the blow, but he instinctively grabbed for his gun. To his surprise, his fingers found his holster empty.

"That was your gun I smacked you with, Marshal," said Jason. "See what a fix you're in here? That's the way I felt that night in Ellsworth."

Kern only stared at him, blood running down his face from the split welt on his throbbing cheekbone.

"Now, we're going to start all over again," said Jason Catlo. "This time you're going to tell me everything that's going on here, and don't leave nothing out." He jostled the stunned gunman again to keep him awake.

"I . . . will," Kern said in a strained voice.

"That's good," said Jason, turning Kern

loose and patting his shoulder again. "I'm going to smack you again every once in a while just to keep you on the right track."

Inside the marshal's office, the four gunmen looked at each other every now and then as they heard another thump against the side of the building. At one point, Denton Bender started to turn toward the front door. But Philbert Catlo wagged a finger at him.

"No, no, *Deputy* Bender," he said. "You heard brother Jason say they wanted to be *alone* for a few minutes."

Bender backed off, but Cooper stepped forward and said to Philbert, "I don't give a damn if you go check on things yourself. But somebody needs to go." He hooked his thumb into his gun belt.

Philbert looked at Jennings, who stood crooked-necked against a wall. "Are you ever going to be worth a damn for anything?"

"By God, I'm good right now," Jennings replied in a harsh voice.

Philbert only shook his head. He walked toward the door, saying half playfully to Cooper and Bender over his shoulder, "If I get jumped on by brother Jason, it's your fault."

As the door closed behind Philbert, Cooper and Bender both turned to Jennings.

"Maybe you ought to get the doctor here to take a look at that collarbone, Buck the Mule," said Cooper.

"Thanks. I will," said Jennings. His cordial reply turned dark. He scowled at them. "When I get *damn* good and ready," he added.

Philbert made his way outside and turned into an alley, following a loud thumping sound. He quickly came upon Kern and Jason, immediately noticing the welts and bruises on Kern's face. The marshal stood slumped halfway down the wall. Jason was wiping blood from the marshal's gun butt with a bandanna he'd jerked from Kern's neck.

"Damn," said Philbert, "I hope this is not your idea of a quiet conversation. You can hear that thumping all over town. What's this about?"

"It's nothing, brother Phil, just me bouncing the marshal's head a little to get his memory oiled up." He grinned, reached out and shoved Kern's gun back down into his holster. "We're all done now."

"You did all that to him, and you're giving him his gun back?" Philbert asked.

"Yep, that's what I'm doing," Jason said.

221

"But why?" Philbert asked, astonished, looking at the many welts and cuts on Kern's face.

"Because I'm a complete *idiot . . . ,*" said Jason, "why else?"

"Jesus . . ." Philbert walked over and stuck the toe of his boot into the slumped marshal's side.

"And . . . I've got his bullets," said Jason, opening his hand and showing his brother the six bullets in his palm.

"Take . . . your damn . . . boot off of me," Kern growled at Philbert.

"Sure thing, Marshal," said Philbert. He stepped back, keeping his hand on his gun butt. "Want to let me in on things," he asked Jason, "before those other two decide to come and take a look for themselves?"

"Yeah, I'll tell you," said Jason. "The marshal here just let me know that there's a big mine payroll coming to the Kindred bank for the first time."

Philbert glared at Kern and said, "All that about the *long ride, squeeze this place over time.* That was all bull, right?"

"You've . . . got it, Philbert," Kern managed to say, blood running down both cheeks.

"Well, kiss my . . ." Philbert's words trailed as he drew his pistol, cocked it and pointed it at Kern's head.

"Damn, brother, don't be a fool," said Jason. "Kern is our partner. He's the one the mining people expect to see when they get here with all that payroll money."

Philbert considered the facts, letting out an exasperated breath and lowering his gun barrel. "That helps, *some,*" he said, uncocking the gun and slipping it back into his holster.

"Let's go inside and talk to the others," said Jason. "I want us all to know where we stand."

CHAPTER 16

Gathered inside the marshal's office, Tribold Cooper, Denton Bender and Buck the Mule Jennings all three stiffened in surprise at the sight of Marshal Kern stumbling through the door with his face battered and bloody.

"What the hell . . . ?" Cooper said, his hand going instinctively to the butt of his holstered Colt.

"Easy, Deputy," said Jason Catlo, he and his brother stepping in behind the pistol-whipped marshal. "Don't grab that iron unless you know why you're grabbing it."

Cooper eased down. He dropped his gun hand to his side.

"What went on out there?" he asked, studying the marshal's battered face.

"Honored fellow deputies," Philbert said with his easy smile, "it saddens brother Jason and me to have to say this, but it appears our marshal hasn't been completely

224

honest with us."

Jason gave Kern a shove. Kern caught himself on the desk and stood for a moment with his disheveled head lowered.

"But now he's had a change of heart and wants to tell all," Jason said.

"I — I can't talk," Kern said, trying to work his swollen jaw with his fingers. "You . . . tell them," he said to Jason Catlo.

Bender and Cooper watched warily.

"All right, here goes," said Jason. "I just learned that for all the talk Marshal Kern gave us about setting up a long-term deal for ourselves here in Kindred, his real plan's to rob a big mine payroll that's coming to the town bank for safekeeping."

"Is that right, *Marshal* Kern?" questioned Cooper with disgust. "You've been lying to us?" Again his hand closed around his gun butt.

"Easy, Cooper. It gets better," said Jason Catlo, holding a hand up toward the smoldering gunman.

"You'll like this part," Philbert said with a dark chuckle.

"Don't let . . . them shoot me," Kern pleaded to Jason Catlo.

"I'll do my best, Marshal," Jason said with a dark grin. To the gunmen in the room, he announced, "The marshal wasn't even going to share the deal with us. He has Harry Whitesides and his two cousins coming to town to rob the bank and take the payroll money." He paused and looked Kern up and down with contempt. "I expect we were supposed to get gunned down in the process — make it all look real."

Both Cooper and Bender stepped toward Kern.

"You dirty son of a bitch," said Cooper. "You was going to let us get killed, while you ride off with a nice fat payroll robbery?"

"With that half-blind skunk, Harry Whitesides?" Bender added, enraged.

"Don't blame me for Harry Whitesides," Kern said in his own defense. "It was Hicks' idea to send for him. He said Harry and his cousins were the best bank robbers a man could find in this part of the country."

"That hurts our feelings," said Philbert.

"You know Whitesides?" Cooper asked Bender.

"Yeah, I know Whitesides," said Bender. "I rode with him until he got so bad I was afraid he'd shoot me by mistake."

"That bad, huh?" said Cooper.

Bender shook his head. "He couldn't look straight down and see his feet well enough to count his toes."

"What does that matter?" said Jason.

"Kern here is supposed to have the town disarmed when the payroll arrives anyway." He reached out with his gun barrel and tweaked Kern's nose. "Right, Marshal?"

"Everything depends on the town being unarmed," said Kern. "That was the whole idea. The mine company always sends along two payroll guards. But Whitesides and his cousins are used to killing a couple of guards. It's the townsmen that are getting to be the problem for everybody. Look what happened in Houston, in Northfield."

"Why are you being so honest with us now, Kern?" Cooper asked.

"My, my, Cooper . . . ," said Philbert, shaking his head at the question, "how'd you ever find your way to town?"

Cooper bristled.

"He's being honest because I pistol-whipped some sense into him," Jason cut in. "Just because he tried to jackpot us and get us killed doesn't mean we can't do business with him, does it?"

"Not to me . . . it doesn't," Kern interjected in a stiff, pained voice. "This is a once-in-a-lifetime opportunity."

Cooper and Bender looked at each other, considering the matter.

"Well . . . no, I expect it doesn't to us either," Cooper said grudgingly.

"When's the payroll coming in?" Bender asked.

"It's due any time now," said Kern. "Whitesides and his cousins are tracking it here from the train station at Burkeville. The guards have telegraphed the Kindred bank and told Matheson it's on its way."

"How do you know they telegraphed the bank?" Cooper asked.

"Fuller, the telegraph clerk, told me," said Kern. "He knows it's his patriotic duty to keep the law informed on such matters." Kern managed a pained smile. "Plus, he likes drinking rye with me."

"When Harry Whitesides and his cousins get here, the payroll won't be far behind?" Cooper asked.

"That's the plan," said Kern. "They'll track it in close to town, then ride on ahead and tip me off that it's coming." He looked back and forth with his swollen and bloody face. "I'm betting it'll be sometime today."

As the deputies and the marshal spoke in the front office, Billy Nichols lay in pain on the cell floor, listening, making out just enough of the conversation to know that these men were not what they appeared to be.

He had to get out of there, he told himself.

There was little doubt in his mind they would let the townsmen hang him. They would even kill him themselves when it suited them.

All this for an apple, a handful of stale bread . . . ?

Billy crawled across the dirty cell floor, pulled himself to his feet and examined his surroundings. There had to be something in here he could use to pick the lock on the iron door. *Something, anything . . .*

The pain in his heel and ankle had lessened a little, but he still winced as he tried to put weight down onto his foot. It didn't matter, pain or not, he had to get out of there. . . .

He patted his pockets and found nothing. But as he felt his belt, an idea hit him. *The buckle . . . !*

He hurriedly loosened his belt and yanked it from his waist. With the metal buckle in hand, he reached and took ahold of the iron-barred door for support. But instead of support himself against the bars as he'd expected, he fell forward a step as the unlocked door swung open a few inches.

Billy stood stunned for a moment, staring, wondering if this was some sort of trap. Then he batted his eyes and swallowed a knot in his throat. Trap or not, he had to take a chance. He eased out of the cell, not daring to breathe. Limping badly, he crossed the floor, sidled up to the rear door and squeezed it open silently.

Hearing the men talking in the front office, he stepped out into the silver-gray light of dawn. With no regard for his throbbing foot, or the limp that pulled him a little to one side, he raced away like a jackrabbit.

In the front office, Philbert looked at his brother, Jason. "What's that sound?" he asked.

The six men stood listening intently. Finally, Kern staggered over and looked out through the dirty front window at a single lantern swinging low at a townsman's side.

"It's the townsmen," he said. "Here to get the boy and stretch his neck at first light, I'll wager."

Jason grinned. "*I'll wager* you told them they could have him?" he said.

"I mentioned that I'm so broken up over poor Ed Dandly's death that I don't much give a damn what they do to his killer," said Kern.

Philbert looked over at Jennings and gave a nod toward the back room. Jennings had been standing off to one side, more concerned with the pain in his neck and broken collarbone than he was with the deceiving the marshal, the robbery or anything else. But he caught Philbert's signal and walked away with a grunt toward the cells.

Out front in the street, Dan Marlowe stood at the head of a small gathering of townsmen armed with ax handles and pitchforks.

"All right, Marshal Kern, it's first light," he called out in a loud, clear voice. "It's time we get this gruesome piece of work done. Bring him on out."

"All right, Marlowe," Kern called out in reply. "My deputies and I are with you fellows on this."

But Kern turned in time to see Jennings standing with his big dirty hands spread in disbelief.

"He's gone!" he said, wide-eyed.

"He's what?" shouted Kern, his battered face looking grim and terrible in the thin dawn light. "He can't be gone!"

Running, falling, rolling back to his feet and continuing to run, Billy Nichols weaved his way through the back alleys of Kindred until he stopped and stood for a moment against a telegraph pole to catch his breath. Across the street and thirty yards ahead of him, he saw a dim lantern light in a window of the widow's shack.

He limped along a few more yards, looking back, making sure he wasn't being followed yet. In the shadowy half-light, he saw the group of townsmen moving along in the direction of the marshal's office. He knew what they wanted. They'd come for him — to hang him, he told himself.

Hunched over and crouched, he hurried across the street and on toward the widow's shack. When he reached the side yard, he veered back to the old barn, where he saw the doctor's buggy sitting by the backyard fence. The horse stood with a rear hoof tipped, sleeping in the still gray morning light.

Sara gazed out the window and was startled to see a young man limp over to the buggy and climb up into the seat.

"Sherman, come here, quick!" she said. "Someone is stealing the doctor's buggy!"

Dahl stood up from the table and came to her side, followed by Dr. Washburn, who'd been sleeping in a chair beside the bed.

"Well, I'll be darned," the doctor said. "A fellow would have to be in some awfully dire straits to want to steal ol' Tom."

"I've got a feeling this is connected to the gunshots we heard earlier," said Dahl. "Both of you wait here," he said to Sara and the doctor.

As Dahl slipped away and out the side door, Sara whispered to Doc Washburn, "He better hurry if he's going to keep your rig from getting stolen."

"Don't you worry about my rig, Sara," Washburn chuckled. "Ol' Tom is a heavy sleeper for a horse. If you wake him too sudden, he'll fly into a fit — well, I suppose you'll be seeing it soon enough," he said.

Outside, Billy Nichols loosened the buggy brake and slapped the traces up and down on the unsuspecting horse's back.

"Hee-*iii!*" he called out in a lowered voice, trying to slip away as quietly as possible.

But the startled horse would have none of it. The dapple gray seemed to spring up off the ground with all four hooves spinning. The horse came down with a long, loud whinny, twirling and bucking like a crazed wild mustang.

Billy let out a shriek as the animal reared and sawed, snorted and kicked. The lightweight buggy slung back and forth, bouncing high off the ground, its helpless occupant barely able to stay in the driver's seat.

By the time Dahl had slipped out the side

door and across the yard, the horse had bolted forward, made a wild sliding turn in the dirt and come racing back toward him, the buggy leaning dangerously over on two wheels. The young man in the seat hung on with one hand to keep from flying over the side.

But then, for all its wild gyrations, the horse slid to a sudden, jolting halt at almost the same spot where it had started. Dahl seized the chance to grab the young man by his flailing arm and pull him from the buggy to the ground. He stamped a boot down on his chest and held him firmly in place.

"Don't shoot, mister! Please!" Billy cried out, seeing the long Colt hanging in Dahl's right hand. "I wasn't stealing it!"

Dahl had pulled the gun on his way across the yard, but upon seeing the young man closer, he'd lowered the gun down at his side.

"I see you weren't," Dahl said, "not if the horse had any say in it."

Dr. Washburn came running up beside Dahl. Behind him came Sara. The buggy horse shook out his mane and chuffed and stamped a hoof.

"Settle down, ol' Tom," the doctor said soothingly to the excited animal. He patted the dapple's muzzle and looked down at the young man in the dirt beneath Dahl's boot. "You're lucky he didn't kick your head off, scaring him like that."

Dahl slipped his Colt back into his holster and took his boot off the young man's chest.

"Get up," he said. But seeing the young man struggle to stand, he reached down and helped him to his feet, noting his battered face, the dried blood on the front of his shirt. "Who are you?" he asked. "What happened to your face?"

"I'm . . . Billy Nichols," said the young man. "This is what the marshal's deputies did to me." He touched a cupped hand to his bloody swollen cheek.

"Whatever happened in town during the night, you must've been in on it," Dahl said.

"I — I was," the young man stammered. "I'm not going to lie about it." He looked back and forth from the doctor to the woman, then to Dahl. "I stole an apple and some bread from the newspaper office. But I didn't kill the newsman. I swear I didn't."

"What?" said Dr. Washburn. "Ed Dandly is dead?"

"Yes, he is," said Billy. "He was stabbed in the heart. But I found him that way . . . I didn't do it, you've got to believe me!"

Dahl saw him limp sideways and almost fall. Doc Washburn caught him by the forearm and steadied him.

"What's wrong with your foot?" Dahl asked.

"The marshal hit me with his rifle barrel, said it would keep me from getting shot trying to escape."

"But it didn't work, did it?" Dahl said. "You still managed to get away."

"They — they left the cell door unlocked," Billy said. "If I hadn't gotten away, they were going to hang me, or kill me." He gestured toward the street in the distance. "The townsmen were coming for me. I heard him as I was running away."

"So you came here to steal a horse and make your getaway," Dahl said, finishing his story for him.

Billy looked at the doctor, who stood stroking the dapple's muzzle, still trying to calm the horse down. "I'm sorry I tried to steal your horse, but I didn't know what else to do." He turned back to Dahl. "You won't turn me in, will you, mister? I swear I didn't kill the newsman. But they will for sure hang me for it if they get their hands on me."

Dahl looked him up and down, realizing he was no older than some of the students he'd taught to read and write not so long ago. He pictured the young man standing with an open book in his hands, reading aloud to the class.

"If you broke the law, it's up to the law to bring you to justice," Dahl said. He looked off toward the dirt street where the glow of a single lantern flickered in the grainy morning light. "But I'm not turning you over to the law in Kindred . . . not unless I see that there is some *real* law in Kindred."

Billy let out a breath of relief, steadying himself with the doctor's hand on his forearm.

"Mister, I want to tell you everything I heard while I was lying on the floor of that cell," he said. "Then you be the judge as to whether or not there's any *real* law there."

Dr. Washburn, Sara and Dahl all listened intently while Billy told them what he'd heard. When he'd finished, he stood looking from one face to the other, waiting for a reaction.

Dahl looked at the doctor and said quietly, "I expect now is the time for you to take the womenfolk and go."

"I'm not going, Sherman," said Sara. "I'm staying here, with you."

Washburn saw the look on Dahl's face and knew this was no place for Sara to be if Dahl turned loose against Kern and his gunmen.

"Sara, for the next few days that woman is going to need the kind of looking-after that only another woman can give," he said.

"Sherman . . . ?" Sara said, turning her eyes to Dahl.

"Go with the doctor, Sara," Dahl said quietly. When he turned his eyes to her, she saw a coldness there that she had not seen before. "I don't want you here," he said. Offering nothing more on the matter, he turned and walked away in the grainy morning light.

Sara looked to Dr. Washburn for help, for advice, for something. But the doctor only shook his head slightly.

"Stay away from him for now, Sara," he said. "This is not the time for talking."

CHAPTER 17

Out in front of the marshal's office, Kern faced the crowd of angry and unarmed townsmen. Behind Kern stood the five deputies, each of them holding either a shotgun or a rifle. When the marshal told the townsmen that the young man had gotten away, a roar of curses erupted. Ax handles and pitchforks waved in the grainy morning-light air.

"How in the hell could he possibly get away?" Dan Marlowe asked above the roar of the crowd. "You've got five armed deputies!"

"Listen to me, Marlowe, and all the rest of you," Kern said. "The little bastard got away from us. That's all I can tell you. He's as dangerous as a rattlesnake. Look what he did to me!" He tilted his chin up for the townsmen to see.

"If that skinny kid did all that to you, Marshal Kern," Shaggs the barber called out, "I'm not sure we should give up our guns and rely on you and your deputies for security." He was one of the few who still had a shotgun in his possession. He held it at port arms.

"That's a terrible thing to say, barber," Jason Catlo said, stepping forward beside Kern.

"Easy, Jason," Kern cautioned him in a whisper. "We still don't have everybody's guns yet."

"Shut up, Kern," said Jason. "Now that I'm in charge, I'll show you how to handle these rubes. He stepped toward the barber with a swagger in his walk.

"I don't want no trouble, Deputy," Shaggs said, sounding nervous despite the ancient muzzle-loading shotgun in his hand.

"Of course you don't," Jason said with his winning smile. "That's why you're going to hand me over that gun and keep you mouth shut."

"Don't hand it over, Albert!" said Dan Marlowe. "Once it's gone you'll never get it back."

Jason ignored Marlowe and stared at Shaggs with his hands out for the shotgun. "You know you're breaking the gun law, and you've seen what happened to folks who do that. Now give me the gun."

"No," said Shaggs, "Marlowe is right. How do we know we'll ever get these guns back if we need them or if we want to leave town? You lawmen let a murderer escape from you. How will we ever be able to trust —"

Jason cut him short, snatching the shotgun from his hands. "There, now you're complying with the law," he said. "You want it back?" He snapped the shotgun butt out, delivering a sharp blow into Shaggs' face. "There, you've got it back." He stepped forward and stood over the downed barber, who lay in the dirt cupping his bloody nose.

"Want it again?" he asked, drawing the shotgun back as if to deliver another blow.

"No, please!" Shaggs said.

The townsmen stood stunned for a moment. Just as Jason appeared ready to jam the gun butt down into Shaggs' face again, the sound of a rifle cocking caused him to freeze and look up.

"Is that repeater pointed at me, pilgrim?" Jason asked, shifting his eyes up to where Dahl sat atop his big dun, his Winchester in his right hand leveled down at Jason's head. Amidst all the commotion, he had walked the dun in between the townsmen without being noticed in the grainy dawn light.

Dahl just stared at Jason Catlow without

241

offering a reply.

Getting no answer unnerved Jason a little. He started to turn the shotgun toward Dahl, but something in the mounted gunman's demeanor warned him not to. He noted the thick look of Dahl's corduroy riding duster, how the long coat was buttoned at the collar.

"Marshal, what's the deal here?" Jason asked warily, keeping his eyes on Dahl as he spoke.

Kern cut in, saying, "I told you not to come into my town armed, Dahl. You're breaking the law." He paused for a moment, then said to Jason Catlow and the others, "This is Sherman Dahl. He's the man who wears the bullet-stopping vest."

Dahl kept his eyes on Jason Catlo.

"What are you doing here, *Fighting Man?*" Kern asked in a sarcastic tone.

Fighting Man . . . ? The townsmen stood staring in rapt silence.

"They call him *the Teacher,*" whispered Stevens the mercantile owner. "I've heard of him."

"I came here to report a murder and a rape, if you're all through beating up your local citizens," Dahl said quietly.

"A murder and a rape? In *my* town?" Kern said, speaking loud enough to make sure

242

the townsmen heard him. "You must be out of your mind. With our new gun law, that sort of thing won't be happening here ever again."

The townsmen gave each other skeptical looks. Dahl still had his rifle aimed at Jason Catlo, but was careful to keep the rest of the deputies in his peripheral vision.

"Not only did it happen here in Kindred, Marshal," he said. "It was your deputies who did it."

"Hey, hold on just a damn minute," said Tribold Cooper. He and Denton Bender looked genuinely surprised. Philbert and Buck the Mule Jennings tried their best to be equally stunned by the news. But Dahl saw through them.

"You're making a damn strong accusation, mister," Jason said, still looking up the bore of the cocked rifle at a man who so far refused to say a word to him. Something about Dahl ignoring him had him more than just a little unsettled.

"Who are you saying this murder and raped happened to, Dahl?" Kern asked, needing to prove his concern to the townsmen.

"A couple by the name of Charles and Celia Knox," said Dahl. "Your deputies killed Charles Knox. They tried to kill his wife, Celia, but they failed."

He stared at Jason, his hand steady on the cocked rifle. "After they raped her, one of them shot her in the back. But she managed to make it here, to the doctor's." He gestured a nod and said poker-faced, "She's at the widow's shack recuperating right now."

"He's lying," Philbert said, not wanting to get too bold, while Dahl aimed the cocked Winchester at his brother's face. He and Buck the Mule looked over in the direction of the widow's shack.

"As soon as she's able, I'll bring her over here, Marshal," Dahl said. "She said she'll identify the men who did it."

"Marshal, what's this man saying?" Walter Stevens demanded.

"You've heard everything I've heard, storekeeper," Kern said. He nodded toward Dahl and said, "If something like that happened in my town, I'd want to hear about it now. I'll crucify the men who done it."

Dahl ignored the marshal. He looked at the shotgun in Jason Catlo's hand and said, "Put it in the dirt."

Something about Dahl's tone of voice caused Catlo to do as he was told.

Dahl backed his dun up a step and said, "The next time you hear me cock a hammer will be the last time you hear me cock a hammer."

The marshal, the deputies and the townsmen all stood watching as Dahl turned the dun around and rode away in the lingering swirl of grainy silver light.

"What the hell was that all about?" Dan Marlowe asked Kern.

"I don't know, but I'm going to get to the bottom of it, you bet your shaving mug," said Kern. "Meanwhile," he said, turning his gaze to the rest of the townsmen, "you need to all go home and get ready for work. My deputies and I have to get started catching Ed Dandly's killer."

In the crowded buggy, Dr. Washburn and Sara sat with Celia Knox lying back on the seat between them. Billy Nichols limped along beside the slow-moving buggy, a hand resting on the side rail to steady himself.

As the buggy turned onto a trail leading toward the shelter of surrounding hills, Washburn stopped for a moment and looked back on Kindred in the shadowy light.

"As soon as we get ourselves out of sight, I'll trade you my seat for a while," he said to Billy. "Long enough to rest that bad foot of yours."

245

"Obliged, Doctor," said Billy. "But I'm doing all right here. I'll walk as far as I have to, so long as it gets me away from this place."

"Kindred's not a bad town, young man," Dr. Washburn said. "The folks there are no different from folks everywhere. You can't blame them for getting upset, thinking you killed one of their own."

"I don't blame them, Doctor," said Billy, "but I don't want to hang for something I didn't do either." He paused for a moment and then lowered his head and said, "Although, I have to admit, if I hadn't gone to the man's office with ill intent, I wouldn't have gotten caught up in all this to begin with."

"It's good that you see that," the old doctor said quietly.

"I not only see it, Doctor," Billy said, "I'm feeling terrible over it. I went there to rob that man. I was carrying a club. Who can say I wouldn't have killed him had he tried to put up a fight?"

Sara sat listening quietly, Celia half cradled in her arms as the horse pulled the buggy slowly onward.

"Be thankful that things didn't happen that way, young man," said the doctor. "And be thankful that you've got enough of a

246

conscience to feel bad about it."

"Oh, I've got a conscience, Doctor," Billy said, "and believe me, it's bothering me something fierce." He looked back toward Kindred as the buggy ambled on toward the hill trails. "First I think how bad it would be to hang for something I'm innocent of doing. But then I think how much worse it would be for my immortal soul if I hung for something I was guilty of."

"It's not often I hear a man as young as you concerned about his immortal soul," the doctor said. "I see somewhere along the way, you received some good upbringing."

"Yes, sir, Doctor, I did," said Billy. "I was raised by Christian Illinois folks for a while after my parents died. They taught me right from wrong." He looked back again toward Kindred.

"What is it you're thinking, Billy?" Dr. Washburn asked, seeing the troubled look on his face.

"Nothing," Billy said. He turned back toward the trail ahead of them and limped on.

But less than an hour later, Sara glanced down alongside the wagon and noticed that Billy Nichols was nowhere to be seen.

"Yep, he's gone, Sara," the doctor said, not appearing surprised as he guided the buggy along the rocky trail.

"This doesn't seem like something an innocent man would do, running off like that," she said.

"It depends on what he's innocent of," the doctor said, turning to her. "Depends on what he's running *from* and what he's running *to*."

The townsmen that had gathered on the main dirt street of Kindred had returned to their homes and businesses to start the day, and the commotion of the early morning had finally ceased. Kern sat inside the marshal's office beside his four deputies, grappling with his recent loss of control. In spite of the fact that Jason Catlo had pistol-whipped Kern and taken over the operation for the most part, the marshal still had a stake in the game.

"Murder and rape . . . ?" Kern said flatly to Jason Catlo.

"Don't go making a big thing out of it," Jason said with a shrug. "We met the couple on the trail coming here. Things got a little out of hand."

"Jesus . . ." Kern shook his head.

Philbert chuckled and put an arm up around Kern's shoulder. "Don't you wish you asked for letters of reference?"

"I'll know better next time," Kern said, staring at him.

"Maybe you Catlos and your idiot friend here think this is funny," Tribold Cooper chimed in, "but Bender and I have a lot on the line. We're not laughing." He held a hand resting on his gun butt.

"What'd you call me?" said Jennings with a dark glower on his face.

"Easy, Buck the Mule," said Philbert, raising a hand toward the crooked-necked gunman. "Cooper, we can fix this Dahl fellow's clock any time we take a notion to. You heard him, the woman's just over at the edge of town. We can *walk* over, kill the woman and him too while we're there."

"Didn't you hear the townsman say who this Dahl fellow is?" Bender questioned. "He's the one they call *the Teacher.*"

"Uhhh, the Teacher!" Philbert said with widened mocking eyes. "All right, I admit, that does scare the hell out of me." He paused for a moment and grinned. "But I can't get too rattled over a man who wears a bullet-stopping vest —"

Jason cut in. "He told us the woman is alive and waiting to identify us so we'd come to kill her. He wants a fight. You have to admire that quality in the man." He looked at Philbert, then at Jennings, waiting for a response.

"So we'll go kill him and be done with it?" Philbert asked, shrugging again.

"Yep, we will," said Jason.

"Even though the Knox woman might not even be alive?" Philbert asked. "She looked awfully dead when we saw her."

"What are you talking about?" Jason shot him a look. "When did you see her?" he asked.

"Buck the Mule and I saw her on a gurney at the doctor's office," Philbert said.

"And you never mentioned it?" asked Jason.

"We would have," said Philbert, "but we haven't had a chance. There's been so much going on here."

"Damn it," said Jason.

"The doctor had already dropped a sheet over her face and pronounced her dead," said Philbert. "We didn't figure it was worth worrying about."

"Hold it, what's this?" Bender said, looking out the dusty front window. As sunlight wreathed the horizon, four riders nudged their horses along the dirt street toward the marshal's office.

"That's Harry Whitesides and his cousins," said Kern. He almost let out a breath of relief.

"Yeah?" said Jason. "Who's the fourth man?"

"Beats me," said Kern. "Whoever it is, I'm betting he hasn't raped and murdered anybody on his way here." He gave Philbert a scorching look.

All five gunmen crowded near the window, looking out at the approaching men.

"If the woman is alive, we're still going to go kill her, aren't we?" Jennings asked Jason Catlo, excitement in his voice.

"Hold your socks, Buck the Mule," Jason said. "We'll kill her and *the Teacher* soon enough. Let's get this payroll deal taken care of first."

PART 3

Chapter 18

Councilman Lyndon Matheson stood before a group of troubled townsmen who had gathered privately in the Great Western Bank and Trust building.

"Gentlemen," said Matheson, "I think we've seen enough out of our new marshal and these thugs he calls his deputies. I propose we set into motion the proper procedure for repealing this law by whatever democratic means —"

"Stop all the jawing," said Fannin, cutting the councilman off. "You said so yourself that it would be a long and complicated process getting this law stricken off the books."

"Meanwhile, Kern and his bullies will continue to ride roughshod over us. They do whatever suits them. We can't stop them," said Shaggs.

"Gentlemen," said Matheson, "we must follow the rule of law. Yes, the law is slow-moving and ofttimes highly suspect and questionable. But let's remind ourselves that we are not uncivilized creatures of the —"

"Shut the hell up!" shouted Stevens. "That's the same kind of oily *politician* talk that got the gun law voted in to begin with."

"It's the voice of *prudence and reason,*" Matheson persisted. "And I'm proud to say that I adhere to it."

"It's the voice of *soft soap and bullshit!*" said Fannin. "I wish you'd choke on it."

"Gentlemen, please!" said Stevens. "Fighting among ourselves isn't going to help. We all believe in the law. But the law is not infallible. This time it was wrong. We voted in a bad law — we've just witnessed first-hand how rotten *the law* can be if we the people don't have the guts or the guns to keep it working for us instead of against us!"

"What are you suggesting we do, Stevens?" a townsman called out. "Kern has all the guns."

"Not all of them, he doesn't," said Stevens. "There're still a few around who didn't turn theirs in." He paused for a moment and said, "I might even know where there're a few others."

"Yeah," said a voice, "we should be gathering the ones together who still have guns. The rest of us can get ours back from Kern.

All we've got to do is tell him we're leaving town for a few days. He's got to give them back to us. That's the law too."

"Kern is no fool," said Stevens. "He'll know something's in the works if we all start showing up saying we're leaving town for a few days."

"But he has to give them back if we're leaving town and need them while we're traveling," said Shaggs.

"Kern doesn't *have* to do anything, law or no law," said Stevens. "He's armed, we're not." He threw up his hands and said in disgust, "How could we ever have been this stupid?"

"Now's not the time to dwell on *how*," said Fannin. "We were stupid enough to fall for it. We gave up the one right that kept all our other rights in check. Now we've got to get it back."

Getting back to business, Dan Marlowe turned to Stevens and asked, "What do you mean you might know where there're some other guns?"

Stevens looked from face to face. The townsmen stared anxiously back at him.

"I had a mixed crate of a dozen used guns come in from Denver last week. Some revolvers, some repeating rifles."

"Oh," Matheson said with a judgmental

look, "and when were you going to report these guns?"

"I just did," said Stevens, the trace of a sly grin slightly visible on his face. "It had slipped my mind until now."

"Well, thank God you remembered," said Fannin. "To hell with reporting them. Let's get them distributed and take this town back from Kern and his thugs!"

The townsmen began to get excited, except for Matheson, who only shook his lowered head.

"Take it easy, gentlemen," said Stevens. "Of course we'll get them distributed. But let me remind you that there are only a dozen. They are in high demand. I want to be fair, but I have to charge what we know the market will bear, given the circumstances."

"You son of a bitch," said Fannin. "You saw the possibility of this gun law going sour. You ordered guns and hid them back so you could turn a profit on our misfortune."

"No, sir, I did not," Stevens said, raising a finger for emphasis. "I saw a potential business venture and I seized it. It's what any wise businessman would do, gentlemen." He looked all around. "Now who wants to be armed and who doesn't?"

Shaggs said with contempt, "Shouldn't you be asking who can afford to be armed and who can't?"

"Well, thank you, barber," Stevens said with a smug grin, "but those are *your* words, not mine."

"To hell with you, Stevens," said Shaggs. He turned and started toward the rear door.

"Wait, Shaggs," said Fannin. "So what if we have to buy his guns at a marked-up price? At least it'll get us out of this mess."

"Do what suits you," said Shaggs, reaching for the door handle. "But why buy this weasel's guns when we can buy ourselves a *gunman?*"

The townsmen looked at each other for a moment. "Shaggs is right," Fannin said. "Keep your guns, Stevens." He stood up, dropped his hat atop his head and headed for the rear door himself. "We'll all remember what kind of a bastard you are when this thing is finished."

Three more townsmen stood and followed Erkel Fannin out the door.

At the hitch rail out in front of the marshal's office, Harry Whitesides stepped down from his horse, stamped his boots on the ground and stretched his back. A brown stub of a flattened cigarette butt lay between his thin lips. Beside him, his cousins Ted and Lyle Sloane stepped down from their horses and examined their surroundings, rifles hanging from their hands.

The fourth man, Odell Trent, peeled off his trail gloves and stuck them behind his gun belt. He popped his knuckles, loosening his fingers.

"Where is this damned bank?" he asked, sounding tense and restless.

Whitesides just looked at him through a pair of dark-tinted spectacles.

"You'll want to settle yourself down some before I go introducing you as my pal," he said.

Trent unfolded his fingers and let out a deep, tight breath.

"I'm just eager to get to work," he said.

"Admirable though that may be, Odell," said Whitesides, "it's not the best way to present yourself under these circumstances."

"Sorry, Harry," said Trent sincerely. "I'll remember that."

The Sloanes just stared at him.

Whitesides turned his dark spectacles to the marshal's office as the front door swung open and Kern stepped out into the first rays of early-morning sunlight.

"Morning, Marshal Kern," Whitesides said.

"Morning, Harry. . . ." Kern looked back and forth along the street. He gave Whitesides a nod and gestured for him and the others to come inside.

As soon as Bender closed the door behind the five of them, Kern stepped over between Jason Catlo, Cooper and Jennings and looked at Whitesides.

"Who's this with you and your cousins, Harry?" he asked.

"I might ask you the same question, Marshal," Whitesides said, looking the Catlo brothers and Buck the Mule Jennings over with careful scrutiny.

"You first, Harry," Kern said firmly. "You know I don't like last-minute surprises."

"Nor do I," said Whitesides, his right hand resting on his belly gun, holstered straight across his waist. He jerked his head toward his friend and said, "This is my pal Odell Trent. I'm vouching for him. We needed another man for the job, and I brought my pard here along for good measure."

"Yeah . . . ?" Kern looked the man up and down. "So, Mr. Trent, are you a rooting, tooting outlaw?"

"I can get the job done," Trent said coolly. "Don't you worry about that."

"Who'd you ride with before?" asked

Cooper. "Anybody I might know, or heard of?"

"Could be," Trent said a little testily. "Who do you *know?* Who have you *heard* of?"

Whitesides cut in before things took a wrong turn between the two.

"Odell here is not what you call an ol' hand at robbing," he said. "But he's a good man and a graduate of the Chicago School of Optometry, and I figure we all got to start somewhere." He looked at the Catlo brothers. "Now, who are these two fellows —"

"Hold it, Harry," said Kern, looking Trent over carefully. "He's *a what?*"

"You heard me," said Whitesides. "He's a graduate of the Chicago School of —"

"All right, that's all for me," said Jason Catlo. His hand streaked up with his Colt cocked and ready to fire. Whitesides did the same, in spite of the fact that Catlo had a head start on him.

"Both of you hold it!" Kern said, seeing that Philbert Catlo and Buck the Mule Jennings had both drawn their guns in Jason's defense. The two Sloanes and Odell Trent raised their guns in turn. Bender and Cooper stood with their hands on their gun butts, not sure what move to make next.

"All you jakes listen up," said Whitesides,

moving his aim back and forth slowly from one man to the next. "I did not ride all this way to get drawn upon by the ones I come to work with."

"Easy, Harry," said Kern. "Everybody's tight as wire here. We've had lots going on."

"So have we, Marshal . . . ," said White-sides, not giving an inch.

"I understand," said Kern. He looked back and forth with his hands chest high. "But let's all pull down our cannons and clear the air some." He gestured toward Jason and Philbert Catlo. "These are the Catlo brothers." He glanced toward Jennings. "And this is Buck the Mule Jennings."

Whitesides looked at all the welts and cuts on Kern's face, then at Jennings' crooked neck and drawn-up arm and shoulder.

"What's happened to this bunch, Marshal?" he asked Kern.

"We've had some problems, Harry," said Kern. "But everything is going the way it should now."

"Oh . . . ?" said Whitesides. "Where's Hicks?" He glanced around. "Where's Newman, Carver and Garrant?"

"Dead, dead, dead and dead," said Philbert.

"What the hell's this one talking about?" Whitesides asked Kern.

"It's the truth, Harry. They're all four dead. Shot down like dogs," said Kern.

"Then I guess we need to get cracking, kill the men who shot them down like dogs." He nodded for his cousins and Odell Trent to lower their guns. Then he uncocked his Colt and slipped it down into his holster. "Where will we find them?"

"He's staying at an abandoned house outside of town," Kern said.

"He . . . ?" Whitesides cocked his head to one side. "You mean *they?*"

"No, Harry, it was one man killed them," said Kern. "A fellow named Sherman Dahl — a hired gunman, calls himself a *fighting man.*"

Whitesides considered it and shrugged. "Well, I expect he's got a right to call himself that if he killed those four hard-heelers."

Cousin Lyle Sloane said, "I've come very near to killing Ned Carver any number of times myself. But damn, all four of them?"

"This Dahl is sort of a private bounty collector, I take it?" cousin Ted asked Kern.

"That's the way I see it," said Kern. "I would have helped those four ol' boys out, except I didn't know about it until it was over. By then I figured I best lie low and not tip my hand about what was getting

264

ready to happen here."

"That was pretty good thinking, Marshal," said Ted Sloane.

"Yes, considering everything at stake here," said Whitesides. "But I'll tell you what. The payroll is coming here this afternoon. We can go call this gunman out, shoot a few bullets into his head, then come back and get ready for our big haul." He looked all around with a broad grin. "Is everybody with me?"

"We're all with you," said Kern, his swollen face throbbing in pain. "But before I shoot anybody, I want to knock back a couple of shots at the saloon."

Whitesides gave him a hard, narrow stare. "Are you saying you need to get your courage out of a bottle, Marshal?"

"Hell yes," said Kern, "if there's any in there to get."

Whitesides and the others chuckled.

"I knew there was something I liked about you, Kern," Whitesides said.

CHAPTER 19

Dahl had made his way back to the widow's shack, cleared away the morning dishes, poured himself a second mug of strong coffee and walked to a chair he'd set near a side window. His rifle stood leaning against the window ledge. He sat down and sipped the hot coffee, preparing himself for a visit from Kern's deputies.

It was only a few minutes later when he saw men walking toward him from the dusty street, the tops of their hats seeming to appear, disappear, then reappear in a glittering sea of sunlight. This wasn't the direction he would have chosen, Dahl told himself.

But here they come. . . .

He stood and pulled his corduroy duster on over his bulletproof vest. Buttoning the coat all the way up, he slipped his right hand into a wide pocket and grabbed the handle of his big Colt, making sure his reach would be unobstructed when he needed it. Then he took a last long sip of coffee and walked bare-headed out the rear door.

Using the cover of sunlight, he circled wide of the bushy rock-strewn yard. He walked down out of sight through a low stretch of brush, and moved back up onto the main trail only a few yards from where it merged into the dirt street running the length of Kindred.

Dahl hurried forward from bush to rock, now approaching the men from behind as they drew nearer to the widow's shack. By the time they had stopped and stood in the front yard, he was no more than twenty feet from their backs, closing the distance with each silent step.

"Sherman Dahl," the man in the lead called out to the dilapidated house. "I'm sure you know why we're here. We came looking to —"

"Drop the weapons," Dahl said, standing so close the men heard his rifle cock as if it were on their shoulders.

"Oh my God —" Shaggs shouted. "Don't shoot, sir! Please don't shoot!"

A long oaken fork handle flew down from his hands as if it had turned red hot.

A pick handle fell from another hand, and a battered ancient squirrel rifle hit the dirt from another.

Dahl saw now that these were not Kern's deputies. These were townsmen, and he identified the purpose of their visit before any of them opened their mouths.

Still he asked in a quiet tone, "What can I do for you gentlemen?"

Shaggs stammered in reply to Dahl, "I — that is, we, are not here looking for trouble, sir." His eyes were fixed on the Winchester rifle in Dahl's hands, its barrel still pointed loosely at him and the others.

"I understand," Dahl replied. "Now, what is it I can do for you?" He wanted to get them out of there quick so he could be ready for Kern and his deputies.

"We were hoping to employ you to stand up for us against the marshal and his deputies, sir," said Shaggs.

He nodded at the pick handles, hayforks and the squirrel rifle relic lying in the dirt. "As you can see, we are sorely pressed to defend ourselves."

"Because you handed your guns over to the law," Dahl said flatly. "Now you see that the law isn't working in your best interest."

"Well, yes, sir," said Shaggs. The others nodded their heads in agreement as he continued. "Once we heard what you said about these men murdering a man and raping his wife —"

"How do you know these men did it?" Dahl asked, cutting him short.

"How do we know . . . ?" Shaggs looked all round, bewildered, seeking support. "Well, you told us the woman identified them, sir."

"Yes, I told you," said Dahl, "but you don't know me from Adam. You're taking my word for it, because it happens to match up with what you need right now."

"How can you say that, gunman?" said Fannin, speaking more boldly than Shaggs.

"You want someone to get your guns back for you, after all of you foolishly gave them away," said Dahl.

"Is that so bad?" asked Fannin, hearing what he took to be a trace of contempt in Dahl's voice. "We have a problem, and we're willing to pay you to solve it. You're a gun for hire. Isn't this what you do?"

"What I do is kill people for money, mister," Dahl said to clear the air, seeing how these men were only talking around the matter without mentioning the shooting, the killing, the hard specifics of his services.

"I'm sure we all understand what it is you do, Mr. Dahl," said Shaggs. "So let's get down to price and see how much it will cost us to have you *retrieve our guns,* so to speak."

Dahl shook his head. They still didn't get it. They still couldn't say they wanted to pay him to kill men for them. But he had no time for explanations.

"There are some things I won't do for money," he said flatly. "Getting your guns back is one of them."

"But, sir, it's a legitimate request," said Shaggs.

"Yes, it probably is, from your standpoint," said Dahl. "But from my standpoint, anybody stupid enough to give up their right to carry a gun probably shouldn't be carrying one in the first place."

"Now, see here . . . !" said Fannin. He took a bold step forward, but then he stopped, seeing Dahl's rifle and realizing he had nothing to counter it with.

"Take it easy, blacksmith!" said Shaggs to Fannin. "We need this man with us, not against us!"

"I'm not against you," said Dahl. "But I'm not with you either. I figure if you men can get your guns back on your own, you deserve them. Otherwise, you'd best learn how to live under somebody's boot. It's all you'll get from now on."

The townsmen stood in stunned silence

until Shaggs finally said in a huff, "I can see we were once again eager to put our trust in the *wrong* person."

"People who don't *trust* themselves usually have good reason not to," Dahl said. He lowered his rifle and took a step back in the direction of the stretch of brush he'd stepped out of.

"Yeah . . . ?" Fannin moved forward now, wanting the last word. "You can take your wise advice and stuff it up yourself. I never heard of a gunman who won't take money when it's offered to him."

"Now you have," said Dahl. "I won't take money from fools." He let the bite of his words sink in.

"Let's go, Erkel," Shaggs said, taking the blacksmith by his powerful arm, stopping him from advancing any farther.

"But here's something to consider if you want to *take* your guns back," Dahl said. "I won't take money to kill the kind of men who did what was done to that woman and her husband."

The townsmen stopped and looked at each other.

"You mean . . . you were going to kill these gunmen anyway?" Shaggs asked.

"Just as soon as I can, just as hard as I can," said Dahl. "If there're any guts left in you, you'll all be armed by nightfall."

From out in front of his bank, Matheson had stood watching the townsmen approaching the widow's shack through a short brass-trimmed sporting lens. In the circle of vision he had seen Dahl step up from the low stretch of brush and slip in close behind the men unexpectedly. "Very clever move, Mr. *Schoolteacher* . . . ," he'd murmured under his breath.

He continued to watch as the townsmen nervously spoke to Dahl. Their faces appeared in the circling lens as if they were standing only five feet from him.

Beside Matheson, a townsman asked, "What's going on over there, Councilman? Can I take myself a little look-see?"

"No," Matheson said sharply. "This lens is the property of the Great Western Bank and Trust Company. I would be violating a sacred employer's trust if I were to simply hand it over to anyone who wants to take a little *look-see*." He collapsed the lens between his palms with finality.

"Well, excuse the living hell plumb out of me, Councilman," the townsman said as the banker turned with the lens tucked under his arm and left the street. "I never thought men who handle other people's money to be on such high moral ground."

"That only proves that you are even more ignorant than I first suspected," Matheson shot back over his shoulder.

The townsman cursed under his breath.

Another townsman said to him, "Don't take it so hard, chappy. His nasty attitude will change soon as it gets close to next election time."

Jake Jellico had unlocked the doors of the Lucky Devil Saloon and Brothel only a few moments earlier. Sunlight streamed in as he stood cleaning up behind the bar. When he saw Kern, his deputies and four new men walk through the doors, he stopped what he was doing and immediately snatched up shot glasses and a fresh bottle of rye and stood them all in a row along the bar top.

"Morning, Marshal Kern," he called out, his voice already reflecting his worried state. "I'm getting ready to boil some coffee."

"No coffee, just rye," said Kern.

"Oh yes, of course," said Jellico. He hurriedly wiped down a length of bar top with a damp towel as the men lined up along the rail.

"Well, well, Marshal," he said, looking closer at the men. "It's like you and your men are all loaded for bear."

Whitesides grabbed his forearm as he made a swipe with the towel.

"What the hell does that mean?" he asked, staring at the saloon owner through his darkened spectacles.

Jellico froze, staring back wide-eyed, on the verge of panic.

"I — I — It just means —" he stammered mindlessly until Kern cut in.

"Pay no attention to our saloon owner, Harry," Kern said. "He is the most scared man you're likely to ever see in this business."

"Is that a fact?" Whitesides turned Jellico's arm loose. But he continued to stare at him through his dark spectacles. "A man that scared ought not make comments about who's *loaded* for what, is my thinking."

"And you are absolutely right, sir," Jellico replied. He rounded a finger beneath his starched shirt collar and gave a nervous smile to Kern.

"A new deputy, Marshal?" he asked.

"No, why?" said Kern.

"Oh, just wondering is all," said the shaken saloon owner. He jerked up the bottle and began filling shot glasses with a trembling hand. "I just saw these four are wearing guns, and with the new law and all,

I guess I just assumed that they are —"

"What the hell's this man jabbering about?" Whitesides demanded, cutting Jellico off.

"I give up," said Kern. He turned to Jellico and gave him a threatening stare. "Why don't you just keep your mouth shut and pour whiskey? Nobody came here to watch you sweat."

"Yes, sir, Marshal," said Jellico.

"Yeah, and pour it fast," Whitesides said. He tossed back his shot glass of rye in a gulp. "I hate whiskey that takes too much time between the bottle and glass. It loses its personality."

"I couldn't agree more, sir," said Jellico.

The men tossed back their rye as soon as it filled their glasses.

"Fill us again, Jake," said Kern, banging his glass down onto the bar top. He said to Whitesides and the others, "One more round while I go to the privy. Then we get to work." He stepped back from the bar, walked to the rear door and went outside.

Whitesides and the others finished their drink, then finished another before Kern walked back in, adjusting his gun belt.

"It's about time," said Whitesides as Kern sidled back to the bar and lifted his shot glass. "We thought you'd got a foot stuck."

"It's not stuck now," said Kern. He managed a tight grin on his lumped and swollen face, threw back his drink and set the empty glass down on the bar.

"Put all these on my account," he said, circling a finger above the empty glasses and the half-consumed rye bottle.

"Yes, sir, Marshal Kern," Jellico said. As he gathered up the empty glasses, he said, "There sure has been lots of excitement in Kindred, poor Ed Dandly getting killed and all."

"Yes, there has been, Jake," Kern said. He pushed his empty glass away. "And the day is just now off and running."

As the gunmen left the saloon, adjusting their gun belts and checking their rifles and sidearms, the Catlos and Buck the Mule Jennings fell in alongside Kern.

"Can I kill the woman again?" Jennings asked.

"Merciful Moses . . . ," said Kern. "What do you feed this idiot?" Kern asked Jason under his breath.

"What'd he say?" Jennings asked, only catching a few of the murmured words.

"Nothing," Jason said to Jennings.

"If you'd killed the woman right the first time, we wouldn't be doing this, Buck the Mule," Philbert said. "This time I better kill her myself —"

"For God's sake, why don't both of you save your breath?" said Jason. "The woman's not there. That's just this man's way of drawing us to him."

"I knew that," said Philbert, sounding a little embarrassed.

"Woman or no woman," Kern said, "this Dahl fellow has been a thorn in my side ever since I first laid eyes on him." He reflected for a moment, then said, "There're other towns all over the frontier who've banned guns on their streets." He lowered his voice. "Hell, everybody still carries what they want to. They just carry a smaller caliber and they keep it out of sight."

"Then what's the point in the law?" Jason asked.

"It works on folks' minds," Kern said, tapping his forehead. "Any time I want to, I can reach out and grab somebody carrying a gun, and he knows he's in the wrong from the get-go. It's a way to let everybody know the law is above them." He grinned and added, "And *I am* the law."

"And you're not carrying no puny, little small-caliber pocket gun. You legally carry the biggest, baddest gun you can lay hands on." Jason grinned. "That makes you the biggest dog on the walk, at all times. Anybody doesn't like it, it doesn't matter. They're outgunned anyway."

"Hey, I see you do understand this thing," said Kern.

"It's not hard to figure," said Jason. "I think you've jumped on a sweet deal here."

"Yes, but damn it," Kern said in reflection, "why have I been saddled with this so-called *Fighting Man,* just when things are starting to go my way?"

"Maybe you haven't been living right," Jason offered with a smug grin.

They walked on.

From a front window of Marlowe's realty office, the townsmen watched Marshal Kern and his deputies closely.

"Maybe if this goes the right way," Fannin said, "we won't have to break in and take our guns back."

"Don't count on it, Erkel," said Shaggs. "The odds aren't favoring that happening today."

They all stared intently as the ten gunmen walked toward the far edge of town.

CHAPTER 20

A warm morning wind rippled across the brittle tops of brush standing in low stretch of rocky ground at Kindred's edge. As the wide street narrowed into a trail, the wary marshal fanned out his deputies with a wave of his gloved hand.

"He'll be waiting to ambush us in the brush before we even get to the shack," he said in a lowered voice.

Whitesides stared at Kern and jacked a round into his rifle as he asked, "How do you know so damn much about what he's going to do?"

"Trust me," Kern said grimly. He gave another wave of his hand and said, "Everybody spread out now. Comb the brush. Run him out and kill him."

On Kern's other side, Bender and Cooper moved away, circling wide of the others and stepping down into the wind-whipped brush. Kern, Jason Catlo and Whitesides spread out a few feet and walked straight ahead, down into the brush, seeing Cooper and Bender covering the left flank. On their right, the Sloane cousins and Odell Trent walked slowly, circling the brushy lowland on their way toward the run-down house.

A hundred yards away from both the widow's shack and the low-lying stretch of brush and rock, Sherman Dahl lay prone behind a rock so small it barely offered him the cover he needed. But that was all right, he told himself. If this went well he wouldn't need the cover for long.

If it didn't go well . . . ?

Then it wouldn't matter, he thought as he adjusted his rifle sights and looked down the barrel toward the gunmen spread across the swaying brush.

Out of habit and experience, he had repositioned himself as soon as the townsmen left. In most cases, a surprise position was only good once. Then a wise fighter picked up his guns and his billet and moved on — find the next surprise, he'd reminded himself.

He lay silently watching and listening while the ten gunmen searched for him through the brush and rock. Ten to one were not good odds and his immediate objective was to change the odds as quickly as possible. There were only three men he wanted to kill. But these other seven became his targets the minute they stepped into the street with the Catlos and Jennings.

So be it. . . . He slipped his finger inside the trigger guard and settled down with the butt of the cocked Winchester resting in the pocket of his shoulder — prepared for his shot the very second it presented itself.

In the brush, Jennings and Philbert Catlo stopped searching and looked over at the others who were still moving forward, thirty yards away. Kern and Whitesides walked along ten feet apart.

"How does he know this *Teacher* fellow isn't waiting for us inside the shack?" Jennings asked Philbert.

"You get no argument from me," Philbert said. "I haven't seen him be right about anything since we met up with him."

"What if Jason is wrong too, about the woman not being there?" Jennings questioned.

"Watch your language, Buck the Mule," Philbert cautioned him. "That's my brother you're getting ready to talk about."

"I'm not speaking ill of him," said Jennings. "What if he's wrong? What if that woman *is* there inside the shack, getting better and better every day?"

"Just biding her time?" Philbert finished for him. "Waiting for her chance to slip a noose around our necks?"

"Yeah, that's all I'm getting at," Jennings said.

Philbert thought about it for a second. He looked back and forth across the stretch of brush. Then he directed his gaze at the front of the shack just ahead of them, dust stirring on the breeze in its barren front yard.

"I hate to say this, Buck the Mule, but you might be right." He chuckled under his breath and gestured toward the trail above the low-lying brush. "Follow me," he said quietly.

"Are we going on to the shack?" Jennings asked, suddenly sounding excited.

"Yeah, why not?" said Philbert, stepping up toward the open trail.

"Oh boy!" Jennings said, his voice almost childlike. "If she *is* there, I get to kill her!" He hurried, trying to pass Philbert on the narrow rocky path.

"Hold up, Buck the Mule! Damn it!" Philbert exclaimed as the two crested the edge of the trail. He grabbed the big gunman by his shoulder.

"Uuumphh . . . ," Jennings grunted aloud,

stopping abruptly, moving up onto his tip-toes.

Philbert felt the hot spray of blood fly out of the big gunman's back and splatter him in the face. At the same second he heard another rifle shot explode and echo off along the distant hills.

The big gunman twisted full circle and crashed down onto Philbert just in time to keep Dahl's next shot from hitting him full in his chest. The two rolled back down as one into the brush. When they came to a halt, Jennings' heavy limp body lay atop Philbert, pinning him to the ground.

"He's out on the dirt flats!" Kern shouted, diving to the rocky ground inside the brush. He returned a quick wild rifle shot in Dahl's direction.

"He's killed Philbert and the idiot!" shouted Bender, he and Cooper both dropping to the ground themselves. They also fired toward the resounding rifle shot.

"I can't say I'm *real* sorry to hear that," Whitesides said to Kern, crawling up beside him. He held his fire, looking all around through the brush. "This sneaking sumbitch has us where we can't get a look without topping that edge like a bunch of turkeys."

"Yeah, turkeys at a turkey shoot," Kern replied angrily. He parted the brush with his rifle barrel and stared as best he could toward the edge of the trail lying above them.

Dahl let fly another rifle shot. From the sound of it, he had moved again.

"Damn it to hell! He won't sit still and fight," Kern growled.

"Philbert, are you all right?" Jason called out to his brother desperately.

Another shot exploded from Dahl's rifle, then another. As soon as he fired the second shot, he hurried off to a new spot behind another small rock.

"I'm all right, brother . . . but I'm stuck under Buck the Mule!" Philbert called back to him. "He's dead and he's bleeding all over me!"

Kern returned four shots blindly, then called out to the brush, "Cooper, Bender, you're the nearest to him. Go get him onto his feet."

Another rifle bullet ripped through the air, this time coming from closer to the widow's shack.

Cooper and Bender stood into a crouch and hurried through the brush. When they came upon Jennings' bloodly body lying atop Philbert, they dragged the dead gunman off him and watched Philbert gasp for breath in the blood-soaked dirt.

"Let's get out of here," Tribold Cooper said, still crouched, dragging Philbert to his feet.

"I'm ready!" said Philbert, his face, clothes and hands coated thickly with Jennings' blood.

"Wait for us!" said Cooper, seeing Philbert running upward to the edge of the trail.

"Not today," Philbert called out over his shoulder. He chuckled. "It's every man for himself before he gets settled in and reload —"

He never got the words out of his mouth. As he topped the edge of the trail, a bullet from Dahl's Winchester thumped into his left shoulder, just above his heart. The impact flung him down the short sloop and back into the brush.

Tribold Cooper, who had been right behind him, dropped to the dirt and stuck his rifle above the trail's edge. He fired repeatedly, as fast as he could lever new rounds into the chamber.

"Damn it all, Bender, is he singling out the Catlos brothers?" Cooper called down behind him to where Bender knelt over Philbert, stuffing a bandanna into the gaping high shoulder wound.

"It looks that way to me," Bender said, working fast, seeing Philbert struggle to

285

hold on to consciousness.

"I'll . . . kill . . . the bastard," Philbert managed to say in a broken voice.

"Right now, you best be careful he doesn't kill you first," Bender said.

From a flat spot behind a low stand of barrel cactus, Dahl turned over onto his back and began reloading his rifle.

Two down, one to go . . . he told himself. After that, the fight was over, as far as he was concerned. That is, unless Marshal Emerson Kern and the rest of his men wanted to pursue the matter further.

Stage guards Bert Frost and Art Sealy both sat upright atop the big Studebaker stagecoach when the gunshots began exploding outside Kindred less than two miles away. The two gave a curious look toward the distant gunfire and sat with their shotguns across their laps.

"Pull her down some, Oates," Frost called out to the driver, above the squeak, groan and rattle of the big heavy rig. "Let's figure out what this shooting is all about before we ride smack into something."

The stage had bounced, bucked and swayed along the dusty trail since daylight. But upon hearing the guard's order, the driver, Calvin Oates, pulled back on the traces and slowed the six-horse rig down to an easy pace.

"You fellows will have to tell me what you want to do," said the driver. "I'm paid to drive, not to figure out gunfire."

The guards didn't reply. They continued looking in the direction of the shots ahead and to their left. Art Sealy stood up and balanced himself unsteadily, as if standing would afford him a better view.

"For a town that's no longer armed, they sure are raising lots of hell. They've got a new town marshal too, I've heard."

"Sit down, Art," said Frost, "before you break your danged neck." He continued to stare and listen. "Maybe they all got together for one last *hoopla* and shoot up all their bullets. Maybe it's the new marshal doing all the shooting."

"That makes no sense," said Sealy, rocking back and forth, almost losing his footing as the stage rolled on at its slower speed.

"That was a joke, Art," said Frost. "Now sit down before I knock you down. All you're doing is aggravating me."

Sealy dropped back onto his haunches. The stage rolled on.

"Do you suppose it's got anything to do with this?" he said, pointing down with a gloved finger at the inside of the coach beneath them. The big rig housed three large, leather-trimmed canvas bags filled with banded stacks of dollars and assorted gold coins. The tops of the bags were each drawn tight and fastened with a padlock.

"If I could answer questions like that, they'd be paying me more," said Frost.

Sealy just nodded.

Frost turned sharply to the driver and shouted, "Calvin, dang it! Will you please slow this rig down! Give us time to think this thing out."

Oates pulled back harder on the traces and called out to the horses, "*Whoooa,* boys, you heard the man."

The stage slowed almost to a halt. Then the driver gave the traces enough slack to keep the rig moving.

"That's more like it," said Frost. He rose onto his knees and stared long and hard in the direction of the shooting. The stage rolled along an upward grade, affording a better view of Kindred and the small shack that stood on its edge.

"It looks like the shooting's all coming from that brush field," said Sealy, also up on his knees, the wind licking at the fringe of his buckskin coat. "We can easily keep clear of it."

"All right, Art," said Frost, "let's get down inside where we belong." To the driver he said, "Oates, soon as we get inside, you pour it on these horses, get 'em flying, and keep 'em flying." He leaned forward and put a gloved hand on the diver's shoulder. "Don't slow us down until we're on the street. Understand?"

"Hell yes, I understand," said Oates without looking around. "Slow down . . . speed up. You don't know what the hell you want." He listened until he heard the two climb inside and slam the door behind them. Then he slapped the traces to the horses' backs and put them up into a run.

From the low-lying brush field, Kern saw the big stagecoach come up into view far to his left, running hard toward Kindred at the head of a long stream of rising trail dust.

"There goes the payroll stage, Harry," he said, a gleam coming into his eyes.

"Yep, just like I told you it would be," said Whitesides, who was positioned near him. "We best hope all this shooting didn't scare them off."

"They heard it, for sure," said Kern, keeping low, lest a rifle shot reach out and nail him the way it did Philbert and Jennings. "That's why it's running to town like its wheels are on fire."

"You don't think they'll bypass us, do you?" said Whitesides.

"No, Harry," said Kern. "It's too far to any place else. They've got to stop here. But all this gunfire will have the guards up on their toes."

The two looked off in the direction of Dahl's last shoots. "I'd hate to come this far and have this gunman scare all that money away," Whitesides said in an ominous tone.

"We're not taking a chance on that happening," said Kern. He raised his head up a little and called out to the others spread out through the brush, "All of you, pull back. We've got business to attend to."

From his position behind a low rock less than thirty yards from the widow's shack, Dahl lay with his rifle leveled and ready. He'd heard Kern call out to the deputies. He watched closely as the men slipped back through the brush toward town, staying low in a crouch. Denton Bender rose clearly into Dahl's gun sights for a few seconds, but Dahl didn't take the shot. He wanted Jason Catlo — no one else, he reminded himself.

He rose a bit and gazed off at the looming trail dust left behind the speeding coach. It had already ridden out of sight, onto the main street in Kindred.

Business to attend to . . . ?

He stared toward the street, wondering just what that business might be. He waited until he saw the last of the deputies move back into town. Then he stood and dusted his knees and elbows. Unbuttoning the corduroy duster, he fanned the lapels to let in some air. Then he turned and walked back toward the widow's shack.

CHAPTER 21

By the time Kern and his deputies had walked back onto the main street, the stagecoach had stopped out in front of the bank and hurriedly taken the bags of payroll money inside. Only Calvin Oates remained outside, inspecting his horses before pulling the rig around to the livery barn and unhitching the animals.

Kern looked around at Jason Catlo and Odell Trent, who carried the badly wounded Philbert between them. Philbert's arms hung limply across their shoulders.

"I'm taking brother Philbert to the doctor's," Jason said to Kern. "Don't do *nothing* until I get back," he warned.

"Go on, then," said Kern, no longer interested in Philbert's condition, or in Jason threats, which carried far less influence now that he was the only one left of the three. "Don't be surprised if the doctor won't answer the door after what Dahl ac-

292

cused you of."

"I'll take my chances," said Jason. He and Trent veered away toward the doctor's office, the toes of Philbert's boots dragging in the ground between them.

Farther back, the Slone cousins dragged Buck the Mule's big body by its heels.

"Think seeing all this is going to upset the stage guards?" Whitesides asked Kern, sunlight glinting off his dark spectacles. He gestured toward the wounded Catlo, and at the streak of blood trailing in the dirt behind Jennings' body.

"Jesus, Harry . . . ," Kern murmured, looking back at their gruesome followers. "I think this would upset most anybody in their right mind."

"Get rid of them," Whitesides said quietly.

"Good idea," said Kern. "All of you go on to my office and wait for us," he said back to the others without hesitation. "We'll come get you when we get ready to do business."

"What do you want us to do with this one's body, Harry?" Lyle Sloane asked Whitesides. "He weighs more than a freight train."

"I don't give a wicked damn what you do with that idiot," Whitesides said. "I don't even know why you dragged him this far.

Nobody asked you to."

"Well, I'll be damned," said Ted Sloane, as he processed Whitesides' words. He dropped his hold on Jennings' boot; so did Lyle. The two turned and walked away behind Cooper and Bender toward he marshal's office.

"Morning to you, driver," Kern called out to Calvin Oates, who stood rubbing the lead horse's muzzle, curiously watching them approach.

"Morning," Oates said flatly, eyeing the two up and down. He'd seen the others break away with the dead and the wounded.

"I'm Emerson Kern, the new town marshal," Kern said, stopping eight feet away. "I expect you're wondering what all the shooting was about out there," he said with a disarming smile.

"No, *sir,* Marshal," Oates said. He offered nothing more on the matter.

"Well, I know you're busy," said Kern. "I suppose your guards are in the bank?"

"Yes, *sir,* Marshal," said Oates.

Kern and Whitesides turned toward the bank. But they were met by Frost and his short double-barreled twelve-gauge shotgun, as he stepped out the door onto the boardwalk.

"What can I do for you, gentlemen?" he

asked stiffly.

The two men stopped abruptly. "I'm Town Marshal Emerson Kern, sir," Kern replied. "We're here on business."

"Bank's closed for a few minutes," Frost said. "You'll have to come back when it reopens."

"No," Kern said, "I'm going inside *now.* This is legal business. Point that scattergun in another direction."

"It's not pointed *yet,* Marshal," said Frost. "It's just making up its mind." But he did turn the gun barrel slightly and give the marshal the trace of a smile. "I'm Bert Frost," he said. "We heard all the shooting, coming in. Was that somebody giving up their gun?"

Kern smiled at the slight sarcasm. "I see you've heard about our new gun law," he said.

"Everybody has," said Frost. "I was telling a young couple about it a while back. They said they couldn't wait to get here and see for themselves." He looked around as if he might see the couple. Then he looked back at Kern and said, "How's all that working out?"

"Slow but steady," said Kern. "Changes take getting used to." He nodded at the bank and said, "Now let us pass."

"Can't do it," said Frost, "the bank is closed temporarily."

Kern remained patient, but said, "Carrying something of value, are you?"

"That's for you and the banker to discuss when the bank opens," Frost replied. "We just haul the goods."

"Are you being difficult, mister?" Whitesides said out of the blue. He stared at Frost through the two black circles covering his eyes.

Jesus . . . Kern gave him a stunned look.

"This man is the town marshal," Whitesides said before Frost could offer a response. "Now get the hell out of the way if you're not the one to talk to. Else I'll take that shotgun and stick —"

"Hold it, Harry!" said Kern, seeing trouble about to erupt between the two.

Frost bristled up like a bulldog, the scattergun gripped tightly, as if he was daring Whitesides to the make a move.

But just in time, the door behind Frost opened and Lyndon Matheson squeezed his way out, looking back and forth between the men.

"Good morning, Marshal Kern. Is there anything I can do for you?" Matheson asked.

"Yes, there is, Councilman," said Kern. "You can tell your stage guard here to get

296

his bark off and let us in. I came to see what's going on."

"Going on . . . ?" questioned Matheson. "Why, just business as usual, Marshal, I can assure you." He gave Frost a look and said, "Please allow our new marshal to enter, Bert. We don't want to appear unwelcoming, now, do we?"

"No, sir," said Frost. He stepped aside and allowed the two men to walk into the bank. But he and Whitesides shared a dark stare until Matheson followed the two inside. As the door closed, Frost turned back toward the empty stagecoach. "Asshole . . . ," he muttered under his breath.

Inside the bank, Matheson escorted the two men toward an ornately carved oaken partition. Beyond the barred teller window, Art Sealy stood over the bags of payroll money with his shotgun cradled in his arm. He watched Kern and Whitesides closely, in spite of the badge on Kern's chest.

"I dared not mention it outside on the street, Marshal," Matheson said quietly, even though the bank was closed and empty, "but this bank has been chosen as a new relay point for the Derning and British Mining Company's quarterly payroll disbursement." He gave an oily smile.

"Oh . . . ?" Kern sounded mildly surprised.

"Of course there was no way you would have known that, Marshal," said Matheson. "We — That is, *I* thought it a bit much to put on you, so soon after you took office."

"I think it's something I *very much* needed to know," said Kern, feigning ignorance. "How can I protect the town and its interests if I'm not told everything?"

Whitesides and Sealy stood in silence as the two conversed.

"My apologies, Marshal," said Matheson. "I assure you it will never happen again."

"Humphh," Kern grunted. He walked closer to the barred teller window. He looked in and down at the bags lying at the guard's feet. "I take it the keys to those locks are someplace safe?"

"Oh yes, indeed they are," said Matheson. "Would you like to know where?"

"No," said Kern. He grinned. "So long as they're somewhere in safekeeping, that's good enough for me."

As Matheson stood up close beside him, joining him to peer down at the bags, Kern looked back at Whitesides and gave a guarded smile.

"Stick 'em up, Councilman," he half whispered.

Matheson stiffened and froze, feeling something hard pointed into the center of his back. On the other side of the teller window, Art Sealy's grip tightened on his shotgun. Behind Kern and Matheson, Whitesides almost snatched his Colt up from its holster.

But Kern had timed everything. He raised his finger from Matheson's back and wiggled it in his face.

"Got your blood pumping, didn't I, Councilman?" he said.

"Good Lord, Marshal!" said Matheson, his face flush. He looked around and back and forth as if coming to from a bad dream. Then, with a sigh of relief, he gave a shaky smile and said, "I blame myself for that. I've heard all about your keen sense of humor."

"And now you've seen it firsthand," said Kern, grinning. He raised his fingertip and blew on it as if it were a gun barrel.

Sealy uncoiled and lowered the barrel of his shotgun. Whitesides shook his head and eased his hand away from his gun butt.

"Before I forget, Councilman," Kern said, "you need to tell *Kit Carson* here that it's all right to let me in there when I want in." He gestured toward Sealy in his fringed rawhide coat, his long hair hanging shoulder-length, his fringe-cuffed gloves stuck down in his waist.

"*Kit Carson?* Oh, I get it," said Matheson, catching himself. "Mr. Sealy, please extend every courtesy to our new marshal. Assist him in any way. If anyone questions it, tell them to see me." He turned to Kern and said, "There, Marshal, how's that?"

"I couldn't ask for more," Kern said, beaming.

Sealy just stared at them through the teller window.

The Sloane cousins had walked away and left Jennings' body lying in the dirt. Two townsmen who had been watching the gunfight had slipped onto the street long enough to pull the big body to one side. They leaned Jennings against the wall of the town apothecary building, out of the traffic for the time being.

Walking past the body on their way to the marshal's office, Kern gave a sidelong glance at Buck the Mule and shook his head.

"This won't do, Harry," he said to Whitesides walking along with him. "Your cousins can't leave a man lying dead on a town's main commercial street."

"It's better than he deserves," said White-

300

sides, "if it's true what the man said he did to that poor woman and her husband."

"I'm talking about the *smell,* Harry," said Kern. "As bad as Buck the Mule smelled alive, imagine what he'll smell like in a day or two."

"Are we going to be here that long?" Whitesides asked.

Kern just stared at him.

"All right, I'll get the Sloanes to move the nasty sumbitch," Whitesides said grudgingly. "I can't say I'm sorry he's dead."

"He was too stupid to live," said Kern, getting back to his old self now that Jennings was dead and one of the Catlos badly wounded. "I have little doubt that they all three did what the *Teacher* said they did. But that means nothing to us. We're one step away from taking the payroll money and cutting out of here." He smiled to himself, walking straight ahead.

Inside the marshal's office, Philbert lay on a bunk in one of the cells. Jason and Odell Trent had pressed bandannas and bandages on his upper shoulder, front and back to stay the bleeding.

"You'd better not let him die, *Eye Doctor,*" Jason said to Trent, the two of them looking down at Philbert, watching his

301

bloody chest rise and fall weakly with every thin breath.

"Don't call me *Eye Doctor,*" said Trent, not giving an inch.

"Why?" asked Jason. "I understand you kept Whitesides from being blind as a bat. Didn't you make his dark spectacles for him?"

"Yes, I did," said Trent. "But I'm no eye doctor. I used to grind and fit spectacles. Don't make more of it than that." His right hand rested on his holstered Colt.

Jason started to say more on the matter, but the front door opened and Kern walked in, followed by Whitesides.

"All right, men," said Kern, "the payroll is here, just like Harry said it would be. Everybody rest up, we're taking it this afternoon before the bank closes for the day."

"What about my brother, Philbert?" Jason asked.

"What about him?" Kern asked, not really caring. He looked back into the cell and saw Philbert trying to sit up on the bunk. "Was the doctor in, or just not answering his door for you?"

"No," said Jason. "He was gone sure enough. I kicked his back door and found some bandages, some laudanum and what-not. The bullet went through clean. But he's bleeding like a stuck hog."

"Too bad," said Kern. "If he's up and able, he's still in this thing. If he can't ride, we're not waiting for him."

"Yes, we *are* waiting for him," Jason said with firm resolve.

But Cooper, Bender, Whitesides, the Sloane cousins and Odell Trent all stepped forward as one.

"Like Kern said," Whitesides interjected, "if he rides, he's *in.* If he *can't,* he's not."

Jason backed off. But he kept his gun hand close to his Colt.

"What about this *Teacher* . . . this *Fighting Man* we said we'd kill?"

"What about him?" Kern repeated.

"He killed Buck the Mule, he's ruined my brother. We can't let him get away with it."

"It appears you Catlos and your idiot friend angered him," said Whitesides. "He doesn't seem to be out to kill me or my men."

"We're all supposed to be in this together," said Jason.

"Hunh-uh," said Whitesides. "You've confused us with those knights of old. We're in this for what we can get, nothing else."

Jason's face twisted in rage.

"Here's the deal, Jason," Kern cut in. "If

303

this Dahl fellow gets in our way, he's dead. Otherwise, we take this payroll and ride off shouting high hell to Mexico. We've already seen this man is a rifle fighter. He won't show his face close up. That means it could take us forever to flush him out and kill him."

"So forget about him," Whitesides put in. "He's a coward anyway, fighting behind a bullet-stopping vest."

"I'm not forgetting about him," said Jason, "not after what he did to brother Philbert."

"If you want to come back and kill Dahl after we're through here, you do it," Kern said. "We'll have nothing but respect for you."

"I'll even make up a song about it, if that will make you feel better," Whitesides said, a grin creeping slowly across his face. Light glinted off his dark spectacles.

The men stifled a laugh, recognizing the anger in Jason Catlo's eyes.

"I'm going in there and getting my brother patched up and ready to ride," he said. "We're not getting cut out of our share."

CHAPTER 22

From a front window of the mercantile store, Stevens and the other townsmen stared out through the waning afternoon, watching the deputies walk their horses from the livery barn to the hitch rail across the street from the bank. Philbert lay atop his horse, bowed forward in his saddle, his right hand gripping his bloody left shoulder.

"What on earth are they all doing at the Li Woo Laundry House?" Shaggs asked. He looked at Walter Stevens as if the mercantile owner might have an answer for him.

But Stevens only shrugged. He'd been busily counting the money he collected from the sale of the used firearms he'd convinced several townsmen to purchase.

"Maybe they're doing the same thing anybody would be doing there," said Dan Marlowe. "Picking up clean shirts." He looked back down at the battered old Spencer rifle in his hands, a recent acquisition

305

thanks to Stevens.

"Walter, are you certain this thing will even fire?" he asked.

"It'll fire, Dan," Stevens reassured him. "Just make sure you know how to fire it."

"So, Stevens, what's the tally?" said Fannin. "How much did you make selling us all of this worthless junk?" He worked the stiff action of a single-shot breech-loading carbine in his hands.

"Don't want it, Erkel?" asked Stevens. "I'll be glad to refund your money." He reached for the rifle. Several pairs of eyes followed him — men who were ready to make a bid on the iron relic, in case they weren't able to retrieve their guns from Kern's office.

"No, that's all right," Fannin said, jerking the rifle back out of Stevens' grasp. "I'm keeping it. I was just curious is all."

Stevens looked all around at the gathered townsmen, some with his used guns, some still holding hickory implement handles, hay rakes, chains. He folded the cash and stuffed it down into his shirt pocket.

"Anybody else wants their money back, now's the time to say so," he said. "Just remember, if we get in there and see that the guns have been hidden someplace that we can't get to, you'll be caught short."

"Damn snake . . . ," a townsman growled

306

under his breath.

"Once I button this shirt pocket, all deals are final," Stevens called out.

"Let's get on with it," Fannin said grudgingly. "The sooner we butt in the marshal's office and get our guns back, the sooner we can throw this junk away."

"*If* we can get them back . . . *if* they're even there," a townsman grumbled.

"It'll be a cold day in hell before I ever give up my guns again," said Shaggs. "They say these gun laws work in some places, but I don't see how. From now on, the only *gun law* I'd support will be one that makes it illegal *not* to carry at least one gun at all times."

"Hear, hear, on that," said another townsman. "I never before realized how much carrying a gun makes everybody walk a little straighter."

"More polite too," said Shaggs.

From the window, a townsman kept watch on the deputies until they hitched their horses and Kern and one of his deputies walked across the street and through the front doors of the Great Western Bank and Trust Company.

"All right, the marshal and two of them are going to the bank," he said. "This might be our best chance!"

"I've got the ax," said Shaggs. "Let's go."

The men filed out the back door and hurried along the alley toward the rear of the marshal's office.

As soon as Kern and Lyle Sloane were inside the bank, Whitesides, Ted Sloane and Odell Trent walked across the street, leading their horses, and stood a few yards away from the bank's doors.

"I don't trust this, cousin Harry," said Ted Sloane. The two watched as a hand inside the bank turned the sign from OPEN to CLOSED with the flick of a wrist.

"Easy, Teddy boy," said Whitesides. "You're just nervous wondering what you'll do with all that money." As he spoke he fidgeted with his dark spectacles, adjusting them up and down on the bridge of his nose.

"You heard what Kern told us," Trent said to Ted Sloane. "This is going to be *slick as a whistle;* not a shot fired, eh?"

"Yeah, I hope so," said Sloane.

"Damn it," Whitesides said, still struggling to get his spectacles to suit him.

"Are you all right, Harry?" Trent asked in a concerned tone. "Can you see everything? Do you need me to bend the wire a little —"

"Damn it, Odell, I'm good," Whitesides

said. He jammed the spectacles down onto his nose and twisted the wire-rims sharply. The three turned back toward the closed doors of the bank.

But as they stared at the doors, sudden blasts of pistol fire resounded from inside the bank.

"Damn it to hell!" Whitesides shouted. He jerked his Colt up from his holster; his dark spectacles fell from his nose. He snatched them from the dirt and shoved them back onto his nose.

"Oh, shit!" he cried out as one of the lenses broke away from the wire frame and fell to the ground.

Teddy Sloane and Odell Trent jerked their guns up and fanned back and forth, ready to shoot anyone who might dare venture forward. Across the street, Cooper and Bender both drew their guns. So did Jason Catlo. Philbert sat swaying in his saddle, turning loose of his shoulder and trying to draw his Colt.

The bank door flew open and Kern emerged with a bag of money in either hand and another bag at his feet. A wide circle of blood covered most of his chest.

"Harry, quick, they've shot me and Lyle!" he called out in a strained voice; he wobbled in place, nearly falling. "Come get this money!"

"You heard him, come on!" Whitesides said to Trent and Ted Sloane.

Even as the three got to the open door, Kern managed to throw one bag after the other to them.

"Where's Lyle?" said Ted Sloane, looking frantically past Kern until he saw Lyle's body lying sprawled in the floor near the teller window. Bullet holes glistened on his bloody chest.

"There's nothing you can do for him," Kern shouted, giving the gunman a shove. "Now get out of here!"

"What about you?" Whitesides asked.

"I'll be all right, Harry, if this bullet doesn't kill me," said Kern. "I'll tell them I walked in on a robbery. They're unarmed. They can't argue about it. Now go! I'll catch up to you later."

Without another word, Whitesides and the other two ran to their horses carrying the heavy canvas bags full of money. As they struggled and lifted the bags up behind their saddles, Cooper and Bender jumped atop their horses.

"We're not letting those money bags out of our sight, Denton," Cooper said, he and Bender turning their horses in the street.

"I hear you, Tribold!" said Bender, ex-

310

cited, his blood racing.

Jason reached for his horse's reins. Philbert sat bowed in his saddle, finally getting his Colt raised and cocked. But before Jason could get atop his horse, he turned at the sound of Dahl's voice booming along the empty dirt street.

"Jason and Philbert Catlo," Dahl called out from thirty yards away.

"Well, well now, look who's coming here, brother Phil," said Jason. He turned loose of his reins and let them drop to the dirt.

Whitesides, Ted Sloane and Odell Trent stopped hurriedly tying the canvas bags down behind their saddles.

Whitesides turned a crooked half-blind stare toward Dahl and his long corduroy duster, walking steadily toward them.

"Damn it, all I see is a blur," said Whitesides. But even as he spoke he held his rifle at port arms, ready to throw it to his shoulder and fire.

"Stand fast, Harry! *Please!* Before you shoot one of *us*," Trent said, speaking for him and the remaining Sloane cousin.

Jason called out to Dahl, "How did you know I was coming to kill you first thing from here, *Teacher?*"

"Just a lucky guess," Dahl said flatly, walking forward, no rifle, only a big Colt in his right hand, hanging down his side.

"We don't have time for all this, Catlo," Whitesides called out, looking back and forth, seeing off-balanced shadows and images, but unable to identify anything clearly.

"We're *making time* for it, Whitesides," Jason replied, staring at Dahl as he spoke. "You saw what he did to my brother and Buck the Mule."

Whitesides called out to Trent and Ted Sloane, "Stay out of this, men. Let the Catlos take care of their own business."

In the middle of the street, Cooper and Bender both heard Whitesides.

"Good idea," said Cooper. The two settled their horses, rifles in their right hands, ready if they needed them.

"I suppose you've got your bullet-stopping vest on today, *Teacher?*" Jason called out.

"Not today," Dahl said quietly.

"You're lying," said Jason. "Not that it matters. It won't help you at all. We're going to shoot your damn head off anyway."

Dahl stopped fifteen feet away; he unbuttoned his corduroy duster slowly. He was bareheaded; a hot breeze licked at his hair.

"Hey, you're really not wearing it, are you?" said Jason. "Look at this, brother Phil, he's crazy as a June bug."

"I see it," Philbert managed to say, struggling to keep himself seated in his saddle. He coughed with great pain and said, "Why is he not wearing it?"

"Yeah, *Teacher,*" said Jason. "Why is it you're not wearing it?"

Dahl said flatly, "Sometimes I wear it, sometimes I don't. Today, *I don't,*" he added.

"Oh, I see," said Jason. He gave a thin smile. "It's just all about how the day suits you."

Dahl just stared without replying.

"Yep, that's how it is. . . ." Jason shook his head with disapproval. "You're one of *those kinds* of people, I just knew it."

Atop the roofline overlooking the street, Billy Nichols watched the gunmen, both the ones on horseback and the ones on the ground, all of them faced off against Sherman Dahl. He gripped the bloody gun butt in his right hand — the big Colt that he'd taken from Buck the Mule's corpse when he'd slipped into town a half hour earlier. Though Kern told Whitesides to have the Sloane cousins move the body, Jennings still sat leaning in the same spot, his lifeless eyes staring blankly.

With a good loaded gun in his hand, Billy felt a newborn confidence coursing through him. Dahl was the only man he'd met lately

313

who'd treated him with any decency, any kindness, any trust. He wasn't about to leave him facing this many men alone. Especially not *these* men, the ones who had beaten him, kicked him around, would have gladly seen him hang for a crime they knew he didn't commit.

Make your play, you dirty sonsabitches . . . he said to himself, his anger growing, replacing any remnants of fear, as he stared down onto the street. Below him he could hear Dahl speaking with calm, cold determination.

"It's time I settle you Catlos up for the woman and her husband," Dahl said.

"Who's paying you, Teacher?" Jason said. "With a man like you, gun work is all about money."

"Not always," said Dahl. "I'm through talking. Bring your gun up. Let's have at it."

"When we're damn good and ready, *Teacher,*" Jason said. "I expect if I take a notion to, I'll stand here until hell freezes —"

Dahl's first shot stopped him cold. The bullet ripped through his chest and out of his back. It bored deep into Philbert's calf, the wounded man sitting on his horse behind his brother.

Jason slammed back against Philbert's

horse and hit the ground dead. Philbert let out a sharp wail as the bullet nailed him just above his boot well. His spooked horse reared on its hind legs; Philbert, in his weak wounded condition, struggled to stay in his saddle. His Colt wobbled limply in his hand.

"Damn you, *Teacher!*" he shouted, leveling the Colt as his horse touched back down. He pulled the trigger; his shot went wild.

Dahl's shot hit him squarely in the chest.

Philbert's Colt roared again on his way out of the saddle and to the ground. His second stray bullet whistled past Whitesides' head.

Unable to see clearly, Whitesides mistook the shot for Dahl's.

"To hell with this! Kill him!" he shouted. He swung his rifle up and began firing, his target any blurry image that moved in front of him. Following Whitesides' order, Trent and Ted Sloane swung their guns up and fired at Dahl.

Dahl had already started to back into an alleyway, having completed what he'd set out to do. But he looked up along the roofline on hearing Billy Nichols call out to him.

"I'm with you, Mr. Dahl!" he shouted, firing the big Colt as he slid and slipped and scooted down toward the edge of a slanted tin roof.

"It's that damn kid! Shoot him!" shouted Tribold Cooper. He and Bender dropped from their horses and turned their fire onto the roofline.

Oh no . . . ! Dahl saw the Colt in Nichols' hand firing wildly as he tumbled off the roof to the ground, right into the midst of the blazing gunfire.

Running down the street from the alleyway beside the marshal's office, the townsmen rushed toward the bank ready to put up a fight, all of them with guns in their hands.

The townsmen had chopped through the thick rear door of the marshal's office, and managed to reclaim their firearms just in time to hear shots erupt from the direction of the bank. They charged toward the gunmen like a platoon of soldiers, yelling and firing. Gray smoke filled and loomed along the dirt street.

"The deputies are robbing the bank!" shouted Shaggs, seeing the three canvas bags on the gunmen's horses. Stevens and Fannin were running right beside him. "Stop, you thieving bastards!" Shaggs shouted.

The townsmen saw Dahl run over to the fallen young man and pull him to his feet.

They carefully directed their fire away from the Teacher and toward the deputies.

"I'm okay!" Billy Nichols shouted as he gained his footing and began firing once again.

The two turned their fire toward Whitesides, Trent and the remaining Sloane cousin. Whitesides cursed and screamed, still firing blindly as bullets from the townsmen sliced through him and drove him backward. He crashed through the bank door and fell dead in a spreading pool of blood. His broken spectacles flew off and slid four feet before coming to a spinning halt.

In the middle of the street, Bender fired as he fanned his hat back and forth trying to clear away a swirling cloud of gray-black smoke. He aimed his fire toward Billy, but a shot from Dahl's Colt stopped him dead. He fell backward in the dirt beneath a red mist of blood.

Fannin and Stevens ran up close to Tribold Cooper, firing as one, any animosity between them over the price of the used firearms now wiped away. Cooper fell dead beneath their relentless hail of bullets.

Through the looming smoke, Dan Marlowe looked all around, his eyes burning and watering.

"Hold your fire," he shouted, seeing that the last two gunmen still alive had just crumpled onto their knees in the dirt. Ted Sloane knelt wobbling in place, supporting himself on the tip of his Colt barrel, which was jammed into the dirt. A quick shot from Marlowe pitched him backward in the dirt.

Beside Sloane, Odell Trent knelt on one knee, his other knee cocked, trying desperately to push himself up. His bloody hands were empty; his rifle lay three feet away. That he was still kneeling and conscious was somewhat miraculous, given the state of things. His chest was riddled with bullet holes. Red-yellow matter dangled from a gaping hole in the side of his head.

"Who are you, mister?" Shaggs called out, sliding to a halt in front of him, his rifle aimed and ready.

"I — I don't know," Trent answered in a thick dreamy voice. "My brain's . . . blown out."

"Yes, it is," said Shaggs. He pulled the trigger. Trent fell backward, his arms spread wide, as if he'd been preparing to fly when the bullet stopped him.

Erkel Fannin looked around at the carnage in the smoky street, and then glanced down at the gun in his hand. Smoke curled up from its barrel and caressed the back of his hand like the breath of some wild, terrible demon. He looked in stunned surprise at Walter Stevens and whispered, *"Lord God . . ."*

CHAPTER 23

Out in front of the bank, Dan Marlowe and Walter Stevens untied the canvas bags of money and dropped them to the dirt at their feet. The door to the bank stood open wide, but no one had ventured inside when Dahl and Billy Nichols walked over.

"That's the boy who killed Ed Dandly," Dahl heard a townsman whisper.

"No, it's not," Dahl said. He looked into the shadowy bank, seeing Harry Whitesides lying sprawled in his own blood.

"It sure looks like him to me," the townsman said.

The other townsmen looked on in silence, wanting to hear what Dahl had to offer on the matter.

"It's not him," Dahl said more firmly. "Take my word for it." His big Colt dangled in his hand, still curling smoke.

But the townsman persisted.

"You mean it's *not him,* or *he* didn't do

it?" he asked cautiously.

Dahl turned to him with both his big Colt and a cold stare pointed squarely at him.

"Both," he said.

The inquiring townsman backed off; the rest of the townsmen nodded at one another, satisfied with Dahl's answer.

Dahl turned back to the open door and looked inside.

After a short, tight silence, Walter Stevens cleared his throat and said, "At least we saved the mine's payroll money, fellows." He looked all around and gave an amiable smile.

"Don't count on it," Dahl said.

He turned and walked to the canvas bags and stooped down over them. Pulling a wicked-looking knife from his boot well, he sliced open the top of one of the locked canvas bags, turned it upside down and shook it.

"My goodness . . . ," said Fannin. He and the other townsmen watched stakes of chopped and bound newspaper spill out onto the ground, followed by a flow of steel washers the size of silver dollars.

"What the hell is this?" Stevens asked with a puzzled expression.

"It's sure as hell not payroll money!" said the blacksmith.

"It's a trick," said Dahl. Without hesitation he walked back to the open bank door and made his way inside, Billy Nichols shadowing him. Behind Nichols the townsmen ventured in, looking all around, seeing the door leading into the enclosed room behind the barred teller windows standing wide-open. They stepped around Lyle Sloane's body, lying on the floor near the teller counter.

Beyond the wall, Dahl looked down at the two dead guards, Frost sprawled on the floor with a checkered napkin tucked down in his collar. Sealy sat slumped back in a chair, a checkered napkin spread across his lap. Both guards had white foamy spittle on their lips.

"Poisoned!" said Stevens, staring, repulsed by the sight, but unable to take his eyes away.

"My God!" said Shaggs. "Who would do something like this?"

"Take your best guess," Dahl said. He slipped his big Colt back into its holster, turned and walked toward the door, Billy Nichols right behind him.

"My best guess?" said Shaggs, hurrying along beside him, out onto the street. "My best guess is that Emerson Kern has orchestrated this entire thing! He has deceived us,

misled us and has now stolen our money!"

"It wasn't your money," said Dahl, walking to the middle of the street through the blood and carnage.

"I meant the *bank's money*," said Shaggs. "But it's our money too —"

"It's not the bank's money either," Dahl said. He stooped down, loosened the gun belt from around Tribold Cooper's waist and pulled it free.

"It's not?" Shaggs said. He spread his hands. "Then whose money is it?"

"It belongs to the Derning and British Mining Company," Dahl replied.

"How — how do you know that?" Shaggs questioned, appearing both impressed and bewildered.

"It says so on the bag," Dahl answered. He reached out with the toe of his boot and pointed to the letters on the stiff canvas.

"Oh . . . ," said Shaggs.

"And you can't blame Emerson Kern for all of this," Dahl said.

"No, you're right, sir," said Shaggs. "I blame Mayor Coakley. He's the stupid son of a bitch who allowed this to happen. Him and his damn *gun law*."

Dahl stopped and looked squarely at Shaggs. "If he's a stupid son of a bitch, what are the rest of you?" he asked, his sharp stare hitting all of the armed townsmen standing in the street.

"Sir . . . ?" the barber said.

"You're the ones who voted him in. You set the stage for everything else that happened here," Dahl said with finality on the matter.

Shaggs and the others squirmed.

"Be that as it may," Walter Stevens said, stepping forward, "what will you charge us to hunt him down and bring him back here?"

"Like I told you before, there're some things I won't take pay for doing," Dahl said. He turned to Billy Nichols and handed him Cooper's gun belt, an empty slim-jim holster hanging on it. "Put this on. Sooner or later you'll get tired of carrying that Colt in your hand."

Stevens started to say, "But what if we —"

"I'll bring him back to you, no charge," said Dahl. "But don't count on him being alive."

"No, of course not," said Stevens. "I have a feeling you'll find poor Lyndon Matheson somewhere along the trail. I'm almost certain that Kern took him hostage."

"Don't count on that either," said Dahl. He looked off toward a trail leading up into the hills. "Bankers have a way of coming through these things unscathed."

Billy adjusted the gun belt around his waist and shoved the Colt down into the holster.

"Can I ride with you, *Teacher?*" he asked.

Teacher . . . Dahl looked him up and down.

"Have you got a horse?" he asked.

"Well, no. . . ." The young man looked down at the ground, embarrassed. "I don't have much of nothing."

"Don't worry about it, you're still young. You've got time," said Dahl. He turned and called out to the townsmen gathered around them, "This man needs a horse. Anybody got a horse for our friend here?"

Nearly every hand went up.

"See how it works?" Dahl said to the young man. "Show folks what you stand for. The good ones will always stand with you."

"I'm learning," the young man said. He nodded and fell in beside Dahl, following him to the livery barn.

At the edge of an upward-reaching hill trail outside Kindred, Kern stood with his rifle in hand, the tip of its barrel pointed at Lyndon Matheson's side.

"I like the sound of things," he said, staring back toward Kindred. "The townsmen have gotten their guns back by now, but they're not shooting at us."

Matheson pushed the straying rifle barrel away from him. "Will you watch where you're pointing that thing? I hate guns."

"Oh, really?" said Kern. He turned his eyes to the tall, regal-standing banker. "I'm not surprised. I noticed how scared you are of them when I pretended to stick one in your back," he said.

Matheson frowned. "I thought you had lost your mind and deviated entirely from our plan."

"No," said Kern, "I just did it to get a rise out of you." He chuckled. "I wouldn't do nothing to change our plan. It was too perfect." He touched his fingertips to the circle of dried blood on his shirt. He'd wiped the blood from Lyle Sloane's chest onto his own after shooting the unsuspecting gunman.

"It was until now," Matheson said, gesturing at the trail behind them, where the buggy sat with a length of wheel broken away from the spokes. An extra horse stood hitched to the rear of the buggy. Two large laundry bags from the Li Woo Laundry House lay in the small rear buggy seat. The three canvas bags of payroll money had been emptied into them.

"We sent the townsmen off chasing Whitesides and the others, and here we are — not a shot's fired at us," said Kern.

"Thank goodness for that," Matheson said.

Kern looked at him again. "Because you *really* hate guns," he reiterated for the banker, teasing him.

"Yes, *really,*" said Matheson.

"And why is that?" Kern asked.

"Why indeed . . . ," Matheson chuffed. "They're loud, vulgar and crude. Civilized mankind has no place for such monstrous, *deadly* weapons."

"*Vulgar and crude,* eh?" Kern looked at the rifle in his hand, turning it back and forth.

"Precisely," said Matheson.

Kern smiled to himself. "Not at all as refined or dignified as, say . . . *poison?*"

Matheson just looked at him stonily for a moment.

"We really should get busy and change the wheel," he said. "You'll find tools in the undercarriage, along with a spare wheel."

"Oh, will I?" said Kern, noting how Matheson had just passed the physical labor off onto him. "You bankers must think of everything."

Matheson gave a smug grin, standing with

his hands folded behind his back, his swallowtail coat stirring slightly on a warm breeze.

"I had the blacksmith install a spare wheel for just such an emergency as this," he said. He swept a hand back toward the buggy. "So, have at it, and we'll soon depart from this terrible frontier."

"Hunh-uh," said Kern. "You change the wheel."

"You must be joking," said Matheson. "I'm a banker and a politician. I wouldn't know where to start."

"I'll show you," said Kern.

"No, I refuse to do it," Matheson said.

Kern eased the gun barrel back around, pointed it at his chest and cocked the hammer.

"I know how *vulgar* this must look, but here's a *nasty* ol' gun pointed at you, Mr. *Banker-Politician*," Kern said. "Now, unless you've got some leftover *poison* you'd like to point back at me, you better do like I tell you."

Kern followed the banker to the buggy and stood back and watched as Matheson took off his black swallowtail suit coat with a sour look on his face. Matheson folded his coat neatly and laid it in the buggy beside the two laundry bags stuffed with money. He rolled up the sleeves of his white shirt, loosened his collar, lay down on his back in the dirt and crawled under the buggy.

"It's not here," he said.

"What do you mean, it's not there?" said Kern, stooping for a better look.

"That blasted Fannin!" said Matheson, crawling back from under the buggy, dirt and black grease streaking his white shirt.

Kern stared at him.

"I specifically told that imbecile to mount a spare wheel under this buggy. I even paid him to do it!" he raged.

Kern shook his head. He looked off the trail back toward Kindred and let out a breath.

"You're starting to try my patience, *Lyndon*," he said, a sense of warning in his voice.

"It's not my fault that Fannin didn't do as he was told," said Matheson.

"I wonder if a rifle shot would tip anybody off that we're up here," Kern said, thinking out loud.

Matheson looked worried. He scrambled around on the ground picking up pieces of the broken wheel.

"What the hell are you doing?" Kern

asked, his thumb slipping over the rifle hammer.

"I once watched my father fix a buggy wheel," Matheson replied, fitting a broken length of rounded wooden rim on the wagon spokes sticking down into the dirt. "I believe I can piece this together well enough to get us up the trail. There's a place Dr. Washburn has up there where he goes to get drunk without making a spectacle of himself. I'm certain he has spare wheels there."

"Here's the thing, *Banker-Politician,*" Kern said calmly. "I can shoot you, put the money bags on the buggy horses and ride my horse out of here."

"Is that the wisest thing for you to do, Kern?" Matheson asked.

"Yeah," said Kern, "I'm thinking maybe it is." He eased the rifle barrel back at Matheson. But then he looked toward Kindred once again, let out a breath and said, "All right, work fast. Get this thing rolling, or I'll leave you here looking up at the sun."

CHAPTER 24

Once the wheel was repaired enough to ride on, Matheson drove the buggy up along the hill. To take some of the weight off the buggy, Kern followed on horseback, making sure not to let the laundry bags out of his sight for a second. At the top of hill, where the land leveled off some, Matheson pointed Kern toward a narrower path veering off along a hillside, covered heavily with pine and spruce.

"This winds about two miles in and stops just before the door to the doctor's cabin," he said.

"After you," said Kern, wagging him forward with his rifle barrel. "I prefer keeping an eye on you from behind, rather than looking back over my shoulder."

"I've done nothing to make you distrust me, Kern," the banker said indignantly.

"Right," Kern said, "and you did nothing to the coach guards except to serve them lunch — their *last meal,* as it turned out."

"That was part of our plan, was it not?" said Matheson, his coat still off, his sleeves still rolled up. A black streak of wheel grease stained his cheek.

"Yep, it was," said Kern. "There's just something sneaky and unnatural about poisoning a man. I can't say why, but it makes my skin crawl."

"Oh, *what . . . ?*" said Matheson. "I suppose it's much more wholesome to blow a hole through a person's heart with a big slug of lead?" He slapped the reins to the buggy horse and rolled on.

As the buggy pulled forward, Kern's hand tightened on his rifle.

"Lyndon, I don't see us lasting together very long in Mexico . . . ," he murmured under his breath.

A short time later, the trail widened out onto a flat clearing in the rocky hillside. There, built on stilts beside a runoff stream, stood a cabin made of pine, tin and adobe. Around its side sat the doctor's buggy, a canvas thrown over it as protection from pine needles and rain.

"Now, here we have a man who *truly* likes to drink alone," Kern quipped in a guarded voice.

"Finding the doctor here is both a blessing and a curse," said Matheson. "He can help us put on a new wheel. But I'm sure he's going to have many questions about these Chinese laundry bags."

"We thank him for helping with the wheel," said Kern. "But if he has too many questions, I'll be obliged to close his shop."

"Come, now, Kern," said Matheson. "You can't go around shooting everyone. Sooner or later, it has to stop."

"Yeah? Where'd you hear that?" Kern asked, staring at him.

Matheson shook his head and eased the buggy forward, the patched-up wheel thumping, creaking with each turn.

"At any rate, we've nothing to hide here," he said. "Doc won't know a thing about what went on in town. He has no reason not to trust us — you being our new marshal, me the councilman and bank manager."

"And we'll play it just that way, if we can," said Kern, laying his rifle across his lap and moving his hand away from it.

"Hello, the house," Matheson called out, stopping the buggy a few yards away and rising a little from the seat. "Dr. Washburn . . . it is I, Councilman Matheson. The marshal and I need some help here."

■ ■ ■ ■

Peering out the front window and down a long flight of split pine stairs, Sara Cayes turned to Dr. Washburn, who had awakened from a nap in a cushioned rocking chair. He'd left his shoes sitting by the rocker and walked over beside her in his stockinged feet.

"What should we do, Doc?" she asked.

Washburn lowered his wire-rimmed spectacles, rubbed sleep from his eyes and sighed as he put them back on. He looked out through the wavy window glass, noticing the crooked buggy wheel and dried bloodstain on Kern's shirt.

"If they need help, I expect we'd best help them," he said. "It is our marshal and one of our councilmen."

"But what about Kern's deputies?" asked Sara. "We don't want them to know Celia is here." She tossed a glance over her shoulder at Celia Knox, lying in a small feather bed, a quilt pulled up over her in spite of the day's heat.

"No, we can't risk letting Kern know she's here," said the doctor. "I'll see what they want. As far as they know, you're here with me."

"Yes, of course," said Sara, liking the ruse, "and we want to be alone." She smiled. "So be cross with them, get them away from here."

"Yes, ma'am, I'll do my best," the doctor said, looking her up and down.

"Dr. Washburn," Matheson called out again, "are you all right in there?"

"I'm coming," the doctor called out, cracking the door open a little. "Let me get my trousers on."

Washburn hurriedly unbuttoned his trousers, dropped his suspenders off his shoulders and stripped his shirt from his back. He mussed his hair and started to swing the door open.

"Wait," said Sara. She ran to the bed and came back with a spare blanket. She threw it around his shoulders and gave him a slight shove.

In the buggy, Matheson had started to step down and climb the steps up to the front door. Kern had stepped down from his saddle and followed suit. But they both stopped in their tracks when they saw the front door open. Doc Washburn stepped out onto a plank porch and stared down at them.

"What the bejesus are you doing up here,

Councilman Matheson?" he asked in a growling voice, walking down the steps to keep them from coming up. "Where do I have to go to get away and relax?" he demanded.

"Our apologies, Dr. Washburn," said Matheson. "As you can see, we've had a wheel problem not far from here. I remembered your place here and . . . well, I thought we would go through your barn and see if you might have a spare buggy wheel."

"Yeah, we never expected that you'd be here," said Kern. "Imagine our surprise to see your buggy sitting there."

Washburn looked back and forth at them, noting that there was no hole or rip in Kern's shirt, only the smeared, dried circle of blood. He let out a breath and jerked his head toward a small barn around the side of the house.

"All right, there should be a wheel or two in there. But you'll have to get it yourselves and put it on. Unless one of you is hurt, I'm a little busy right now." He stared at Kern, but made no gesture toward the dried blood.

"Yeah?" Kern asked, suddenly looking suspicious. "Busy doing what?"

"That, Marshal, is none of your business," said Washburn. "I told you where the wheel is. Get it, put it on and go away."

Kern didn't like his tone. "Listen, old man
—" he said, getting more suspicious, swinging down from his saddle.

But before he could say anything else, the
three of them heard the door swing open.
They looked up the long flight of steps.

"Dr. *Freddie,* are you going to be all day?"
Sara called down, wearing nothing but a
thin sheet she held loosely up over the front
of her body.

Good Lord . . . ! Washburn thought, gazing
up at her, his mouth agape.

"Uh — *Yes!* I'm coming. I'll be right
there," the old doctor said. He looked back
at the two, noting Matheson's stunned
expression and the smug, amused smile on
Kern's face.

"Gentlemen," Washburn said gruffly,
"need I explain myself any further?"

"No, Doctor!" said Matheson. "We understand, don't we, Marshal?"

"Oh yes, we understand," said Kern. They
looked up the long steps in time to see Sara
turn around and walk bare-bottomed back
inside the house. "You get on back up there,
Dr. *Freddie,*" Kern said with a grin.

"Help yourself to any tools, wheels, whatever you need," said Washburn, turning
around and hurrying back up the steps.

"All this time," Matheson said, "I thought the old fool came up here to drink alone."

"Let's get busy," said Kern. "We don't know how long it'll be before we'll have townsmen on our tails."

Back inside the house, Dr. Washburn stood puffing and panting from the climb up the steep stairway. With a hand clasped to his chest, he stared at Sara, who was now back in her clothes.

"How did I do, Doc?" she asked.

"Lord, gal . . . you did fine . . . *absolutely fine,*" he said, bug-eyed, trying to catch his breath. He couldn't get rid of the picture of her — the pale, creamy flesh he'd caught only a glimpse of when she had turned and walked back inside. *"Jesus . . . ,"* he added.

"Here," Sara said, seeing his condition, "let's get you seated. I'll get you some water."

"No . . . ," said Washburn. "Make it rye whiskey. I could use a drink . . . soon as I get my lungs back."

Once she'd helped him sit down, Sara went to a cupboard and took out a bottle of rye the doctor kept for times when he was alone. She poured a water glass half full and brought it to him.

"Thank you, young lady," he said as he

took the glass and held it ready for a drink. "Did you . . . see the laundry bags on Matheson's buggy?" he asked.

"Laundry bags?" she asked. "How do you know they're laundry bags?"

"They're from . . . the Li Woo Laundry House," said Washburn. He'd begun to catch his breath. He sipped the rye. "I saw Chinese writing on the sides."

"Oh . . . ," said Sara. She considered it for a moment, then asked, "Why would Matheson haul his laundry around out here?"

"The short answer is, he *wouldn't*," said Dr. Washburn. "These two are up to something. I can feel it all over me." He took another sip of rye. "I don't know what's in the bags, but something told me not to ask." His expression no longer hid his worry. "And the blood on Kern's shirt . . . he never mentioned it," he said.

"It's not his?" Sara said.

"No, but it's *somebody's*," said Washburn.

They both took a quick glance toward the bed where Celia lay sleeping.

"What are we going to do, Doctor?" Sara asked quietly.

"This woman is still in no shape to be traveling just yet," the doctor said. "I don't think there's much we *can* do for now. We'll just have to sit tight and hope they'll fix their buggy wheel and get on away from here."

"What can I be doing?" Sara asked, nervous but determined to keep her wits about her.

Washburn looked around at his medical bag sitting on a nightstand beside the bed.

"You'll find a Navy Colt tucked down in the side of my black bag, Sara," he said. "Why don't you get it and bring it to me? Then go lock the front door."

"I will, right now, Doctor," Sara said.

She started to walk away, but the old doctor stopped her. He handed her the glass of whiskey. He'd only taken a couple of short sips from it.

"You best pour this back in the bottle and put some coffee on to boil. I want to stay alert until these two are cleared out of here."

Outside, Kern and Matheson rummaged through the doctor's horse barn and came out with a dusty spare wheel and some axle grease. Rolling the wheel out of the barn toward the buggy, Kern looked curiously up at the front door of the house.

"Did you notice anything peculiar about how he acted, Matheson?" he asked.

"No, I can't say that I did," Matheson replied, walking along beside him, carrying a bell jack and a large can of grease. "Why, did you?"

"Yes, I did," said Kern. He looked at the two laundry bags, clearly visible inside the buggy. "How come he didn't question you having these two big bags of money in the buggy with you or the blood on my shirt?"

Matheson gave him a condescending look. "Maybe he didn't notice the blood. Maybe he didn't know the two large bags are full of *money*. Maybe he thought it was *laundry,* like anybody else would, given the Li Woo Laundry House words and markings on the sides."

"Damn it, Matheson, you know what I'm saying," said Kern. "Of course he didn't know it was money. But who wouldn't at least ask you why you're carrying two big bags of dirty laundry around with you, this far from Kindred? I would have asked," he added. "Wouldn't you?"

Matheson set the can of grease and the jack down beside the buggy. He looked up the long set of stairs leading to the closed front door of the cabin.

"If I had a dove like Sara Cayes lying naked in my bed, I would not have asked us *anything.* All I would have said was *leave!*"

Kern thought about that, staring up at the door. Finally he let out a breath and nodded to himself.

"Yeah, I suppose so," he said. "We're lucky he didn't unload a shotgun on us, getting here at a time like this." He chuckled and said, "Do you suppose they're . . . ?" He made a fist and nudged his forearm back and forth.

Matheson responded to the marshal's crude gesture by shaking his head in disgust. He stooped and slid the bell jack under the buggy, near the axle. He tried to wiggle the top of the bell jack but found the threads seized on it.

"You'll have to help me lift the buggy onto the jack, so I can take the wheel off and put the other one on," he said.

Kern laid the spare wheel in the dirt, stepped over and helped him raise the side of the buggy onto the jack.

"This should do the trick," said Matheson, spinning the buggy wheel a little to make sure it had cleared the ground. "Would you please pass me the mallet and wrench?"

But Kern had gone back to staring at the front door with a suspicious look.

"Excuse me, Marshal," said Matheson, "the mallet? The wrench, please?"

"Hold on," said Kern. "I want to check things out a little." He turned to his horse and redrew his rifle from the saddle boot.

"Wait a minute, Marshal," said Matheson. "What could they possibly be up to that has bearing on us? We need to attend to business and get out of here."

"Shut up, *Councilman*," said Kern. "When we leave here, I don't want their fingers pointing in our direction." He walked away toward a thin path winding up around the side of the stilted cabin.

"For God's sake, don't harm them," Matheson said in a lowered voice.

"Don't worry. They'll hardly feel a thing, Councilman," Kern replied over his shoulder in the same lowered tone.

From the edge of the front cabin window, Sara Cayes said over her shoulder, "Here he comes, Doc. He's walking around, up into the rocks." She sighed. "I suppose my little playacting didn't work."

"I think you gave a *stunning* performance, Sara," the doctor said. The Navy Colt lay across his lap. He sat in the rocking chair that Sara and he had lined up perfectly with the front door.

"What do we do now?" Sara asked, sounding afraid. She knew the marshal was coming, that there would be no way out for the three except to face and defeat him.

"Once he's up around the boulder behind us, he can jump three feet and be on the roof," Washburn said. "But he still has to come through the front door."

"But what should I do, Doctor?" Sara asked, willing to take whatever action necessary.

"Stay out from in front of me, young lady," said Washburn. He picked up the Colt and turned it in his thick hand. "Once he learns he's not the only man with a gun, our new marshal's life is going to turn *disappointing,* to say the least."

CHAPTER 25

Sherman Dahl and Billy Nichols had followed the buggy wheel tracks and hoofprints to the spot on the high trail where the spokes had separated from the rim. But they only stopped there for a few minutes, long enough to give their horses a drink, pouring tepid water from two canteens into a broad-brimmed hat Shaggs had given Billy for the trail.

When they set back out on the trail, they followed the tracks and hoofprints until their horses stood inside a sparse stand of pine. They looked up and saw the cabin perched on a large boulder-strewn hillside a hundred yards ahead.

"Look at this," said Dahl, his eyes on Kern, as the marshal climbed around the accessible side of a huge rock seated against the rear of the cabin.

"Marshal Kern!" said Nichols. He fidgeted in his saddle, his hand gripping the butt of the big Colt on his hip.

Dahl looked at him and said, "Not from here, Billy. All you'll do is let Kern know we're onto him." He nudged his big dun forward. "Come on, let's get around this turn. Then we'll have him — maybe have them both."

Beside the buggy, Matheson worked hard and fast, sweat streaming down his face. He'd gotten the old wheel off by the time he glanced up and saw Kern crossing the boulder toward the rear of the cabin.

"Hurry, Lyndon, hurry . . . !" he murmured to himself.

This was his opportunity to get away from Emerson Kern and keep all of the payroll money for himself, he thought. He flung the patched wheel aside, grabbed the can of grease and smeared a large glob of it around the protruding end of the axle.

He could have taken Kern's horse, but by the time he'd loaded the bags behind the saddle, Kern was bound to see him. He couldn't risk Kern getting him in his rifle sights. Besides, he was not typically a horseback rider. He was more of a buggy man — even still, more of a Pullman traveler, he thought with a faint smile.

Riding in style . . . ! Oh yes, from now

on . . . ! he thought.

He hurriedly wiped his hand on the dirt to get rid of the grease. He picked up the spare wheel and wrestled in onto the axle. He picked up the large wheel nut and the wrench lying beside him.

"Hurry! Hurry, damn it . . . !" he growled to himself.

Inside the cabin, Sara stood beside the bed where Celia Knox had awakened and tried to sit up a little.

"What — what's wrong?" Celia asked, feeling, *sensing* the tension in her quiet surroundings.

"The marshal from Kindred is snooping around out there, Celia," Sara whispered, reaching down and fluffing a feather pillow up behind her shoulders.

"The marshal?" Celia said. "You mean the one whose deputies . . . ?" She hesitated to finish. "I'm getting up from here," she said. She started to swing around onto the side of the bed, her face still battered and swollen.

"I know you can, but don't," Sara whispered, pressing her back down. "It's important that you stay quiet. They mustn't know you're here."

Celia leaned back stiffly against the pillow

and nodded, her eyes widening in terror.

"Yes, I understand. I'll be quiet!" she whispered in reply.

In his rocking chair, Dr. Washburn jerked the gun up, startled, as he heard a loud thump on the rear of the tin roof.

Sara turned facing him and froze in place; Celia lay fear-stricken, not daring to breathe.

"Here comes our honorable marshal now," Washburn whispered. "When he gets in front of that door, I've got him."

Sitting alert, the doctor cocked the Navy Colt and held it in his right hand, the gun butt resting on his crossed knee. He and Sara's eyes followed the much quieter sound of Kern's boots on the tin roof as the marshal tried to slip across the roof unnoticed.

After a tense, silent moment, their eyes turned to the sound of Kern climbing down from the roof onto the narrow walkway surrounding the cabin. Another moment later, they heard him try to pry open a closed shutter for a peep inside.

"Don't worry, ladies. He can't see in," Washburn whispered.

Their eyes followed Kern's softened footsteps around the side of the house to next window, then the next. Sara remained tense and frozen as she stood beside the bed; Celia lay with the same terrified expression on her healing, but still battered face.

Dr. Washburn finally broke the tense silence by calling out, "Marshal Kern, we know you're out there. If you wanted to see what's going on in here, you could have climbed the steps and come to the door."

"Damn it to hell . . . ," Kern murmured to himself. "All right, Doc, open this door. I want to see what you and the whore are up to."

"Shame on you, Marshal," said Washburn. "You know what we're up to. I did everything but spell it out for you."

"Huh-uh, Doc," said Kern through the door. "I mean what you're *really* up to. I don't buy the story of you two in bed together. The picture doesn't sit well with me. Not that pretty little thing with an old geezer like you."

"Well, you can go straight to hell, Marshal," said Washburn, feigning anger. "This young woman has been my very special friend ever since —"

"Open this damn door, Washburn, or I'll bust it the hell down!" Kern shouted. He began slamming his shoulder against the door over and over.

While the whole cabin shuddered from

the impact and the door strained on its hinges, Celia rolled up onto the side of the bed and looked at Sara.

"Don't stop me," she said. "I better get up from here."

"Yes, maybe you should," Sara said, not sure how long the door could take the beating. "Get up and get under the bed before he breaks in and sees you." She grabbed Celia and pulled her to her feet.

"Ladies, trust me, I've got him," Washburn said with confidence as Kern continued to shoulder the front door loudly.

No sooner had the doctor spoken out to the women than the door burst open and Emerson Kern stumbled inside, trying to catch his footing and raise his rifle barrel at the same time.

"Take that, you bastard!" the doctor shouted, firing round after round from the Navy Colt.

Out of five of the .36-caliber shots fired, four hit their target. Each bullet hit Kern like the sting of some large, terrible insect. He jerked back, forth and sideways with each shot; his rifle flew from his hands.

Washburn let out a yell of frustration when his last shot had fired and the Colt's hammer fell on an empty chamber. He sat stunned, seeing Kern still on his feet, wobbling unsteadily in place.

When Kern's rifle had hit the floor, Sara leaped across the room and dived onto it. She grabbed it by its barrel and rolled onto her feet just as Kern snatched his Colt from his holster and aimed it at Washburn.

Seeing Sara rise up with his rifle, swinging it back like a club, Kern turned his Colt toward her. But before he could fire he caught a glimpse of a wide black ribbon of steaming hot coffee fly out of a pot in the hands of a woman he'd never seen before.

Kern screamed as the scalding coffee hit him in his chest. But before he could do anything to help himself, his scream was cut short by the force of his rifle butt striking him in his chest. The hard blow sent him flying backward out the front door and tumbling head over heels down the long, steep stairs.

Rounding the last turn toward the cabin thirty yards away, Dahl and Billy Nichols veered their horses away from each other as Matheson came charging between the two of them in the buggy, Kern's horse hitched to the rear of the rig, running hard behind them. The councilman stood in a crouch, slapping a long buggy whip to his horse's back.

Matheson only tossed them both a wild-eyed gaze as he sped away. Grease smeared his face and his white shirt. Part of his stiff white collar batted in the wind.

"Go get him, Billy," Dahl shouted across the rising dust the fleeing councilman left swirling between them.

"What about Kern?" Billy asked, already turning his horse in pursuit.

"I'll get him," Dahl said.

Before Nichols was even out of sight around the turn in the trail, Dahl had already heeled his dun on toward the cabin. He saw Kern getting up from the dirt at the bottom of the steep stairway. He saw him stagger back and forth like a drunk, ranting and screaming curses toward the open door high above him. Kern's fall had torn away half of the handrail from the stairs. Miraculously, through it all, he'd managed to hang on to his Colt.

Through the open door, Sara saw Dahl riding into sight, and immediately she felt her eyes well.

"We're going to be all right," she cried over her shoulder. "Sherman is here!" But then, seeing Kern raise his Colt and turn it toward Dahl, she screamed, "Sherman, *look out!*"

Kern took careful aim at arm's length. But Dahl swung the dun hard to the left and hurled himself from the saddle in the opposite direction. He heard the first bullet slice through the air dangerously close to his head as he left the saddle. When he hit the ground, he went into a roll with bullet after bullet kicking up dirt behind him.

He stopped rolling, prone on his stomach, both elbows supporting him. His Colt bucked once in his right hand. He watched Kern flip backward and land facedown in the dirt.

Dahl stood and walked forward, his smoking Colt waist high, cocked, ready to fire again.

Kern struggled up onto his knees and scraped his gun up off the ground. Dahl took note of his fiery red chest. Blood ran from bullet holes in his forearm, his thigh, his shoulder and his belly. A bullet graze ran back along his head above his right ear.

"You . . . damn . . . people," Kern said, gasping for breath. He started raising his Colt again.

"Don't do it . . . ," Dahl warned.

"Don't . . . *do* . . . *it?*" Kern chuckled sadly. "You . . . must be . . . joking." He leveled the gun.

Dahl's Colt bucked again. The shot exploded in a streak of orange-red fire. Kern flipped backward again. This time when he landed he didn't move.

Dahl stood over Kern. He thumbed open the loading gate on his Colt and let shell after smoking shell fall to the dirt. As he reloaded, he looked up and saw Sara coming down the stairs two and three at a time, with very little handrail left to hold on to.

"Is everybody all right?" he managed to ask her as she threw herself into his arms.

"Oh yes! *Yes, yes, yes,*" she said, her arms going around him, pressing her body to his. "We're all three fine!"

Dahl felt her warm tears on his throat. He held her for a moment. Then he pushed her back slightly.

"Let me look at you," he said. "He didn't harm any of you, did he?"

"No," Sara said, "but he might have — would have, that is, if we hadn't fought back."

"How's the woman doing?" he asked.

"Oh, she's much better," said Sara. "She's up out of bed."

"That's good news," said Dahl.

They both looked saw Washburn and the woman staring down the stairs at them.

"Hello, Mr. Dahl," said Dr. Washburn. "You arrived at a good time. Much obliged."

"You're most welcome, Doctor," Dahl said. Bareheaded, he touched his fingers to his forehead courteously.

Celia Knox stood with a smile on her battered face.

"Ma'am, I'm glad to hear you're feeling better," Dahl said.

Celia nodded. With the same pleasant smile on her face, she gestured down at Kern lying dead at the foot of the stairs.

"I threw scalding coffee on that dirty son of a bitch," she said.

"*Oh . . . ?*" Surprised by the woman's language, Dahl looked at Sara.

"She really did," Sara whispered. "It was terrible, you should have heard him scream."

"I bet," said Dahl. He looked back up at Celia. "Well, that's real fine, ma'am . . . Good work."

CHAPTER 26

Dahl and Sara turned toward the sound of the buggy rolling back into sight, Matheson slumped on the driver's seat. A large bloody welt ran across the side of his forehead. Billy Nichols rode along on his horse beside the buggy, leading Kern's horse by its reins.

"You won't *believe* this," Nichols said to Dahl as the buggy rolled to a halt a few feet away. "These bags are full of money." He stopped his horse and gestured for Matheson to get down from the buggy. Once standing on the ground, Matheson looked at Kern's body and shook his head in disgust.

"I believe you, Billy," said Dahl. "The banker here poisoned the two guards and unlocked the payroll bags. He rebagged the payroll money. The deputies were going to ride off with newspaper trimmings and the townsmen on their trail. These two were taking off with the real money."

Nichols looked taken aback by Dahl's knowledge of the incident.

"I guess I was wrong, you do believe it," he said.

Dahl saw the young man's disappointment in not being the one to break the news.

"But you're the one who caught him and brought him back," Dahl said quickly. "I'd say the town of Kindred owes you a debt of gratitude."

"It's not Kindred's money," Matheson said sorely. "Anyway, I'm both a bank manager and an elected town leader. I have every right to be out here protecting this money. Once the townsfolk hear how this all happened, I know —"

"Save it for the townsmen, then," Dahl said, cutting him off.

"The townsmen, *ha!*" said Matheson. "What was I just thinking? There's no explaining anything to those idiots in Kindred. They do well to find their mouths with both hands and a wooden spoon."

"Be sure to mention that to them," said Dahl. "Maybe it might make them go easier on you."

Matheson gave him a puzzled look. "What is your position in all of this, mister? Aren't you some sort of hired gun?"

"Yes," said Dahl, "I'm some *sort of* . . .

hired gun."

"What I mean is . . . ," Matheson said, stepping over closer and lowering his voice. "Isn't there a way for us to — you know — end this to everyone's satisfaction?" He looked back and forth between Nichols and Dahl. "There is a great deal of money in those bags, sir. If you get my meaning."

Dahl looked at him. Then he looked at Nichols, then at Sara, who had taken a step back when the buggy rolled up.

"I get your meaning," he said to Matheson. Nodding toward Sara and Nichols, he said, "Why don't you two walk up there and take the doctor and the woman back inside?"

Sara hesitated. Nichols looked stunned.

"It'll be all right," Dahl assured them both. Seeing Nichols hang his head in disappointment, he said, "Go on, Billy. This is the way it's done."

Matheson grinned with satisfaction. He and Dahl watched on in silence until Sara and Nichols had climbed the stairs and followed the doctor and the woman inside.

"I've got to hand it to bankers and politicians," Dahl said to Matheson. "You always find a soft place to land when the storm's over." He gave a slight smile.

Matheson returned the smile and spread

his greasy hands.

"What can I say?" he said. "We all have to make allowances for —"

"Except for this time," Dahl said, cutting him off again. His smile was gone, and a cold, hard look had come into his eyes.

"Pardon me?" said Matheson, not believing what he'd heard.

"This time, there's no soft place to land," Dahl said quietly. He looked toward Kern's Colt lying in the dirt three feet away from Matheson. "Grab the gun and make your play."

"Whoa, hold on," said Matheson, his hands went chest high. "I was under the impression we were coming to a deal here."

"We are," Dahl said. "You just heard it."

"I'm no gunman, sir," said Matheson. "We can each have half of this money, to do with as we please."

"Or *one* of us can have it all," said Dahl. "To do with *as we please*." He nodded at the gun in the dirt. "Grab it. That's the deal."

"I'm a banker," said Matheson. "I don't take foolish risks . . . and that's what this is. I'd never make it to the gun. You'd kill me first."

"You need better odds?" said Dahl. He

slipped his gun into his holster. "How's that?"

"Uh-uh," said the banker, "I'm not a fool. I don't take the broad risk — I leave that to the other party. I always take the minimum risk for the greatest return." He managed a thin smile, liking the banter, the negotiating.

"Then how's this?" Dahl lifted his Colt from his holster and unloaded it, letting one bullet after the other drop in the dirt at his feet.

"That's better, but still . . . ," Matheson said hesitantly.

"Now grab the gun," Dahl said. "This is the best odds you'll get from me. The deal won't get any better . . . only *worse* from here."

But Matheson didn't understand how that could be. He'd taken the deal this far. What else could he get? He looked at the bullets in the dirt, the empty Colt in Dahl's hand. This was turning out better than he could have hoped for, he thought. Still he pressed for more.

"No, I'm not going for it," he said. "I need more than this. Give me something else." He gave a thin, nervous smile. "Call it stronger security, better collateral if you will."

Dahl shook his head slowly. "You turned down my strongest offer." He looked at the empty Colt in his hand. Then he pitched it over ten feet away.

"Well, well . . . ," said Matheson in surprise. A confident gleam came to his eyes. He looked at the bullets on the ground and at the big Colt lying far out of Dahl's reach. *The gunman just gave it up,* he told himself. He had to make a move now. This was a deal to his liking — no risk, all gain.

Dahl didn't move an inch as he watched the banker leap to the ground, grab Kern's Colt and scramble around in the dirt toward him.

What's this? He hasn't moved . . . ! Matheson thought, cocking the Colt, raising it. *Why hasn't he moved . . . ? This fool . . . !* He threw the Colt out at arm's length and aimed it. *Not my problem . . . ,* he thought. *I have him . . . ! It's all over —*

But his thought stopped suddenly as Dahl's right arm sprang up from his side. A small, two-shot Marston hideout pistol jumped out of Dahl's duster sleeve into his hand . . . and fired, all in one motion.

"You turned down the better deal," Dahl said. The banker's dead eyes turned up toward a gaping hole in the center of his forehead. "Greedy, I guess . . . ," he murmured, shoving the hideout gun back up in his duster sleeve and snapping it into place on a small spring-loaded metal track.

Hearing the shot, Sara ran out the front door of the cabin and hurried down the stairs. A few feet behind her, Billy Nichols walked down a little slower, seeing that Dahl wasn't wounded.

"Oh my God, Sherman! Are you all right?" Sara said, her voice trembling. This time, instead of flinging herself into his arms, she stopped warily at the foot of the stairs and looked down at the banker's body lying in the dirt.

"He went for Kern's gun," Dahl offered, seeing the questioning look on her face.

"I — I see that," Sara said. "But I never thought I'd see a gun in Lyndon Matheson's hand."

"Well, now you see it," said Dahl. "Unless you think I put the gun in his hand."

"No, I didn't think that," said Sara. "I know you wouldn't do something like that. . . ." She paused for moment, then asked, "Did you?"

"No, I didn't," Dahl said. He gave her a look and a smile. He stepped over and picked up his Colt and walked to Sara and Billy Nichols, picking up his bullets on the way. He saw the look in Nichols' eyes as he reloaded his Colt. "All right, maybe I did put the gun in his hand, in a manner of speaking," he said. "I can't deny I wanted him to grab for it."

Billy Nichols nodded, satisfied. "But he made his choice," he said in Dahl's defense.

"Yes, he made the choice, Billy," Dahl said. "Much obliged."

On the upper porch, Dr. Washburn stepped out and looked down.

"Does anybody need me down there?" he called out to them.

"We're good, Doctor," Dahl replied.

Billy sensed that Dahl and Sara wanted to be alone.

"I'll take these horses over and water them down," he said. "Then I'll dig holes and bury these two if you want me to."

"No, these two are going back to Kindred, along with the payroll money," Dahl replied without taking his eyes off Sara's.

"All right," said Nichols, leading the buggy horse away with one hand. He guided both his horse and Dahl's with his other.

"This is all done," Dahl said. "I'm able to leave anytime."

Sara let out a breath and said, "You've been able to leave for a while. I'm obliged you stayed and helped everybody out." She looked him up and down. "Is that something most hired gunmen would do, for free, I mean?"

"Fighting man," Dahl corrected her. "It is if I want to."

Sara smiled. "And now you're leaving . . ."

"If I want to," Dahl said.

"Do you . . . want to, that is?" Sara asked.

"I don't think so," Dahl said. "I can go home, but there's no home there."

"Then stay here," Sara said. "Make this your home. If you want to, I mean."

"Would you like me to do that?" he asked quietly.

"Yes, I would," she said, "if that's what you want."

"It is," he said. He stared into her eyes. She saw something leave him, something that she knew he had kept masked from the world — something cold and distant in his demeanor that had been there only a moment ago, and now was gone. Whatever it was, she was glad to see it vanish.

"What about the fact that I'm a whore — I mean, a dove?" she corrected herself. "Should we talk about that?"

"If we need to," he said. "Do we need to?"

"I think so," she said. "I *am* a dove. I have been for a while now."

"Do you want to be?" he asked.

She shook her head. "No, not anymore,"

she said.

"Then don't be," he said. He tipped her chin up to his face, standing close to her.

"I won't," she said.

"All right, then," he said, smiling. "I'm glad we talked about it."

"Me too. That was nice," she said.

They turned, arms around each other's waists, and stepped around the two bodies lying in the dirt. They walked along the rocky trail for a few yards, feeling a cooling breeze blow in off the far green hill line.

ABOUT THE AUTHOR

Ralph Cotton is a former ironworker, second mate on a commercial barge, teamster, horse trainer, and lay minister with the Lutheran church. Visit his Web site at www .RalphCotton.com.

DISCARD